"I was bored," Elayna returned without thinking.

"You're lying." His gaze on her was fierce, angry—at her or at himself? "You shouldn't be here. Not in my hut, not in this wood. Not anywhere near me. I should have gotten rid of you in the beginning. I should have—"

In those impenetrable eyes of his she saw something more than pain then. She saw loneliness and need, and it chipped away at something inside, something that held her heart fast and safe. But not now.

"Why didn't you?" she asked, her voice wispy, her breath barely there.

"I want to be rid of you. I want it more than anything except—"

Elayna wanted to run away, but there was no place to go, and he was holding her so very tightly in his arms.

"What do you want?" she cried, not at all knowing what she wanted herself.

You. She thought he said *you.* But she wasn't sure, because at that very instant, the storm that had threatened on and off since the day before returned with a loud rumble.

And the next instant, he was covering her mouth with his.

Dear Romance Reader,

Last year, we launched the Ballad line with four new series, and each month we'll present both new and continuing stories set everywhere from medieval England to the American West—the kind of passionate, romantic stories you love best, written by the most gifted authors. At the back of each book, we'll tell you when you can find subsequent books in the series that have captured your heart.

This month, the fabulous Suzanne McMinn returns with the second installment of her *Sword and the Ring* series. **My Lady Runaway** is determined to escape marriage to a cruel nobleman, but she never expects a face from her past to become her knight in shining armor. Next, Lori Handeland continues *The Rock Creek Six* with **Rico,** a man who has a way with women—until he meets the one woman who refuses to believe that love is possible.

In the third entry of rising star Cindy Harris's charming *Dublin Dreams* series, a widow meets her match in a brooding attorney and wonders if she can convince him that a true romance is certainly not **Child's Play.** Finally, reader favorite Alice Duncan concludes the smashing *Dream Maker* series with **Her Leading Man,** as an actress who dreams of medical school learns that even the smartest men can be stupid when it comes to love. Enjoy!

Kate Duffy
Editorial Director

The Sword and the Ring

MY LADY RUNAWAY

Suzanne McMinn

ZEBRA BOOKS
KENSINGTON PUBLISHING CORP.
http://www.zebrabooks.com

For all the great staff and teachers at Acton Middle School, and especially for the ones who kept me sane through their generous mentorship while I was writing this book: Cortney Brewer, Janie Green, Connie Leonard, Suzanne Young, and Connie Youngblood.

PROLOGUE

France
February 1348

He had noticed her first at the Saint Valentine's feast.
The Château Voirelle was occupied, but that didn't stop
the villagers and castlefolk from celebrating the last of
winter's chill and the coming promise of spring. If anything, the celebration was greater, as if tradition could
overcome the years of war.

They danced beneath the watchful eyes of soldiers. They
flaunted, they rebelled. They enchanted.

She wore a garland of small-leaved branches festooned
with winter berries over her artfully upswept plaits, and
on her sleeve, a red cloth heart had been sewn as a sign
of her devotion to Love.

After the feast of rare roast beef and chestnuts and
cream, she joined the pairing circle with the villeins. She
seemed to take no pride in her superiority as the sister of
the lord's wife, a daughter of a highly placed French lord
herself.

For this night, there was no villein or noble, no captive

or captor. And eventually, for a few hours, there were no French or English.

Guests sat on chairs facing one another in a large circle. The appointed Lover stood within it, and when it was she, his heart went wild. Jealousy. He hadn't expected it. As she began to walk round and round, the rush of possession was unique to him. She began to chant the Valentine's rhyme, her sweet voice carrying even to him.

"Choose from the East. Choose from the West."

Beyond the circle, across the hall, her eyes caught his. She'd noticed him in his dark corner, in his shrouding black cloak and his separateness. She'd noticed that he was staring. He almost turned away, embarrassed, but he couldn't. Why should he? Was he not a man too? Did he not deserve love? Had he not been too long denied?

The long years of rigid adherence to service reared huge in his mind. He deserved love. He deserved her.

He started to move toward her, led by feet with a will of their own—

"Choose the one you love . . ." She let the last line draw out. "The best!"

And her gaze left him, sudden and sharp, and she reached out her hand to another. The man said something to her, and she laughed shyly, as if she were embarrassed and yet flattered at the same time. They exchanged kisses on the cheek, as decreed in the game, but when they walked arm in arm from the circle, into the firelight and shadows, they were no longer playing a game.

That night was only the beginning. He watched day after day as she fell in love. He approached her, spoke to her, tried to explain to her that what she was doing was wrong.

She didn't understand. She didn't listen.

She avoided him.

He tried to ease his pain, first in drink, then in other women. There were so many of them in the village below Voirelle—young, plump, eager. He denied himself no

more. He had been good and pure and all that cruel
happenstance of birth had demanded.

These other women understood. They gave themselves
willingly, and the first time he killed one, it was an
accident.

He had been thinking of her, his beloved, and somehow
he had squeezed the poor goosegirl's neck.

It was not his fault; it was her fault, his beloved's.

She would have to be punished.

CHAPTER ONE

England
October 1353

She was free.

Elayna of Wulfere peered carefully from beneath the scratchy woolen blanket under which she hid in the back of the minstrels' cart. She'd waited, eternal damnations it had seemed, although she knew it could have been only half the day, before daring to peek. She'd been jostled by ruts in the road, bitten by fleas who'd made their home in the blanket before she had, and worst of all, she'd had to listen to the small troupe enjoy their midday meal with gusto while her stomach growled.

They'd tossed the food satchel back into the cart—onto the top of the blanket.

Even through the wool—damp from the light, misty rain that had plagued them for hours—she could smell the wonderful aroma of Cook's mutton pasties, and for a moment she longed for the home she'd left, for her brother and his wife, Belle, and

her three younger sisters, Gwyneth, Lizbet, and
Marigold. Even more she missed Venetia, Damon
and Belle's two-year-old daughter, and their new
baby boy, Ryen.

She pushed the feelings aside determinedly.
Awaiting her at Castle Wulfere were more than
Cook's fine foods and her sisters' mischievous
smiles.

Awaiting her there was the man who planned to
wed her, and her no doubt now-furious brother
whose well-meaning attempts to see her settled had
served only to drive her away.

Her muscles ached from the cart's jostling movement. Her skin itched from the rough blanket and
her stomach bunched in hunger—but she felt a
sense of excitement just the same. She smoothed
her hand around the heavy satchel she'd brought
with her. It contained clothes and toiletries, coin to
get her started, and her collection of bound poems.
There were also her own writings—her poetry, her
songs, and especially her journal—along with blank
sheets of parchment, ink, quill pens, and erasing
knives. She had everything she required to prove her
value as a copyist.

She reached up to touch her hair beneath the
blanket, feeling the clean edges of her newly shorn
chin-length locks. The cut made her feel light,
unshackled. There was no turning back. She wore
clothes filched from Gwyneth, who'd long ago convinced Belle to let her keep her own wardrobe of
boy's tunics to wear when she practiced at swords.

Elayna had never been tempted to don them . . .
till now.

No more ribbons, no more gowns. No more
rouge and perfume.

Surprisingly, she didn't think she would miss any
of the lady's accoutrements she had always enjoyed.
Her breasts were bound—the only discomfort in

her new, otherwise liberating costume as a young man. For the first time, she felt a connection with her boyish sister, Gwyneth, whose past antics had inspired Elayna's own desperate scheme.

The first thing she had to do was convince the minstrel troupe to let her travel with them, at least until she could find other means of transportation. This was the sticky part. People were afraid of her brother. She planned to wait until they were well away from Castle Wulfere before revealing her presence—well enough away that they wouldn't take her back.

For now, she wondered if they would notice if she took that last pie. Over the edge of the blanket, she could see it almost falling out of the satchel. One last, splendid pie. Abandoned, calling to her. Liberation was hungry work.

Glancing at the cloaked, hooded figures on the cart's driving seat, she considered her course of action. The only noise was the splash of the wheels hurtling across yet another muddy rut in the road . . . and the sound of her stomach growling.

Elayna made her decision, snagged the pie, and pulled it under the cover. Even the sour odor that permeated the filthy blanket couldn't dim her desire for it. She stuffed in the first bite, then the second. She was licking the last crumbs off her fingers, peeking out from the blanket again, when she saw one of the minstrels turn, reach his hand back toward the satchel. He wanted that last pie! *Damn the saints.*

She had decided to take up swearing now that she was posing as a man. Now seemed as good a time as any to start.

Elayna burrowed under the blanket in her narrow position between the back of the cart and the minstrels' bags of instruments and other belongings. She lay perfectly still while the minstrel's muffled grumblings went on from the cart front.

"Who ate my other pie?" he demanded in a snarling, short-tempered voice she barely recognized.

Performing after the evening meal last night at Castle Wulfere, Drogwyn and his brother and sister-in-law had seemed so much more good-natured. At Castle Wulfere, Drogwyn had seemed downright charming—he was a juggler and a lute player, and he'd had the women nearly swooning from his good looks and smiles and flatteries. His brother Alan had sung beautiful love songs, and Alan's pretty wife, Marilette, had told fortunes.

She'd held Elayna's hand and told hers.

"I see great love," Marilette had said, her blue eyes serious as she'd studied the lines of Elayna's palm. She'd also held Elayna's brooch between her hands, pressing it against her heart as if it spoke to her there.

"What?" Elayna had asked, surprised. It wasn't what she'd expected to hear and it took her off guard. She'd gone to the fortune teller with a more pressing concern. She had already decided to run away with them, to hide in their cart at dawnbreak. Would she make it away safely? Would she find work as a copyist in the city? Would anyone discover that she was not a boy? Those were the answers she sought. And yet the fortune teller appeared to have no inkling of these great changes to come in Elayna's life.

"Love." Marilette had lifted her deep gaze to Elayna's. "He was your first love, and he will be your last."

Elayna felt a tightness in her chest then. Images flashed in her mind against her will: *Castle Wulfere. She'd been only three and ten. Graeham was older by several years. He was a knight now and he looked differ-*

ent. She was different too—feeling the first fluttery stretches of womanhood. And he was most certainly a man. She had known him all her life, and yet now it was as if they began anew. He had arrived to participate in the tournament that was part of the summer festival. Her father had been ill, but all those worries seemed to recede for this brief time, this week when she'd met Graeham again. He'd asked for her token, and she'd given it to him, and then she'd kissed him and her world had turned on its head.

For that April sennight, she walked in a dream. Because her father was ill, there had been no one to notice when she sneaked away to the meadows and the gardens. They held hands and whispered secrets about nothing. Sometimes they just looked into each other's eyes and smiled.

The last night of the tournament he'd showed her the ring he had purchased for her from one of the many peddlers who had attended the festival. It was delicate but ornate, gold with a deep garnet in its center.

Red fire, he'd said. Red fire for the Penlogan red dragon, his family's heraldric emblem.

She had never seen anything so beautiful.

He would talk to his father, he promised, and then hers. Their fathers were close friends and neighbors—but his was far away, at war in France. It would take time. There would have to be a messenger sent. But word would come by return courier and the arrangements would be made. Their fathers would both be overjoyed, he assured her.

For now, their plighted troth—binding as it was— would have to remain a secret. Their secret. Somehow, the secrecy made it more special. They lived in their own world. There were only the two of them.

She gave the ring back into his keeping, in waiting for the day they would wed and he could place it on her finger forever and she wouldn't have to hide it. "Keep it, hold on to it, know it is my heart," she told him. She

*was afraid he would forget her. She was afraid it was
all too good to be true.*

She had been right.

"There was someone," she said slowly, frowning.
Her throat was tight. "But you don't understand.
He's dead."

"There must be some mistake." Marilette looked
affronted. "He can't be dead. He will be your husband. But you will not know him in the beginning,
and you will lose him before you find him. Great
love comes with great tragedy."

There was no point in arguing. Elayna had risen
abruptly and walked away. Obviously, the woman
was a fraud. If she couldn't give her any useful tips
about her future, why couldn't she at least have
provided her any one of the number of simple
sham fortunes everyone else had received? Marilette had told Gwyneth to place rosemary inside her
pillow. By morning, it would be creased, pushed,
disarranged, and if she stood afar, she would see
her lover's face in the folds. Not that boyish Gwyneth *wanted* to see a lover's face in her pillow. In
fact, she'd sworn to sleep on the floor for the next
moon to avoid it. But at least the fortune had made
sense. It sounded like a thousand other fortunes
Elayna had heard distributed. But the one she had
received was like nothing she'd ever heard. It was
more riddle than fortune, and it irritated her.

She didn't need a fortune teller, she reminded
herself. She'd make her own fortune and her own
future, not wait for someone else to make it for
her. She'd had the one piece of blind luck she
could hope to have three years before, when her
then-betrothed, Lord Harrimore, an ancient and
decrepit miser from the cold, bitter northlands,
had died on the way back from paying court to
her at Castle Wulfere. The betrothal to Lord Harrimore had been her father's idea. She'd been too

numb at first to protest it, then her father had been too ill. After her father's death, and then Lord Harrimore's, Damon had let her have a say in her own marital plans, at least for a time.

She'd spent the next few years rejecting every betrothal offer that came her way. Damon had despaired of her.

"Love is something that grows between a man and wife," he'd said to her only recently. "At some point, you're going to have to give it a chance. You can't keep saying no. You are growing old for marriage, Elayna."

She was all of eighteen.

Belle was more sympathetic, but she supported her husband. "Damon and I were strangers when we wed," she reminded Elayna often.

It was true; Damon and Belle, strangers at the time of their marriage, were blissfully happy. There was excitement, emotion, attraction between them. Their love was obvious.

Elayna felt none of those things toward the men who'd paraded through the gates of Castle Wulfere in search of a bride. No spark, no tingle. No hint of excitement, emotion, attraction. No sense of destiny. She'd sent them away empty-handed. None of them had made her feel anything.

None of them had been Graeham.

Even now she had to remind herself not to think that way. Graeham couldn't have been her destiny; he was dead. She wasn't sure what her destiny was, but she knew what it wasn't. Out there, somewhere, was the life she was supposed to live. She had examined her talents for clues.

Her writing was what had sustained her, kept her from going mad when Graeham had gone. She had always listened avidly to the visitors who came to Castle Wulfere—priests, peddlers, physicians, musicians. She'd learned of the world outside her sheltered home, a world where the demand for books—for writers and especially for copyists—was increasing. Never had she thought to join this world, not really. She was, after all, a woman. Worse, she was a noblewoman. But she had dreamed, especially lately. . . . There was something inside her, something stretching, pushing. She hadn't figured it out yet, and then she'd run out of time.

Ranulf of Penlogan had cornered her in the tower stairwell and reminded her that he'd saved her brother's life during the wars in France. He'd earned the lordship of Penlogan when he'd uncovered Wilfred of Penlogan's crime—a crime that had left her brother falsely imprisoned in a French dungeon until Ranulf had brought Wilfred to justice. Graeham had been Wilfred's son, and he had followed up his father's perfidy with his own—defying the truth of his father's execution and the king's order to turn over Penlogan. In the end, Graeham had died and left Ranulf to claim Penlogan.

And now her.

She felt betrayed all over again when Ranulf made his proposal.

"I have thought long and hard about choosing a wife." Ranulf bowed over her hand and kissed it. His lips felt smooth and hard on the thin skin of the back of her hand. She'd pulled her hand away, and felt a shiver creep up her spine. The stone stairwell inside the keep was always cold. "I have thought long and hard about you."

"Perhaps you haven't thought long and hard enough," she countered, trying to keep things light. She didn't want to hurt his feelings.

"We've known each other a long time. I've watched you grow up."

"Then you should understand."

"You don't wish to wed me." He furrowed his

brow. He stood very close, and she had the uncomfortable sense that if she tried to walk past him, he'd stop her.

"I don't wish to wed any man. Haven't you noticed?" How could she explain to him that she could especially never wed him?

It wasn't his fault that Graeham had died. It wasn't fair to blame him. It was Graeham who had wanted revenge more than he'd wanted her.

But Ranulf didn't know that she had ever cared for Graeham. No one did. Graeham had died before he could ask her father for her hand, and she had tried very hard to forget him.

She had not spoken his name since she'd learned of his death.

"I've noticed," Ranulf responded to her question.

"So you understand."

"Yes."

She wanted to feel relieved, yet somehow she didn't.

"Think you I'm not good enough, Lady Elayna?"

"No!" Had she hurt his feelings? She looked at him again, disbelieving. No one would believe that Ranulf of Penlogan was not good enough for anything or anyone. He was renowned for his daring.

The thought made her wonder why he wanted her. He could court any woman. . . . *But she was near, and she was Damon's sister. And she was very rich.*

Were the rumors of Penlogan's debts true? Ranulf had embarked on a massive building expansion and restoration after claiming the castle for his own.

"Then no man is good enough?" he pressed, adamant.

"I didn't say that." She didn't know what to say. She was starting to feel more than annoyed. She was starting to feel scared. What would Damon say

to Ranulf's proposal? He had been patient with
her for a long time, but this was different. This was
Ranulf. He'd never asked Damon for anything in
return for saving his life—until then.

He was going to ask for her. How could Damon refuse?
And how could she? It would be harder than
ever before. Even if she tried to explain about
Graeham— But she couldn't. Damon had spent a
year in a dark prison because of Graeham's father.

She couldn't tell her brother that she couldn't
marry the man who'd saved his life because she'd
once thought herself in love with his enemy's son.

"I'm better than you think, Elayna," Ranulf had
said softly, determinedly. "I'm going to be the most
powerful lord in this realm. You'll see." His voice
had risen and the look in his eyes sent a sense of
hopelessness down her spine. He was determined.
"You've grown up, and you're beautiful."

He touched her hair, sifting it through his fingers. His touch felt strange and possessive. She had
never realized that he was repugnant before. She
had never really thought of him at all.

"I don't mind your reluctance," he said quietly.
"No battle is worth winning if there is no chance
of losing."

She wondered how he could lose, and could
think of only one way. She had left a brief, painful
note, packed her satchel, and climbed into the
back of the minstrels' cart the following dawn.

Voices rose from the front of the cart, breaking
into her thoughts, and she realized that Drogwyn
and Alan were arguing—over the meat pie. Drogwyn was accusing Alan of eating it.

They sounded like children instead of grown
men. She was pretty sure her sisters, at ages nine,

twelve, and fourteen, were more mature than these two brothers.

She hoped it was simply that traveling didn't agree with them rather than that these were their true personalities.

"You fen-sucking puttock," one of them was calling the other, and she heard Marilette intervene. "We can buy more pies, you know. So just shut up."

"*He* can buy more pies," Drogwyn snapped. "*He* has all the money."

"Someone has to hold the coins to prevent you from giving them away to every flea-bitten whore you come across," Alan said.

Marilette broke in with something Elayna couldn't quite catch. She heard a crack, as if someone had been struck, and then Drogwyn was swearing and Elayna pressed herself deeper into the corner of the cart and wondered how they could possibly be the same people she'd witnessed charm the crowd the previous night.

Her doubts mushroomed.

She chewed at her lip and examined her options. She could hide in the cart all day, sneaking out only after they'd arrived at their evening's destination, a huge wedding feast at Glenmorgan Castle.

Dozens of jongleur troupes would be gathering to entertain such a crowd. Surely somewhere among them she would find some gentle, kindred souls who would let her join their troupe, travel on with them to the city. She could even hitch a ride with a peddler, or perhaps hide in a noble guest's baggage. There would be a thousand ways to travel on without these . . . fen-sucking puttocks.

Thinking over her plans made her feel better. She even smiled as she thought that adding to her repertoire of insults and curses might be a side

benefit to traveling with her current hosts. She
might as well get something out of the trip.

The men's voices kept rising as they argued, and
Marilette was screaming at them to stop, when the
cart made a jerking motion to the side. For a horrible instant, Elayna thought the cart was going to
tip over, and she swallowed a cry.

The cart bumped to a halt, tilted down on the
right front side, and she heard Drogwyn and Alan
jump out, their voices coming around the side of
the conveyance with swears and ill-tempered
grumbles.

The right front wheel was stuck in a deep muddy
rut, Elayna picked up between condemnations and
profanity.

"It's your own fault, you and your boil-brained
arguing," Marilette griped as she was heard to
climb down from the bench and come around to
the men. "You would have seen that hole coming
if you hadn't had your hands around each other's
throats."

"Why didn't *you* see it coming, oh, great fortune
teller?"

"Shut up, both of you," Alan said. "Give me a
hand." There were long grunting sounds. "You
too, Marilette," Alan ground out, and Marilette
made some unfeminine sounds before she, too,
joined the men pushing against the stuck cart.

There was more swearing, then the sudden ominous sensation of a heavy body climbing over the
back of the cart, boots stomping onto its wood
bottom.

"What have you got packed in here, Marilette?"
Drogwyn griped.

Elayna could hear sacks of cooking implements
and other belongings being thrown over the side,
clinking and clanking against one another as they
hit the ground.

In desperation, she flattened her body, clutching her satchel tightly, her heart exploding in her chest. He was grabbing things right and left, tossing them out, closer to her all the time.

Marilette shouted at him to stop and jumped into the cart after him.

"You idiot!" she screamed. "You—"

Drogwyn threw out the bag directly in front of Elayna.

CHAPTER TWO

There was no place to go, no place to hide. A rough hand grabbed at the blanket. She couldn't stop the little shriek that came out.

"Here now, what's this?" Drogwyn gaped at her, his charmingly handsome face snarled into a look that made her want to grab the blanket back and hide again—but she couldn't. He had hold of it.

Whatever Marilette had been in the middle of saying was forgotten.

"What's going on?" The fortune teller was half in, half out, of the cart. She swiveled a look at her husband, who was still standing at the side of the cart, then back at Elayna. "Who are you?"

Elayna scrambled to her feet. Drogwyn seemed a lot bigger than he had the night before. He towered over her in the confines of the cart, the misty late-morning clouds hanging above him lending a dreamlike aura to the moment.

"Speak, boy!" Drogwyn advanced, closing the short space between them.

She forced her best smile. "My name is—" She

stopped, realizing she'd almost stated her true name. She had to get hold of her wits. She could scarcely be a boy named Elayna. "Kipp," she blurted out. There was a wheelmaker named Kipp at Castle Wulfere. He was a kind man. "My name is Kipp."

"Kipp of whence?" Drogwyn glared down at her. Elayna didn't have a chance to answer.

"Saints' blood," Marilette breathed. "This is no boy."

Elayna's pulse thumped. "Yes. Yes, of course I am."

"This is not a boy!" Marilette repeated louder. She pushed herself up and into the cart, reaching for Elayna's hair. She grabbed a shorn lock before Elayna could move, tugged her close, and stared into her face. "I never forget a face."

Elayna's heart thumped painfully. She couldn't speak. Her throat closed.

"This is one of the ladies of the castle!" Marilette cried.

"What?" Alan glared at her.

Marilette narrowed her eyes as she tried to remember. "It's . . . Elayna. That's it. Elayna."

"No, no."

"Yes." Marilette reached for the ties that gathered the top of Elayna's short tunic. Beneath, she wore rough woolen hose. Marilette tore the ties apart to reveal the binding that hid Elayna's breasts. Elayna clutched at the tunic, drawing it together as best she could, her breasts covered, thankfully, by the binding that still revealed her lie. "See?" Marilette cried.

"All right, yes," Elayna admitted without choice. She worked to think fast. "I'm but a castle hand-maid, Fayette. I—"

Marilette shook her head. "She's lying. She's the lord's sister, I'm certain of it."

"Hercules, it *is* her." Drogwyn stared at Elayna with a mixture of irritation and interest that made her uncomfortable. She worked to tie the tunic together again, her fingers shaking. "I remember her now." He narrowed his eyes and continued to scrape her with his gaze.

She gave up the pretense. "I need a ride, that's all. If you would just let me—"

"God's eyes, get her out of there," Alan ground out.

"No, no." Elayna's pulse thumped even harder. "I just—"

Drogwyn grabbed her arm.

"The lord will kill us if he thinks we took her," Marilette said, her voice rising slightly. "What are we going to do?"

"Don't take me back," Elayna said quickly. "If you won't let me travel with your troupe, just take me to Glenmorgan Castle. I'll find another troupe there. Please."

"We're not taking you back, you little idiot," Drogwyn said, pulling at her. She tried holding her ground, but his strength was irresistible. He compelled her to the side of the cart, where Alan grabbed her waist and pulled her down, setting her unceremoniously on the side of the road with the piles of belongings they'd thrown out.

She was barely able to hold on to her satchel, and she nearly fell when she hit the ground.

"Let's see if we can get this thing moved now," Alan said. Drogwyn joined him, and they moved quickly to push the lightened contraption out at last, carefully moving the rear wheel over the perilous hole as well.

Elayna watched with a sense of desperation.

They were going to leave her. They weren't going to take her home. They were just going to leave her!

"Please, I pray you, let me go with you to Glenmorgan Castle," Elayna said again, her throat tight and thick. "My brother will never know I was with you—and even if he suspected, he wouldn't be angry with you but with me. He's not as fierce as he seems, you know." He *was* fierce, but he was gentle too. Few people saw that gentleness though, and she realized these minstrels weren't about to believe her.

They were tossing their things back into the cart. Marilette was already on the cart seat.

"Be gone," Drogwyn snarled at her. "Do you realize what will happen to us if we're caught with you?"

Alan climbed into the cart and took hold of the reins.

"I will swear that it was my own doing. My own decision. No one will blame you. I've run away with minstrels before." This was true. She'd run away with minstrels several times during her betrothal to Lord Harrimore, years ago now. She'd never made it much farther than the castle gates during any of those attempts.

She'd thought she'd gotten better at running away. Apparently, she was wrong.

Elayna tried to move around Drogwyn, closer to the cart—closer to Marilette. If anyone would listen to her, she hoped it was Marilette. The fortune teller had been so kind last night, and she was a woman. Surely she wouldn't let them just leave her on the side of the road! "Marilette—"

"I said, be gone," Drogwyn repeated, and he grabbed her arm, pushing her away from the cart.

"Don't hurt her," Marilette cried.

"Get out of here," Drogwyn said in a low, menacing voice.

Elayna glanced at Marilette. The fortune teller looked stricken, afraid—but she wasn't going to

move to assist her, she realized. She was on her
own. They were truly going to leave her.

A roll of thunder filled the air, and she realized
the air had grown heavier. Sprinkles dotted her
face. Rain was coming.

Drogwyn hadn't moved. There was nothing left
to remind her of the charming, handsome minstrel
she'd seen the night before.

A gust came up and she shivered—both from
the wind and fear. The early autumn leaves rustled
loudly in the forest surrounding both sides of the
road.

"Come on, brother," Alan roared from the cart.

"Go," Drogwyn ordered her again flatly.

"I have money. I can pay if you'll let me come
with you." She was thinking of the small leather
cache in her satchel, but Drogwyn's gaze dropped
to the small pouch hooked to her belt.

He snapped it off and emptied out the coins.

"For our trouble." He tossed the purse back at
her feet. "Now get out of here."

She didn't pick it up.

"Go, little girl," he spat out.

Thunder rumbled again, closer now. The look
on his face changed, and he grabbed her arm in
an implacable hold. With his other hand he
squeezed one of her breasts through the tunic and
binding. Her breasts, already tender from the confinement, stung at the harsh touch.

"Go before you make me do something that will
get us all killed," he said under his breath, harsh
and close, then he let go of her. She stumbled
back, almost fell, still gripping her satchel. He just
stared at her for a terrible instant, then started
coming toward her again.

Panic spun in her mind. She turned and ran
into the woods. Branches snagged at her, and she
whipped them out of the way with her arms, heed-

less of how they tore at the material of her tunic. She darted around huge tree trunks that sprang darkly at her out of the shadows of the dense forest.

She tripped, stumbled as her foot slipped in a hole, and landed flat on her face. She hit hard and lay there for endless moments, no sound but the wild beating of her heart, the harshness of her own breath, and the ominous sound of the gathering storm—trees swaying and slapping against one another in the wind, and the low, fearsome rumbles of thunder.

Had Drogwyn followed her? She couldn't see him or hear anyone. She pushed up on her arms, still sitting, her legs weak with exhaustion, listening through the noise of the coming storm with every fiber of her being.

There was no sign of Drogwyn. She was relieved for a tiny beat.

Her lungs burned, and she tried to slow her breathing, stop the panic from rising. She concentrated on brushing off the bits of twigs and leaves and dirt from her dress, wrinkling her nose. She was filthy! Drops of rain splattered down on her, filtered by the thick canopy of the forest. Soon, it would be pouring and she had no shelter. She had to focus on that one thing. Shelter.

Thank God he hadn't taken all of her money. He hadn't realized that she had money in her satchel, far more than had been in the small pouch on her belt.

A sharp noise broke through the sounds of the storm, a sharp snapping, like a stick. Someone stepping on a stick. Drogwyn!

Elayna sprang to her feet, twisting her head to the side. She met glowing red-black eyes—then, as if in some slow-moving dream, the wild boar charged, eerie and terrifying and so unreal.

She came out of her shock, willing herself to

move, to turn and run, but not soon enough. The animal's great tusks tore into her.

Pain burst from her side, sharp and piercing. Her brain ordered her feet to move, to flee, but it was as if they were rooted. Those horrifying tusks came toward her again, and she experienced the sudden, calm feeling that she was about to die.

In that instant, an arrow sliced right between those feral tusks. Elayna stood there, dazed, aware of pain, of wind shrieking through trees, and of a man, solid form and darkness, and the most terrible eyes she'd ever seen. Falcon eyes—sharp and dangerous. Deadly as any wild creature. And yet familiar too. Somehow, fantastically, familiar.

He came at her, and she couldn't move, couldn't run.

Scream, she told herself. *Scream!* But the world was already spinning away.

CHAPTER THREE

Damn her eyes.

He couldn't get them out of his mind even though now they were closed. He knew exactly what they looked like. Gorgeous, huge, with wonderful speckles of gold that lit them up like candles. But the beauty of them wasn't what Graeham of Penlogan-by-the-sea—for that was how he still thought of himself—couldn't get out of his mind.

It was the fact that he knew her instantly, as if the intervening years were lifted away, nothing but a bad dream. He hadn't even seen the boyish hair, the tunic. He'd seen past them to her eyes, her amazing candlelit eyes, so mysterious to him, so relentless. How he'd wanted to walk away from her and the painful past she represented. She made him think of happy times, of treasured freedom, of home and family and everything of a world he'd once thought would be gifted to him as his right.

Everything of a world that had betrayed him.

What was she doing here? How had she gotten here? He had a hundred questions and no answers.

He knelt beside her pallet on the dirt floor of his dark forest hut and pulled back the cloth covering her wound. Light sputtered from the smoky fire in the center of the dwelling. It was a hovel by any standards—but it had never seemed so poor as when he'd carried this beautiful girl inside it and thought she might die there.

He'd cut her tunic from the neck down to expose the vicious gash. He'd cleaned the wound the best he could—but it had bled wildly, her bright life pumping from her body before his eyes. There was blood everywhere—on her, on him. He hadn't let himself think about what he had to do. If he'd thought about it, he wouldn't have been able to do it.

That was when she'd opened her eyes. He'd pressed his fire-hot blade against her side, searing her torn flesh and burning his own hand in the process though he'd barely felt it at the time. He didn't want to feel anything, couldn't let himself feel anything—especially for this precious noble girl who represented everything he had learned to hate.

But he *had* felt—too much. Not the burning of his skin but the torment inside him when her eyes shot open, once, for a shocking, horrible instant, and she screamed.

He'd applied a poultice of herbs, and then bound her with strips torn from her own ruined clothes. He watched her now for signs of consciousness, but there were none. Her breathing was regular though shallow, her skin pale and grayish and more warm than he liked. The wound didn't look as if it was festering, but experience told him that he would have to keep a close guard on her.

If someone had told him he would one day exchange his sword for a spade, not only raising medicinal plants but using them to help others, he would never have believed it. He certainly hadn't started out to become a healer when he'd left Penlogan.

Then, he had simply been hoping to survive.

Now those who had helped him in his darkest hours depended on him to help them. It was surreal to find the skills of his new life suddenly tested on the most painful aspect of his old one.

In the distance, he could hear muffled thunder. More rain, and nothing but the pitiful blaze of the small, smoky fire to provide heat. Elayna alternated between shivering and sweating, and he wiped her face with a piece of damp material he'd torn from her tunic. He reapplied the poultice, rebinding the wound. It would make an ugly scar, and the Elayna he'd known would hate this marring of her otherwise perfect body.

He had always thought of her as petite, but of course he hadn't seen her in years. Her body had matured.

He'd removed the binding that had held her breasts. The beast had ripped the lower portion of it, and it had perhaps saved her from the attack being even worse. It had been soaked with blood. Why she had worn such binding to begin with was a mystery, as was the clothing and shorn hair and her presence in this wild wood at all.

Her freed breasts were heavy and pale, her waist small, her hips full. He could have spent a lifetime looking at her, but he forced himself to drag the thin blanket back over her, covering her.

He couldn't resist touching her face again, and she made a soft sound, almost a sob, turning her cheek into his palm, unconsciously needy—so unlike the stubborn, independent girl he'd known her to be. Emotion pierced him, and he pushed it back. He didn't want her to need him.

She was trouble, and he had enough of his own.

What if she recognized him? It was a troubling thought.

Where was her family? How had she come to be wandering in this rain-soaked forest so far from Castle Wulfere?

He'd felt no compunction about searching her satchel. It had contained clothes—more tunics and rough hose—and parchments, ink, writing tools. There was a bound book of poetry, and another collection of her own writings. It was a journal, a diary of days. He flipped toward the end of it, and his gaze caught on an entry months in the past, a description of the May Day celebration at Castle Wulfere. There were flowing descriptions of flower crowns and hoop-rolling games and green parsley bread, all to celebrate the awakening of earth's spirit. Memories of home seared his mind. He almost missed the last few sentences.

My spirit is here, stretching, and so am I. Why? For what purpose? I wonder. . . . She had stopped, seemingly in mid-thought.

He didn't go on to read any more of the journal. It felt too intimate, too personal, too close. He didn't allow anyone to get close.

She also had money, a lot of it. He didn't know what to make of the satchel's contents, what it said about her journey.

He didn't like to think of what would have happened to her if he hadn't found her. But he liked even less to think of what would happen if anyone found *him.*

Somehow, he had to get her out of there, get her to her family. Yet she couldn't be moved, and he couldn't leave her—at least not tonight. After tending her wound, he'd left her only long enough to go as far as the road, which wasn't far at all if you knew where you were going through the thick, secluded part of the woods where he'd built his hut.

If you didn't know where you were going, it could just as easily have been as far as the sea, for the mist that shrouded this forest rarely let up. His hut sat in a small clearing, allowing him enough sunlight to grow his herbs. But beyond the occasional clearing, a person could be lost forever in these untamed woods where much of the land was low and patterned with bogs that could swallow a man whole.

It was a perfect place to disappear.

Few travelers were foolhardy enough to leave the road. He'd thought there might have been an accident while Elayna had been traveling with her family. Perhaps they'd been set upon by thieves. But there was no sign of anyone or anything—only pouring rain and fog and mystery.

He hadn't wanted to leave her alone long enough to go to the inn in the nearest village down the road. He would have to wait until she was resting more easily, until he was sure this fever didn't take hold.

Was Elayna's brother even now at the inn, waiting, or was he yet in the stormy forest somewhere, searching for his sister?

If so, how had they become separated? And why was he not searching along the road near this part of the forest, where Graeham had found her?

The situation seemed inexplicable, and even as Graeham wished he could leave her long enough to find out if the lord of Wulfere had passed through the Green Stag Inn, he was loath to do anything without thinking it through with care.

The last thing he wanted was for the lord of Wulfere to know that Graeham of Penlogan-by-the-sea was alive.

He felt Elayna nuzzle her cheek needily against

his palm again, her skin soft and hot, too hot. She was getting warmer, and he knew it wasn't from the poor fire. The rough hay pallet provided little comfort, he knew, and the smoky fire even less.

She sighed, and the long, pained sound of it pierced something inside of him again, something he thought had died long ago. He got down on his knees, closed his eyes, and prayed that saving her life wouldn't cost him the one thing that had saved his own.

Elayna awoke with a trembling start. At first she saw only shadows. Misty shadows that made no sense, along with muted *pat-pat-pats* above her and rustling shudders around her. There was a searing pain inside her.

She didn't move. She feared that the merest attempt would be agony. Her breaths came in shallow jerks, and she carefully slowed them—because breathing hurt too. There was a terrible throbbing fire in her side that seemed to radiate outward to every part of her body. It took confusing, blank moments before the memory of all that had brought her there hit her.

Ranulf. Escape from Castle Wulfere, then the minstrels. Drogwyn's hands touching her, his cruel voice ordering her away. The woods. And the boar and the red glow of his eyes. She could have died!

And then she remembered the man with his terrible falcon eyes. He'd killed the boar. He'd saved her. He'd brought her . . . here.

Who was he? Why had he seemed familiar? How *could* he seem familiar?

Those questions seemed impenetrable, and others were more pressing. *Where was she? How long had she been here?*

Beneath her, she could feel rough, lumpy straw,

and she blinked desperately, working to clear her vision, pushing back the tears of pain that stung them. Slowly, she struggled to make sense of her surroundings.

The muted *pat-pat-pats* were created by rain. A steady drizzling rain. She was in some kind of hut, she made out through the misty shadows. There was little to see. A couple of stools, a stack of kindling wood, some kind of metal implements—tools?—atop a large chest, and a few basic kitchen pots and bowls on a rough-hewn table. A string of onions hung by the door. There was another table against the far wall that held a neatly jarred collection—herbs? There was a drying rack, leather pouches, perhaps also containing herbs, and some other pots and utensils that could have been used both for healing and for cooking.

The dwelling itself seemed to be made of some sort of dried grass, the roof thatched, the floor naught but hard packed earth. There was a pile of shiny metal objects in the corner, and it took her some time to comprehend that they were pieces of armor.

A small fire glowed from the center of the dwelling—and with no way for the smoke to escape, it burned her eyes and scratched her dry throat. A crude spit hung crookedly over the low flames, and she could just make out the shape of something sizzling over it.

Sick horror lodged in her throat as she realized it was the boar.

She'd seen boars cooked over spits before, had eaten boar meat before—but this boar had nearly killed her.

Instinctively, she reached for her side, felt beneath the thin blanket at the wrappings that covered her, feeling her nakedness but for those wrappings. Someone had removed her clothes, tended her, nursed her. There was a wooden bowl beside her pallet and a ripped piece of material, hanging half in, half out, of the bowl.

Another memory struck her, dreamy and yet real. A man touching her, speaking softly to her, gently washing her brow, changing her wrappings, comforting her—and his soft voice, soft touch, as inexplicably part of him as his harshness.

That wild, fierce demon-man with his strange familiar eyes had brought her here, tended her, wrapped her wounds. Seen her naked. Knew she wasn't a boy. She pushed at the blanket again, and through the hazy dimness she could make out the material of the wrappings and realized it had come from the tunic she'd been wearing.

She was lucky she was alive, she knew that—but fear gripped her as surely as the pain.

How long had she been here, in this hut, in this stranger's care? Was this even morning? It was impossible to gauge time in the windowless haze of the dwelling. She could have been here for days, or weeks. She had to get out of here!

She tried to sit up, pushing with her hands, pulling at the thin blanket. Agony burst through her, and she fell back, barely holding on to consciousness, a terrible moan filling her ears. She hardly realized it was her own.

Pain burned from her side, spilling across her chest.

A rush of cool air swept her, and misty light stung the backs of her eyelids. She opened her eyes, blinking against the sudden glow—soft, yet much brighter against the darkness inside the hut. Her breaths came in jerky gasps still, then suddenly lodged, trapped, in her throat and she forgot to breathe at all.

He was back.

CHAPTER FOUR

He filled the small doorway, had to bend his head to come inside. He was darkness and light, planes and angles, shape and solid form—nearly as tall as the hut itself with his massive shoulders and powerful body. She could see nothing of his face then—only the gleam of his eyes.

Falcon's eyes, she remembered sharply. It was what she'd thought when she'd first seen him in the woods. Sharp, dangerous falcon's eyes.

And there was no way for her to escape him. She couldn't run—could barely move at all.

He slowly walked toward her, looking taller and bigger with every step. Sheer instinct made her shrink backward, but there was nowhere to go— only the wall of the hut and relentless pain greeted her futility.

As he came closer, the small fire's glow reached him, revealing his face in its pitiful, sputtering light, and she felt hysteria bubble up inside her. He was menacing—everything about him, his penetrating eyes, his unruly mane of hair, the cruel slashes of his brows. His nose was straight, his cheeks angled.

What was he doing in this forest? And what was he planning to do with her?

She almost choked because she'd forgotten to swallow, the humming fear still clawing up her throat, threatening to take over.

Her rescuer was motionless now, staring down at her, examining her with those falcon eyes that suddenly looked somehow dead, as if there were no feeling inside him. He looked capable of anything—lopping off infidels' heads, boiling prisoners in oil, cleaving enemies in twain. *Anything.*

And she was at his mercy.

"You're awake." His voice was as low and burned-out as his eyes, and he moved even closer, putting the fire's light behind him—leaving nothing but hulking shadow and threatening shape as he came toward her.

She felt oddly nerveless, light and heavy at the same time. She realized she was shivering and sweating, and it wasn't only because of him, because of fear. She was sick. She could be dying. She'd seen men die of wounds—not right away, but afterward, slowly, when the wound grew putrid. Fever would set in, and that would be the end of them.

The sickness made her bold, or stupid, she wasn't sure which, and it didn't matter.

"If you're going to kill me," she said, "I would rather you went straight ahead."

Dizzily, she was aware of the slight tightening of his already-hard mouth.

"I saved your life."

His voice seemed to emanate from very far away, though she could see that he'd come closer. He was bending over her now. She felt his warmth, recognized his earthy man's scent, as if somehow she knew it, remembered it from her dreams. Those dreams of gentleness and nurturing. Of kindness. Yet it was impossible. There was nothing gentle or nurturing or kind about this man. She'd never seen anyone so grim in her life.

"I'm not going to kill you," he continued in his low, terrible, dead voice.

The familiarity of his scent was joined by the familiarity of his voice. It seemed more than the familiarity of a dream. His eyes, his voice— She knew him. But how could it be? It made no sense. She struggled to focus on the moment.

I'm not going to kill you.

So what *did* he have in mind?

"That's what I'm afraid of," she whispered wildly, the hot-cold streakiness almost making her lose consciousness again.

He said something else, something she didn't catch, but she realized he was angry. Before she could stop him—as if she could have stopped him from doing anything—he pulled back the blanket and started unwrapping her bandages. His hands felt cool against her burning skin as he reached under and around her with deftness.

It was one thing to know he'd seen her naked. It was quite another to be aware of it as it was happening. Even through the buzzing feverishness, she was embarrassed.

She managed to flail at his arm, pushing away from him, not even caring at the searing rush of pain the movement yielded, hardly feeling it, really. She caught him accidentally on one cheek with a cracking smack and she was terrified because she'd struck him. He grabbed at her arms, taking control of her with fierce, frightening ease, and she waited for him to strike her back, but he didn't, only held her.

"Dammit, lady," he rasped, his low voice coming to life now. "I may change my mind about killing you yet. That's if you don't kill yourself first."

She blinked, her breaths coming in quick gasps. She didn't have the strength to fight him anymore even if she could have stood a chance. But she *didn't* stand a chance, not one—her body was shaking and her vision was starting to blur.

There was a humming in her ears, and she felt as if she were floating, light-heavy and hot-cold. She was aware of his efficient hands and she gave in to them, weary and barely conscious, her energy spent. She was aware of him gently washing her wound, smearing some terrible-smelling unguent on her, then wrapping her again, lifting her as if she were no heavier than a kitten.

She was aware that he left and came back, though she couldn't have guessed how long he was gone— it could have been hours or days, but she realized vaguely that it must have been only moments. Her eyelids felt too heavy to raise, and she knew she couldn't have lifted a hand to fight him again if she'd tried. She heard him set something heavy on the dirt floor, and it was only after he began washing her fevered skin with the cloth he dipped in the pail that she understood he'd retrieved water from somewhere nearby. Cold water that had her trembling harder, but aware, still startlingly aware of softness from hard hands and comfort from a dead voice. She knew that she should have been embarrassed, that she *would* be embarrassed when she was stronger, but that she wasn't strong enough now. She was floating, his hard-tender touch the only thing holding her down.

She knew that somewhere along the way she'd started dreaming, because she wasn't in a hut in the middle of the forest with a terrible warrior anymore. She was at Castle Wulfere with a laughing boy-man who somehow had those same penetrating eyes, that same firm voice, that same passionate mouth.

She was on the wallwalk, pennants flying over the castle, voices rising below them on the crowded tournament fields—but she heard none of them, only his voice, his tender, laughing voice, here in this high corner of the castle. Then he swept her into his arms, taking her into a dark, private shadow. They kissed and whispered promises that she knew would never fail. . . .

Yes, she was definitely dreaming.

The wide sleeves of his cloak flapped in the light wind, black and thick, as he made his secret way between the cottages. The village slept around him, a sleep he had ordained. It was easy; they trusted him. But trust wouldn't save them. There was wickedness in the world. Sin. Stubbornness. And it was up to him to punish it. To punish her.

But she wouldn't die. Every time he thought he'd killed her, he looked around and found her all over again. That didn't stop him from trying. It had become his mission.

The hair-thin crescent of moon overhead shed no light on his path as he stepped into the deeper darkness of the cottage. Tonight, he would try again.

CHAPTER FIVE

"Well, look who's here. Where've ye been, sugar?" The kitchen maid stopped short on the stoop of the Green Stag Inn, almost running into Graeham as he tried to make his way in through the back entrance. Caitrin carried two pails, one in each hand.

She set them both down with a clunk that had the contents—probably used cooking water but possibly refuse of a different sort—sloshing over the sides and had Graeham taking a step back.

Cocking her head, she watched him with her dark, heavy-lidded eyes as she pushed the door shut behind her without looking back, enveloping them in the golden-red autumn light of the stable yard behind the inn. They weren't alone—he could hear the conversation of stable boys putting up horses for new guests he'd seen tramping inside as he'd arrived—but that wouldn't stop Caitrin.

The maid leaned against the door frame, crossed her arms—causing her generous bosom to push at the already-loose ties of her low-cut brown kirtle—and effectively blocked his entrance.

"I missed ye." She uncrossed her arms, thinking to push stray hairs out of her face, tucking them into her snood.

She was young, much too young, to Graeham's mind, though it occurred to him now that she was probably only a year younger than Elayna. He reached out and lifted the ends of the cords that bound her kirtle together and tugged hard, pulling the bodice once again snug across her bosom. She watched him calmly, with a dare in her eyes.

He dropped his hands from her tightened bodice, not taking her up on that dare. The muted sounds of voices and laughter and clattering dishes and the cook's barking orders mixed together to fill the air. The roadside inn was close to the one-time village of Cradawg, which was little more than a wide spot in the forest. Its history was lost in the timeless mists, but there were the remains of an old Roman fortified post nearby to recall days when the post, village, and road must once have held strategic import.

Now there was only a cluster of sod and wood huts whose poor, forgotten inhabitants primarily made their living from working in the Green Stag, serving those unlucky enough to find themselves seeking shelter in the middle of the dark wood at nightfall as they traveled the untended section of road.

Graeham had been one of those unlucky souls passing by at one time. Now he was one of the poor, forgotten inhabitants instead. They'd accepted him, and he was grateful.

He couldn't afford ties though—even to these kind people. He was a part of them, yet separate. It had been that way from the beginning. He'd arrived half dead, never planning to stay—yet with nowhere to go.

Caitrin hadn't given up trying to change his mind

about attachments, at least temporary ones. There had been plenty of times he'd wanted to take her up on her repeated invitations to her obvious charms, but this night he wasn't even tempted. He could think only of the sleeping beauty in his forest hut.

She was casting a spell on him even in her unconscious state.

Either that, or prolonged abstinence was making him lust unwisely. Whichever was the case, he could not give in to the weakness.

He had to find out where Elayna had come from, and even more important, how he was going to get rid of her.

"Where's Meldrik?" he asked.

Caitrin sighed, the late afternoon sun hitting her pretty face, gilding its youthful curves. She tipped forward on her toes and pressed a swift wet kiss on his mouth.

"In the tavern room," she breathed against his cheek, moving to press her lush body against him as if to remind him one last time what he was missing. "In a fine temper because ye haven't been to the inn for two nights." She stepped back and pulled at the ties of her kirtle, letting the bodice fall enticingly open again.

She glanced up at him with a sparkle in her pouty, heavy-lidded eyes and shrugged.

Graeham couldn't resist a smile at her saucy look. Caitrin was, if nothing else, a practical girl. If she couldn't entertain herself with him tonight, he had no doubt she would find companionship elsewhere. She had a crippled, widowed mother and four baby brothers and sisters to support in the village. There was business, and there was pleasure. Luckily for Caitrin, Graeham had an idea that she'd found a way to combine the two. And he knew her youth was not what most men saw.

"Do ye have a good excuse?" she asked. "Meldrik said ye'd better've snapped yer leg in two fer being gone so long with no word. He's been run off his feet with this storm and travelers staying fer days on end with nothing to do but drink—and no one to tend the bar but himself and Jordie."

Jordie was Meldrik's son—and jack-of-all-trades in the inn by age eleven. As with most children in the village, his childhood hadn't lasted long.

"I couldn't be here." Graeham gave Caitrin all the excuse he intended to give her. He didn't plan to give Meldrik much more. As much as he owed the beefy, bighearted tavern master, he wasn't going to tell him about Elayna—and despite Meldrik's bluster, he knew the tavern master wouldn't ask.

Graeham's mind flipped back to his problem. He had to find out if anyone was looking for Elayna. He'd turned over the conundrum in his mind during the past two nights.

The fact that no one was beating the trees searching for her hadn't escaped him. The notion that she'd been lost after her party was attacked had shrunk in his mind.

How could she have been lost in the forest without her family knowing to look for her there?

Lady Elayna of Wulfere would normally travel with a maid, grooms, no doubt in a fine litter and most likely not without her brother or some other worthy guardian to protect her from the brigands that quite often haunted lonely roads to rob and slay travelers. She would be shielded carefully. Not only was she an innocent and a woman, she was of noble birth—a valuable tool of negotation at the bridal bargaining table. And though a hardy band might still venture an attack against even such a well-equipped group, Graeham had found no signs of such a struggle—and nothing Caitrin said now was changing that perception. If a group had been attacked, and sought shelter at the inn, she would have mentioned it without his even asking.

There was little of excitement in the village of Cradawg—and what excitement there was would be turned over many times in the villagers' minds and conversations.

"Tell me about the travelers who've been here these past few days," he said abruptly when Caitrin stooped to pick up her pails again. She straightened and gave him an odd look.

"The usual sort." She gave another slight shrug. "A couple of wagoners. A merchant who took ill. A messenger with his groom." Her mouth twisted a bit at that. "He was a fine one," she added with another of her saucy looks. She went back to recounting visitors. "Oh, and a small band of knights. But they didn't stay the night, just passed through. I didn't even see them, just heard of them—they came through yesterday morning."

Graeham took in the information. The knights could well have simply been passing through on the way to tournament. Or they could have been looking for someone. He didn't want to rouse Caitrin's suspicions by pressing her on that point. She hadn't been here anyway. He wanted firsthand information.

He needed to see Meldrik.

"The merchant's still here," Caitrin went on. "Better now, sitting by the fire, shouting about every little thing that's wrong. Rats under his bed, hard bread, sour ale. Cursed, pock-faced man. The rest are gone. Of course, more stopped today. A group of monks, a pardoner, and a lord and lady on their way to a wedding at Glenmorgan. We've had quite a few of those in the past week. Why're ye asking anyway?"

Graeham reached out and tugged her bodice

strings tight again. "Thanks, Caitrin." He pushed past her to open the door to the kitchen, tipping his hand in passing to the cook, another kitchen maid, and the tavern master's wife—who was busy raking Jordie over the coals for dropping a chicken off the spit.

"Ye better be here to work," Auda broke off to call to Graeham as he passed. "Tydeus is ill, and we need Jordie in the kitchen tonight. Now"—she turned her plump face, glowing with sweat from the heat of the kitchen, back to her son—"don't ye—"

The rest of her tongue-lashing of Jordie was lost on Graeham as he entered the main room of the inn. The tavern room was bursting with people— eating, drinking, talking loudly. The air was ripe with the smell of sweat and ale. A man, the merchant he guessed, sat by the fire, holding court with a circle of well-dressed monks—all heaving great mugs of ale. A lad, either the merchant's son or his servant boy, sat on a stool behind him, chewing on a hunk of meat.

The lord and lady sat at a table in the corner, partaking of a meal Graeham had no doubt had not originated in the inn's kitchen. Often, nobles traveled with their own victuals, which they pressed upon harried innkeepers to prepare. They'd probably traveled with their own bed as well, which their servants would break down and put up at the next inn the following night. Their servants were probably the less fortunate-looking group—a maid and a couple of grooms—who hovered nearby as if waiting to jump to their lord and lady's beck and call.

Graeham stared at the noble entourage for a long while, struck by memories that sucked the air from his chest. Sometimes, he almost succeeded in blocking out the fact that he had lived another life. But he would see someone, even strangers such as these, and it would all rush back.

"Where've ye been? Get yer dog heart behind the bar."

Meldrik, the tavern master, came charging across the tavern floor, a wet towel over one arm, the expression on his face a mixture of irritation and relief. He slapped the towel on the bar. The rough-hewn surface was messy—food crumbs littering across its surface, floating in the occasional spill of dark red wine and brown ale.

Graeham took up the towel and started cleaning. "I'm sorry I couldn't be here." He met Meldrik's gaze.

The tavern master stared at him for a long beat. "I figured ye were gone, Gray," he said, using the name Graeham had lived by since he'd arrived in Cradawg.

"I have nowhere to go, you know that," Graeham said. This conversation wasn't new.

The tavern master sighed and pulled at his red beard as he regarded Graeham. He'd been a mix of father and protective spirit from the day Graeham had arrived, bloody and desperate. It had taken hours for his world to change forever, weeks for him to recover his health, years for him to forge a new life. A life as a fugitive.

He'd been raised to be a knight of the realm.

Somehow, Meldrik seemed to sense it. He knew the man living in Cradawg as Gray didn't belong, and in his own gruff way he made sure Graeham knew that was all right. Graeham paid him back not just by serving ale but by providing the muscle that kept the inn and tavern safe along this lonely road. The Green Stag occupied his nights; his herbal gardening and medicines consumed his days and gave him yet another way to repay those who had made this second life possible. It was easier to focus on the aches and pains of Cradawg than on his own. Tinctures of willow for their hurting muscles, swabs of chamomile for their teething babes, infusions of hawthorn for their pounding temples.

They accepted him on his terms. They never asked about his past, where he'd come from, and Graeham knew it was more than respect for his privacy. They didn't *want* to know Graeham's secrets.

They knew he was an outlaw.

The noise from the fire rose as the monks burst into a roar of joint laughter at something the merchant had said. The merchant pounded the table beside him and barked for more ale. Meldrik's face mottled.

"If that man doesn't leave tomorrow, I'll have to have ye throw him out," Meldrik muttered. "Almost needed ye yesterday, I tell ye true."

"Yesterday?"

"Knights. Thought they were going to knock out the damn merchant's boy."

"What were they fighting about?"

"They were searching for a girl," Meldrik said, shrugging. "Some missing noble girl—run away from her home. The merchant's boy said something about the character of a girl who'd take off on her own, and next thing ye know, the damn knight had him on the floor with his hands round the lad's throat."

Graeham's chest tightened. *Elayna hadn't become separated from her party. She'd run away. It had to be her.*

But why? It wasn't like the Elayna he'd known over four years ago. She'd loved her family, her home. It bothered him that she would have a reason to flee it. He thought about her shorn hair, the binding of her breasts, the masculine clothing.

Had she been planning to fob herself off as a boy? What sort of insane scheme had she embarked upon?

He put down the cloth he'd been using to clean the bar, keeping his face expressionless. "Where did these knights come from?" He didn't breathe, just waited for the confirmation of his tortured hunch.

"Castle Wulfere," Meldrik said. "Thank the saints they've moved on."

Graeham forced his hands to unclench, realizing only then that when he'd dropped them to his sides he'd fisted them so tensely, his blunt nails had nearly drawn blood from his palms.

"And by the time they return," Meldrik continued, "the merchant will be gone. Or sliced in twain. Either one."

"By the time they return?" Graeham picked up on Meldrik's remark.

"They said they'd be back if they don't find the lady elsewhere. They're searching everywhere." Meldrik looked annoyed. "They're offering a reward for any information about her. Wasting their time in Cradawg, that they are."

The night stretched interminably before him. He took the pitcher of ale and crossed the tavern room to fill the merchant's cup. When he returned, Meldrik was haggling with a pair of jongleurs. The inn had only four rooms to let, and they were already taken. The jongleurs accepted a bed of straw in the stable and their meals in return for providing the evening's entertainment.

Caitrin bustled in with generous trenchers of the plain, solid fare the inn served, and the jongleurs set down their instruments—a cittern and a vielle—on the floor by the bar and dived into the food.

The rest of the evening went according to routine. He went through the motions of cleaning, serving, tending the tavern tap. It was simple toil most nights, broken by the occasional brawl for which his fearsome demeanor—cultivated deliberately for the anonymity and distance it provided—came in handy.

But there was nothing routine about the trouble that waited for him in his hut. He took care of one aspect of the problem before he left for the night.

He advised Meldrik to recruit a few lads from the village to take his place. Graeham wasn't sure when he'd be back.

The moon was high in a cloudless black sky when he rode away from the inn. Graeham stopped at the edge of the forest and stared into its thick, haunted boughs, twisted and ancient. It was his haven, his home—at least it had been. Now she was there.

Turning his horse toward his hut, he walked his steed quietly through the whispering trees, one hand gripping the reins, the other holding fast to the bag of goods Auda always sent home with him—bread, cake, chicken, whatever was left over in the kitchen at the end of the evening.

Would Elayna be awake now? She had rested easily all this day, the fever having passed sometime during the previous night. Her wound was healing, though it was no doubt still painful. He knew what it felt to be run through with a sword, if not a boar's tusk.

It would be days before she could travel comfortably, or even move about very much without running the risk of reopening the wound, which only created more complications.

He thought of the knights of Castle Wulfere who'd passed through Cradawg. He had to convince her to go to the inn to await them. Then he would have to disappear for a while, stay out of sight until she was gone.

Damon would be back; that much was clear. Would she wait for him? After all, he didn't know why she'd run away.

The memory of those painful candle eyes flashing at him, the way she'd flailed her arms—in fear of him, but also in foolish courage—snapped across his mind. She was proud and defiant, and if she was anything like the Elayna he remembered, she was stubborn. But this Elayna had been attacked by a boar, nearly killed. If she had any sense at all, she would be cowed by the experience.

He would leave her with Meldrik and Auda to await her brother's men. No one would ever have to know she had been with the son of her brother's enemy.

Unless she recognized him before he could get her out of his hut.

He refused to let his thoughts follow that possibility any further.

The hut rose in the darkness, a shadow looming low among the taller shadows of the trees encircling the clearing. He dismounted, put his horse in the small lean-to barn with a meal of hay, then pushed open the door of the hut, blinking into the hazy, dim light. It smelled like woodsmoke and cooked boar's meat and onions, and something feminine. Her.

At first, he thought she was gone, that it was only the vaporous memory of her that remained, then he realized she'd moved, somehow, despite her injury, and was huddled miserably against the back wall, half sitting, half slumped. And she was holding a knife directly at him.

She didn't look at all cowed.

CHAPTER SIX

He was back.

He'd saved her life, but that didn't ease Elayna's mind as she faced the man who filled the doorway of the hut.

"Don't come any closer." Her voice came out raspy, thin. She clutched the knife she'd found on the floor of the hut by the fire. It was small, probably a knife he used for eating. She couldn't truly resist him—she didn't possess the strength, nor did the weapon. She could imagine him swatting her—and it—aside as if they were nothing.

He just stood there, staring at her. Had he even heard her?

Then he moved, just slightly, one step, and his face came into the glow of the fire. "You shouldn't be sitting up," he said as if she'd never spoken at all. "You need to rest."

His words were kind despite their gruffness, and she yearned to give in to them. But she couldn't, not willingly. Her bluff was all she had.

There was a sack in his hand, and he set it on the

crude table before closing the small space between them. He rose over her, hulking shadow and form.

"I said, come no closer," she repeated.

He knelt, continuing to ignore her. He reached out and, with one deft move, took the knife out of her hand, revealing the futility of her bluff with ease.

"Do you remember what happened to you?" he asked. "You were in the forest. You were attacked by a boar."

She tipped her chin, pretending not to notice how easily he'd disarmed her. "Yes. I remember the forest, the boar." She remembered him too. Or she thought she did. She remembered his touch . . . or maybe she just remembered a dream. She wasn't certain now—of him, of anything.

Could this fierce man have touched her with such tenderness? How was that possible?

"Then you remember that I saved your life. I'm not going to kill you now."

He was frowning at her with impatient irritation. He'd saved her life, but he wasn't happy about it. She tried to tell herself this meant something good. She didn't want him to want her here. She didn't want him to be the living embodiment of every cautionary tale she'd ever been told about strangers . . . demons.

Even though he *looked* like every cautionary tale she'd ever been told about anything.

"Thank you for saving my life." She didn't like admitting she was helpless. She didn't want to trust him—and surprisingly, she realized he didn't want to trust her either.

She didn't know what his problem was, but she knew her own too well. Trusting him could be dangerous. Either he really *was* the embodiment of every young girl's nightmare, or he was something almost worse: a conscientious, honorable man who would march her straight back home to her brother's castle. And despite everything that had happened, she didn't want to go there.

Her rescuer—stranger, demon—pressed his hand against her cheek, then her forehead. His touch, unlike his face, was solid and shockingly gentle. *Tender as a dream.*

The tiny hut seemed to shrink further with his continued proximity.

"You're cool now," he said. "You were taken by fever. I thought—" He returned his hand to his side, didn't finish.

"How long have I been here?"

"This is the third day."

Three days, in this hut, cared for by this fearsome stranger.

She didn't let herself think about what that care must have entailed. It was too humiliating.

"Lie back." He pressed down on her shoulders.

She felt drenched with remarkable fatigue. She fought it, fought the scratchy comfort of the straw at her back. But continuing to hold her body upright, even with the support of the hut's wall, was too hard.

The stranger took hold of the blanket and lifted it away from her side. Instinctively, she reached for the material, holding it so that it covered her private parts, covering her nakedness as best as she could. He ignored her, as if he didn't notice that she had private parts, as if he didn't notice that she was a woman, as if he didn't notice that the rest of her body was even connected to the bandaged gash in her side.

"Where are the clothes I was wearing?" she asked, carefully avoiding looking at him. It was the only way she could pretend this wasn't happening. She'd wanted to dress in the extra tunics she'd brought with her in the satchel, but it had hurt to move that much. She'd tried.

"Had to cut them off to use as bandages. Didn't have anything else."

He spoke as if wasting words on her was more trouble than she was worth.

His touch was as efficient as his speech as he unbound the wound, slipping his arm under and around her, supporting her so that she barely felt as if he'd moved her at all.

"Who are you?" she said, finally forcing herself to look at him again.

He rebound the wound, pulled the thin blanket back down over it.

"My name is Gray." His glance skidded over her briefly.

"Gray of whence?"

"You will recover soon," the stranger said, not answering her question. "But you shouldn't move any more than necessary. I've bound your wound, and it's healing—but too much exertion will reopen it. There is an inn. There you will await your family as you heal. Men have been there already, searching for a missing noblewoman, offering a reward—"

"No!" She pushed up on her elbows—which was a mistake. She fell back, breathing harshly, but in spite of the pain, all she could think of was Damon's men, and Ranulf. "I am not the noblewoman they seek." She cast about for an explanation, anything but the truth. "I'm not a noblewoman at all. I— I was on my way to visit my sister near—near Glenmorgan. She has a new baby, and she's not well. I'm to tend her."

He stared at her with obvious disbelief. "Where is she? Let me send word to her that you are delayed. What happened to your traveling party? How did you end up in the woods alone?"

Her mind felt stupidly blank.

"Do you always travel to your sister's house dressed as a boy?" he added.

She reached instinctively for her hair, feeling the blunt, shorn ends. She had no answers.

The stranger said something under his breath that she couldn't quite catch. She caught the tone though. He was annoyed, but his hands were still gentle. From somewhere the remains of her squire's tunic appeared in his arms.

"I bade you not move." His curt voice was in stark opposition to his touch. He lifted her head to push the balled-up remnants of her tunic behind her, picking up her shoulders and raising her body into a partial sitting position. "You need food, drink." He settled her against the makeshift cushioning and took her chin in his hands now, regarding her with his severe eyes. "You're pale. You've had naught but the small portion of water I could pass between your lips these past days. Take this."

He let go of her to take up a small pitcher she hadn't noticed before. He poured water into a metal cup that he took from beside the fire and held it to her lips.

It was warm but pure. She was more thirsty than she'd realized, and hungry too. But her mind was fixed on her plight.

She pushed his hand away.

"Drink. 'Tis all I have, it will have to do."

She blinked, realizing belatedly that he thought she was rejecting the water. As if she might be expecting fine sweet wine instead.

"I'm not thirsty," she lied.

"Drink anyway." He shoved the cup into her hand.

He turned away, stood, strode across the small hut to a crude table in the shadows against the opposite wall, and opened the sack he'd brought in with him. She couldn't see what he removed from it but knew he'd placed something in the bowl. He returned to the fire and scraped bits of boar meat into the bowl with his knife. The meat had been roasting for days, and she could see the seared flesh shred easily into the vessel.

Her stomach growled despite her abhorrence to the meat itself. It made her sick to think of the boar.

"I don't want to eat that."

"You will hinder me if you're weak, and I've no patience for that." He pushed the bowl at her the same way he'd pushed the cup. "Eat. Then you will tell me the truth. No more of your lies."

"I'm not lying."

"You are lying, Elayna of Wulfere." He pushed the cup to her mouth.

Her name on his lips shocked her. She choked on the liquid he forced on her.

He cursed beneath his breath and wiped at her mouth with a cloth. She hated his assistance, hated her own weakness.

She refused to acknowledge his assertion of her identity right away. *Think!* she demanded of herself. She had to think. It was this stranger and his care, or her brother's men and marriage to Ranulf. Neither option was what she wanted. She felt light-headed. Maybe food would help. Maybe he was right about at least that. She would eat, and then she would think.

She didn't acknowledge that she was simply putting off the inevitable, facing a dire situation.

There was bread and some kind of cake, and of course the meat. She forced herself to pick at the food, even the shredded, seared boar's flesh. It was tender, blackened from days over the fire, but not terrible. It was terrible only if she thought about those wild red eyes coming at her. She didn't allow herself to do that.

He didn't look at her as she ate, though she sensed he was aware of every move she made, every bite she took.

She set the cup and bowl down. She felt a small surge of strength from the nourishment, enough that she could even bear the throbbing pain in her side. Pushing up on her hands, she settled into a more upright position.

He took away the cup and bowl, proving she was right—he knew every breath she took whether he appeared to be paying attention to her or not.

"Now," he said abruptly, "I will have none of your lies. Tomorrow, when the sun rises, we go to the inn. Your brother will return, and you can go home."

"I don't want to go home." She made a quick decision to give up on the lies since they seemed only to serve to irritate him. She would have to depend on the truth, or what measure of it she was willing to give him.

"Why not?" The ruthless piercing of his gaze, the sheared-off tone of his question, stunned her for a moment.

She swallowed hard. This close, she could see the flecks of gold in his dark eyes. Firelight glimmered around him, his powerful body shielding the hut's hearth from her. It made him look fierce and magical in silhouette, the only light in his face burning from the depths of his eyes, alive with a fire of their own.

"I have my reasons."

"Your reasons almost got you killed," he said with no sympathy.

"My brother wants to see me wed." She felt vulnerable and emotional suddenly. She didn't want to explain her feelings to this stranger, this mysterious, dangerous-looking man.

"Is that why you left dressed as a boy?"

"A man," she corrected him. He irritated her too. His attitude reminded her of Damon's, as if she didn't know what was best for her. Protective. Then she shook herself. Why would she sense this stranger wanted to protect her? He wanted to get rid of her.

"So your brother wants you to be wed," the stranger said, ignoring her last assertion. "And what do you want?"

His question surprised her. She wasn't accustomed to anyone asking what she wanted.

"I want—" She didn't even know how to answer that question. The truth was, she wasn't entirely sure what she wanted. *Destiny.* But that sounded too stupid, so she wouldn't say it aloud. Gaining employment as a copyist was a start, a path. She wasn't sure where the path would lead. She just wanted to find out. "Independence," she said finally. He looked like a man who would understand a need for independence.

"To be wed is a woman's obligation to her family, her king."

His tone was dismissive. Why had he even asked what she wanted? She was stupidly disappointed in his response, as if she'd thought for just a moment that he was different from other men. But he wasn't.

She thought of the cache of coins inside her satchel. Money. That was all men cared about. "I can pay." Her remaining money was probably nothing in comparison to Damon's reward, but it would have to do. "Let me stay here—just until I'm well enough to travel." She couldn't believe she was asking this. She was desperate and probably not thinking clearly. She knew that but didn't know what other choice she had at the moment. She couldn't go to the inn until she was well enough to travel immediately. Well enough to outwit her brother's men should she cross their paths.

"I don't want your money," he said.

"You need money. You must." The smoky, firelit hut seemed to fade back into nothingness as his relentless falcon eyes bored into her with unreadable ice.

"I don't need *your* money. Tomorrow at first light I will take you to the inn. You will be well enough to be moved. You can pay for a room at the inn as well as you could pay me, and you'll have a better bed for it. There will be no further discussion." His voice was final. He turned and walked away from her, toward the door of the hut.

Where was he going? She pushed to her feet, not even thinking that she couldn't, forgetting her wound. The pain hit her immediately, bringing it all back, but she made it to a wobbly stand anyway.

"Wait! I'm sorry. It's just that I—" She stumbled, half fell from the effort, dizziness swooping over her.

She didn't see him, just felt him—his strong hands gripping her, his warm breath against her face as he pulled her into his arms, his hard voice brushing her. "God's bones, lady. Will you stay where you're put? Has this injury made you daft?"

He settled her back against the straw pallet again, arranging the makeshift cushion behind her head, his movements both tender and abrupt. The smoky dark straw roof of the hut seemed to spin.

She grabbed his sleeve, fighting the cloud that threatened to suck her in. His piercing eyes were her only hold on consciousness.

A flash of something ephemeral streaked across her consciousness again as she stared up at him.

"You remind me of someone," she blurted out,

staring at him as hard as she could, fighting to hold on, the pain sucking her down into the dark. Even his falcon eyes couldn't hold her back.

Was his grip tighter? She struggled to focus the ephemeral impression.

"Who?" he demanded. "Who do I remind you of?"

His voice was harsh, and yes, he *was* holding her tighter. But it was too late. The sea of darkness was already sweeping her in.

CHAPTER SEVEN

Graeham worked in the silence of the forest, his feet and arms moving in the familiar patterns of swordsmanship, albeit the solo form he practiced now. It was an aspect of his old life that he had carried with him into the new. He had loved the art of knighthood, and carrying that pleasure, in some small way, with him had been the thing that had pulled him through. He had spent years culti-vating not only muscle memory but mental strength, focus. He'd needed that focus here in this wild wood—to forget the past, to forget the pain, to forget the betrayal.

It had taken a few days for one woman to break that focus.

He held his sword out, staring down the gleaming point. *People saw what they expected to see.* He had depended on that truth for so long. No one expected to see Graeham of Penlogan-by-the-sea tending a tavern in Cradawg, living in a hut in the wood. Part hermit. Part healer. *Part ghost.* No one expected to see Graeham alive at all.

Men he'd known all his life had passed through the inn and not recognized him. And it was more than his location that had changed in four and a half years. He'd become a man full-grown—taller, broader. Crueler. Dead.

You remind me of someone.

He tipped his head and opened his eyes to cast a brief, baleful gaze heavenward, wondering what saint was toying with him thusly. He felt the weight of his father's honor, and even his own—both tarnished, both deep. Even if she didn't recognize him, she was trouble. Would he have to take her to the inn against her will?

Or would he have to take an entirely different approach? If she recognized him—

That would be terribly dangerous. For both of them. The question, in that case, would be how he could let her go at all?

Birds twittered in the trees high above him. He'd gone some short distance from the hut to a sweet grassy glade surrounded by the sheltering forest. A stream tumbled over rocks, tinkling as it splattered over the stones and through the secret crevices of its timeworn path. The early morning was pleasantly cool, the air redolent with the still-recent scent of rain. He held his sword in his right hand, moved it downward, then abruptly over his head, his boot pivoting on the soft earth at the same time.

The concentration he normally reserved for this daily physical practice battled with the memory of Elayna's candleglow eyes. He hadn't allowed sentiment in his life for a long time.

The dawning sun gleamed off his blade, and he hated her for bringing back everything he'd sought to leave behind forever.

The bustle of the tournament swirled with color and pageant, the tall towers of Castle Wulfere rising above the crowded field. It had been Graeham's first tourney in which he would participate as a knight rather than a squire. His blood was pumping—everything was brighter, hotter, more real that day.

That was when he'd seen Elayna. She had twined a garland of flowers in her long, dark hair, and the white blossoms stood out like stars over her brow.

"A kiss for luck, sweet Elayna?" He bowed with flair. Newly knighted, he was still more boy than man, but suddenly he wanted her to see the man.

"I am not sweet," she said saucily. "And you will need more than luck to win this day, Sir Graeham."

He straightened and stared down at her, taking advantage of the height he had gained over her now.

He'd always liked the banter between them—but there was a new edge now. They had ever provoked each other as children, thrown together often by their fathers' friendship. Now, with his father and her brother away on the Continent, it had been years since he'd seen her. He'd heard celebrations were rare at Castle Wulfere these days, with her father in physical decline and her mother dead.

He had seen the old lord, and he didn't look well. It was rumored this was one last gasp of glory, a stab at bringing light back into a darkened castle.

Nothing, and everything, had changed—for himself, for Castle Wulfere, and for Elayna. But one thing remained the same—that sauciness. And it was only then that he realized how he'd missed it, and that it had been more than childish play.

"What will I need, Lady Elayna?" he inquired. "Tell me." His voice was quiet, meant for her ears alone. The crowd around them seemed insignificant and far away.

"I think you need your ego clipped." Her eyes glowed. She enjoyed their sparring too.

"And you are just the one to clip it?"

"You will clip it on your own if you take the field with your usual arrogance."

He laughed deeply. Oh, he'd missed her rudeness. She always said what she meant.

"You aren't like other ladies," he said. "I like that."

"Then I shall be like other ladies simply to plague you."

But she was not like other ladies. There were a dozen damsels who would have offered him their token, but he wanted hers. She was different. She always had been.

"For old time's sake," he said, "it would please me to carry your token in the tournament this day."

"For what old times?" she tossed back. "For the old time when we played hoodman blind and you talked everyone into running away to hide, leaving me wandering, blindfolded, alone in the garden? Or the old time when you put a squirrel in my bed? Or the old time when you rigged a pail of water over the privy door? Or—"

"I had no idea you would be the next one to push upon the privy door," he pointed out, laughing. "And you had put flour inside my helmet right before I went out upon the practice field the day before."

He could see her biting the inside of her mouth and knew she wanted to laugh at the memory. Saints, she looked beautiful in that brilliant blue day. Young, still on the verge of womanhood, and yet certainly no longer a child. She was old enough for kissing, and he realized quite suddenly that he wanted to be her first, and quite possibly, her last, and every one in between.

"Fine," she said. "So then we're even. I owe you no token." She turned as if to march away.

"Would it not please you to honor the winner?" he said, pushing her with his arrogance. It was the one sure way to bring out her own.

She turned back, her dark eyes alight with fire that matched his.

"What do you want, sir knight?" she had asked.

"I want a kiss," he had said.

She laughed, but there was something in her gaze, a

*certain spark, a heat, and he knew she felt the same
attraction he did.*

*"Win, sir knight," she said softly, "then you can have
any token you please."*

Something slipped. The sword. Graeham broke
from the past with a sudden sweating jerk. The
cool air brushed his hot brow, and the present
slammed back onto him.

Memories were cruel—the ones he had, the ones
he'd lost. For a long time he'd fought within in
his own mind for control of them. He'd woken in
Cradawg four and a half years ago in a dim, smoky
hut—the home of the old wet nurse of Thomas,
his father's squire. He had been a few weeks and
a lifetime away from Penlogan by then—suffering
from a fever and deep wound. His recovery had
been gradual and agonizing. Thomas had filled in
the missing pieces of that night, but he couldn't
fill in all of them. They'd come back in painful
increments, in flashes that seared his mind, until
the picture of that night was as complete as he
believed it would ever be. There were holes in his
memories that had never been filled.

Everything else had come back, his life before
that night. Elayna.

He had had to learn to forget her. He hadn't
learned well enough.

He had thought that fine week of tournament
at Castle Wulfere was only the beginning. But it
had been the end instead. She should have been
wed to someone else by now. Why she hadn't been,
he didn't know. But she would be soon, apparently,
if her brother had his way.

He gripped his sword more tightly, forcing his
mental slate to clear. The concentration was hard-
won. But the past—and its innocence—was long
gone.

* * *

She was waiting for him in the doorway of the
hut, the thin blanket pulled about her, as if it were
the finest cotehardie, her posture regal. Her chin-
length hair, short as it was, was tangled and wild.
Her eyes were fiercely luminous. Scared.

Fine. Let her be scared, he thought grimly. Yet
the look of her still bothered him.

"What are you doing, lady? Hie thee back to bed
before you faint and I must be bothered to carry
you there. I have food for you to give you strength,
and you must rest. A room at the inn awaits you,
and as soon as you can travel, I will take you there.
Do not even think to pester me with your lies this
morning."

His rudeness brought a flush to her pale cheeks,
and just as he'd known it would, it straighted her
spine, hardened her mouth, though she didn't
loosen her grip on the doorjamb. She was supporting herself, he realized, and that irritated him too.
She should have been abed, but he wasn't surprised
that she was too stubborn to stay there.

He also realized she was still staring at him, as
if she couldn't stop. A prickle of uneasiness crept
down his spine.

"What are *you* doing?" Her voice was cool, but
there was a shake to it that she couldn't hide.

He gripped his sword more tightly and paced
toward her. "If I told you the answer to that question," he said dangerously as he reached her,
"then I couldn't let you walk out of this forest alive.
So if you know what's good for you, lady, you won't
ask. You'll just do what I say." It was deliberate
now. If nothing else, he would scare her away.

"Who are you?"

His uneasiness heightened. "My name is Gray.
I told you that."

"No, it's not."

He felt his heart clench again as she reached up so very tentatively and touched his face as if trying to know him in some way that her eyes couldn't accept.

"I can hardly believe it— It can't be true, but it is, isn't it?" she whispered.

She wouldn't stop staring at him. She whispered one last word softly, and yet it was as if she'd hit him with a mace.

"Graeham?"

CHAPTER EIGHT

He jerked away from her, and she dropped her hand.

"My name is Gray."

All Elayna could do was wonder how she had ever not recognized him, even half aware, injured, and ill. And yet at the same time, she could scarcely believe what she was seeing, thinking. Graeham was dead!

But he was very much alive and there before her.

"No," she argued. "I know you. I don't care what you call yourself. I would know you anywhere. 'Tis my side that was wounded, not my head."

He slanted a sardonic brow, and oh, how familiar it suddenly was. How many times had he cocked his brow that way at her, teasing her.

"Your wits, mayhap, were wounded before you left Castle Wulfere."

"Say what you will, I do not believe you." She spoke calmly in spite of the quiver in her veins. "You're alive. You're—" She broke off, just needing to stare at him some more. His identity had hit her the instant she'd woken this morn, though she hadn't been able to completely accept it till now, till she'd faced him. She'd kept telling herself she'd imagined the resemblance, but— It was not her imagination. "You're Graeham of Penlogan."

And yet he was a stranger. For all that was familiar about him, there was so much that was not. Graeham had never looked like this—cold, harsh, dead and yet not dead at the same time. It was not his body that was cold—it was his eyes.

"You're supposed to be dead," she said, her heart thumping. "How—" She didn't know how to go on, what she wanted to say. There was so much to say, so much to ask.

If I told you the answer to that question, I couldn't let you walk out of this forest alive.

She didn't believe him. He wouldn't hurt her. He'd told her that, and she was more sure of it than ever now that she knew who he was. Graeham wouldn't hurt her. But he didn't want her asking these questions.

"Cease this witless prattle."

He was so close now that she fancied she could feel the warmth emanating from his powerful body. Something quickened inside her.

"It's not witless prattle if it's true." She sounded breathless now. She hated that. She was not one of those demure, breathless damsels. She was strong-willed, or so her brother accused her.

But she was also off her guard, unsettled, shocked.

"It's even more witless if it is true, lady. Don't you see? You're lost in the middle of the wood, alone, attacked." His gaze didn't flinch from hers while he spoke. "Vulnerable to whatever—or who-ever—comes upon you."

Was that a threat? She couldn't tell. She could read nothing in those relentless falcon eyes that were so familiar and so strange all at once.

No, this wasn't the Graeham she'd known. That Graeham had been funny and sweet. This Graeham didn't look as if he'd laughed in a long time.

"You're supposed to be dead."

"I'm alive." He shrugged those massive shoulders. "You reveal your own foolishness. You speak of a dead man to one who is far from that state."

He made as if to move past her into the hut, but she touched him again, just barely, and stopped him. He was even closer now, and it was as if his nearness sucked the air from her chest. There was awareness, a spark of something she hadn't felt in a long time. Something she'd wanted to feel again—but not now. Not with him. He was alive, but—

He had committed a terrible crime. He had killed her own brother's men. He had defied the king. He had committed treason, treachery, betrayal. Murder. She had to remind herself of all of it. How could she forget? And yet she had the awful feeling she could, if she stared into his eyes for too long, if she came too close to him again. If—

"No." She swallowed thickly. "I'm not wrong. I don't know how or why, but I know you. You're Graeham. You're—" She didn't know what she wanted to say. Her mind was reeling.

"My name is Gray." He dropped the sword on the ground behind him and gripped her shoulders, shook her slightly. "Say it. Say you believe it."

"No," she said with a bravado that had been hard won from years of fighting for herself and her sisters, especially during the terrible time after her father had died and they had been alone, before Damon had returned home from France. "I'm not wrong. I don't know how you came to be here, why you're here, but I know who you are."

She tried to pull away from him, but he wouldn't

let her go. Her knees shook, and maybe it was just
as well that he was all but holding her up.

"What are you doing here? All this time, I—" She
stopped, suddenly feeling choked. All this time—
what? She had mourned him, blamed him. Loved
him. And it was all somehow worse to realize that
he had been alive. Anger surged, replacing the
fear and confusion for a moment. "Why did you
do it? Why did you kill Damon's men? Why did you
betray everything the king offered you, everything
that Damon offered you—for what? Revenge?
Why?"

She wasn't caring now how his fingers dug into
her arms. "It was one thing to believe you were
dead—but you were alive all this time."

There was a lump in her throat as huge as an
apple, and she couldn't swallow past it to ask the
last question that burned so hotly in her mind—
and had for years.

How could you love revenge more than you loved me?

"You were alive, and hiding. Why? Couldn't you
face the truth of your father's crimes? Your own
crimes? At least your father faced his judgment.
You pretended to be dead—by your own hand, no
less! You killed those men, burned your own castle,
and fell on your sword. That was what they said!
That was what you wanted them to think! How
did you do it? And all along—you had run away!
Coward! Murderer!" she spat at him, not caring
that his fingers dug into her arms, not caring about
anything but that her heart—that she had thought
had been safeguarded behind a stone wall these
past four years and more—was not safe. It couldn't
hurt this much if it were. He had simply looked at
her, and the walls had crumbled and all the pain
had been revealed.

He watched her with those eyes that seemed so
familiar and so strange at once. So cold. There was

anger inside him that matched her own, maybe even exceeded it, and she couldn't understand it. He didn't deserve anger. He deserved shame.

But there was no shame in his eyes. There was an acceptance suddenly—in his stance, in his expression. A determination that sent a chill down her spine. It was as if something dreaded had come true. He had known she might recognize him.

He had waited. He had given her every chance to back out of it, to claim she knew she was wrong, to accept that he was this stranger, Gray.

She had made a terrible mistake. In her anger and shock, she had not seen it coming.

"You shouldn't be here, and you're too stubborn to see it." He moved his grip from her arms to catch her face in his hands. She felt frozen in place. "If you'd had any sense at all, you would never have left your home, your world, where you belong, where you're safe. But you have left it—you are in my world now, and you don't belong here and you're not safe."

Her feet were rooted. Her knees weren't shaking anymore. She couldn't *feel* her knees. She felt caught up in his hard stare.

It was too late. She couldn't do anything to change the words she'd already spoken. She couldn't pretend she didn't recognize him and that she didn't care.

She'd let her emotions get her in trouble, and there was no way out. She had to brazen her way through whatever was coming.

He leaned forward, closer, still staring at her as if memorizing her features. Relearning them. She found her gaze caught on his beautiful harsh mouth, remembering—

"Why did you run away from your home, lady?" he demanded, his words so soft, they were like breaths that she felt more than heard.

Her heart thumped within her. She jerked herself out of the memories.

How could she explain that she was running away from a destiny that would destroy her soul to a man who looked as if his were long gone?

"I've already explained." She made herself as stiff as she could, not wanting him to feel how much he affected her. She would not explain her spirit's dreams and hopes to the man who'd nearly destroyed them over four years ago. She was just now recovering from what he'd done, all the while that he had let her believe he was dead. "And I am no lady. Not anymore."

His mouth tightened. He moved one hand to touch a curling lock that brushed her jaw.

"Your hair—" He stopped, examined her.

She wondered if he could see all the way inside her. What would he think if he knew her thoughts? Would he make more sense of them than she could?

"You look foolish," he said abruptly. "You should not have cut your hair. You can cut your hair, bind your breasts, dress in tunics. But you are a lady whether you want to be or not."

Her chest tightened and she felt her skin heat. She didn't want to remember that he'd undressed her, that he'd tended her, removed the binding. She didn't want to talk about it, or anything that reminded her of it.

"Thank you so much for that unsolicited counsel," she said. "But I'm not interested in your opinion—of my hair or anything else."

"You'd better get interested." He gave her a little shake, both hands gripping her shoulders again. "This is my world, not yours. And trust me, you are not prepared for it."

"You can stop acting as if you are some mad hermit," she said, staring him down. "You won't hurt me, so stop trying to scare me. I know you, Graeham. You won't hurt me."

She prayed her words were true. Her certainty was diminishing. Hadn't she already pointed out that he was a murderer?

But she knew, too, that she was too weak from her injury yet to flee him. She needed his help, at least for then. She had to believe there was some shred of decency and honor in him. She had to demand it of him.

And later—

She didn't know what to think about later. He'd rescued her, but now she was unsure of where she stood. Now she had recognized him. What did that mean?

What was he going to do with her—or to her?

He stared at her a moment longer, and she felt strange, full of too many conflicting emotions.

"I'm not this man, this Graeham, that you remember. What you knew of him is right—he is dead. And you, lady— What you know of *me* is right too. I'm a nasty son of a bitch. I'm a man capable of murder. You should have left when you had the chance." His eyes looked bleak and endless. "You have no idea what you have done."

CHAPTER NINE

He watched her, dark and unallowable emotions clenching his chest, and he knew he would have to deal with them sometime, but not then. She didn't know yet what she'd done, what it meant, but he couldn't afford to sympathize with her. She could destroy him.

"What—what are you going to do with me?"

She had the nerve to ask.

"To begin with, get in the hut," he ordered curtly, fixing a scowl on his face as he pushed past her into the dim interior of the hut. He didn't want to tell her that he needed time to figure it out.

She was no longer an annoyance, an unwanted guest. Whether she fully realized it or not, now she was a prisoner. He couldn't let her go—but how could he keep her?

The situation was impossible.

He realized she wasn't moving to obey him, and he stopped short, pivoted, impatient. "I must see how your wound fares today."

"I can take care of myself," she objected from the doorway.

She took a step as if to prove her vigor.

He saw her suck in a breath, and he cursed as she did so.

"You're in pain."

"I'm fine," she repeated, but her proud voice was damnably faint.

"You're not fine. You need to rest. You won't get up from that pallet again until I give you leave to rise." He moved to take her arm. She tried to pull it back, but he wouldn't let her. "You need to cause me no more trouble than necessary. You will follow my commands." He stopped before the pallet. "Lie down while I fetch the salve. Your dressing must be changed."

He arranged the wadded remains of her tunic atop the pallet to provide support for her head. "This salve will make your wound heal faster." He turned back toward her.

"Then give it to me. I'll tend my own wound."

He withheld the pot of salve, a part of him annoyed and another part concerned. He wanted to see to her wound himself, to see that she was recovering properly. He was the healer, not she. But there was a part of him that knew it was more than that.

A tight beat passed in which neither of them moved.

"Lady, you are more trouble than you are worth." He was stunned to see moisture welling up in her eyes. She blinked it away furiously. "I will not have any of your womanish tears," he said, pushing on before he was felled by those womanish tears. "You will—"

"I will not," she choked out without even waiting to find out what he was going to tell her to do. "I have no clothes. You've seen me naked, washed

me, tended me—'' She broke off. "Just give me
the salve and let me take care of myself. I am no
physician, but I'm well acquainted with the tending
of wounded. I know what I'm doing." Her candleglow eyes blazed at him, determined.

He felt awkward and at a loss. He had seen her
nude body—there had been no other way. He
hadn't had a chance to think of how much it would
bother her. He had thought too much of how it
had bothered him.

He realized suddenly that she was trembling
where she stood.

She was so much weaker than she wanted him
to know, and the longer they stood there arguing,
the weaker she grew.

"You're working yourself into a state over nothing," he said roughly, shoving the pot of salve at
her.

She took it, still not meeting his eyes, and she
waited. He realized she wasn't going to do anything
else until he turned his back to her.

"Be quick about it." He braced himself against
any feelings at the sound of her soft gasp, followed
by the even more agonizing sound of silence as he
knew she must have been biting her lip bloody to
keep from gasping again in pain as she applied
the salve and redressed the wound.

There was no sniffling, no more evidence of
tears.

Damn her courage. Not that he wanted a bawling
woman on his hands, but her courage was almost
worse.

"I'm finished."

Her eyes were shiny and intent on him as he
turned. She was seated on the pallet, the pot of
salve beside her.

He didn't know what to do next.

"There's meat," he said. The boar meat was

tough and dry now, but he had little else to offer her to break her fast. He refused to feel inhospitable about it. He had not asked for her company.

He scooped some of the meat into a bowl for her.

She didn't respond and he paced toward her, stopping so he towered over her. From this position, she looked defenseless and small, and for that moment he experienced the sudden urge to gather her into his arms and reassure her—of what, he didn't even know.

He had no reassurance, for her or himself.

"Here, eat," he demanded, pushing the bowl into her hands.

"I'm not hungry," she said snappishly. "I can think for myself, thank you very much."

He cocked a brow, knowing a reluctant admiration which he squelched with deliberate care.

"You don't seem capable of it. If you'd been thinking clearly, you'd be at Castle Wulfere right now, breaking your fast with mead and sweetbread at your leisure, waited on by servants who quake at your every command. But you're not at Castle Wulfere. You're in my hut. You follow my rules. I say we eat now—and this is what we're eating. So, eat."

She took the bowl, though she subjected him to a look that told him she didn't care for his attitude.

"You don't have to be unpleasant," she commented. "Have you forgotten all the courtly manners you ever knew?"

"If you want to be treated like a lady, then act like one. Ladies don't travel the countryside alone. They don't run away from their homes, their families, and find themselves living in forest huts with strange men."

He thought she might remind him again that

she was no lady, but she let it slide. She went on her own attack.

"You're not a stranger."

He scooped out a bowl of the meat for himself, pulled up the stool to the fire, and began to eat. He preferred not to look at her. She was relentlessly stubborn, always had been. And she was a distraction, even disheveled as she was. Her fine-boned beauty disturbed him.

How such an irritating, difficult, contentious woman could be so fascinating at the same time was a mystery he didn't want to solve. He had other problems that loomed larger now. Like how to get rid of her and yet keep his secrets.

"What are you going to do with me?" she asked, evidently undeterred by the fact that he'd decided to ignore her.

"What should I do with you?" he returned without glancing back at her.

Was he actually hoping she'd have a solution?

"Help me," she suggested.

He hated the sound of her voice, low, hopeful, as if she couldn't quite stop believing in—what? Magic, miracles, life, love— He didn't know. It didn't matter. He'd stopped believing in any of them a long time before.

"I can't help you," he countered, still refusing to look at her. If the sound of her voice did such awful things to his insides, how much worse was it to look at her? He would avoid it as much as he could, he resolved. "You shouldn't be here. You shouldn't have run away from your home. You shouldn't have gotten yourself gored by that wild boar."

He took another bite of his food and told himself he didn't care that she could have died. His life just then would be a hell of a lot simpler if she *had* died.

Yet he knew that he didn't want his life simpler, not that way.

"You shouldn't be here either, Graeham," she remarked with her irritating persistence. "You shouldn't have run away from Penlogan, feigned your own death. You shouldn't have defended your father's crime—"

He put down the bowl, pulse jumping in his jaw, and he resisted the urge to spin around and roar at the injustice of her words. She believed what the rest of the world believed. A lie.

"You think you know so much about this Graeham of whom you speak?" he asked with a control that cost him. He slowly turned. "Were you there?" He didn't give her a chance to answer. "You think you know so much, lady? Or do you just believe everything you hear? Are you that stupid?"

There was nothing but the crack of the low fire for a long beat.

"Do you think *you* know so much?" Her voice was still low, but her eyes fierce. "I judge you only as much as you judge me. I'm naught but a spoiled girl running from my pampered tower, is that what you think? I should be home in my castle, tended by servants. However empty that life is doesn't matter? Is that right?"

She stopped, as if she had said more than she wanted to. He thought her voice had cracked just a little, but he wasn't sure.

Was there more to Elayna's story than appeared on the surface—a spoiled, defiant aristocrat playing a stubborn game of will with her family? The Elayna he remembered had been a complicated girl—loving, strong, proud, rebellious.

He didn't want to think about the past.

"I don't want to be the judge of you, lady." He turned away from those fierce eyes of hers because he felt things he didn't want to feel when he looked into them. "I just want to be left alone. Most people have the sense to give me my wish."

The remainder of the meal was completed in silence. Not that Elayna wanted to break it. She didn't know what to say to this Graeham. The Graeham she'd known had teased, played with her as a child, loved her as a young woman, promised her a future that he hadn't delivered.

And this Graeham—he made no promises at all. And that was somehow more frightening than anything else.

He hadn't come right out and said she was a prisoner, but she knew it just the same. She was trapped in a web of her own making.

I'm not this man, this Graeham that you remember. They were right about him—he is dead.

His words haunted her. She watched his hard profile. He had changed physically—that much was obvious. She could almost, in brief moments, still question his identity. He had grown—his shoulders and chest were massive. His legs below his short, plain tunic were muscular, long. He was taller, stronger, different in so many ways. Even his face had changed—his jaw harder, his mouth crueler. His eyes burned cold and hot all at once, reminding her of the candle boats they sailed across the pond every Midsummer's Eve—fire floating on water. His eyes were like those candle boats—water and fire. Hot and cold. Life and death.

He'd changed inside too.

She finished eating, and he took the bowl. She would have offered to clean up, but he'd been so insistent about her resting. And the truth was, she was worn out from their confrontation. Not that she would have admitted that to him.

"Where am I?" she asked.

" 'Twas your journey, lady." He'd stoked the small fire, and he sat down again on the low stool, taking with him a small chunk of the wood. He began to use the knife he'd been eating with to whittle at it. "Where were you going?"

She suppressed a huff of annoyance. "I know where I was going. Obviously, I didn't get there."

"Hmm." He flicked at the wood. "And where was that?"

"None of your business." She didn't want to tell him anything. He knew too much about her already. And she knew too little of him.

He looked up from his carving, cocking a brow. "Then it's none of your business where you are now, lady," he replied.

A number of unladylike phrases leapt to her tongue, and she held them back with difficulty. She blew out a frustrated breath.

"Stop calling me lady. Graeham. Graeham of Penlogan." She added the last bit deliberately. If he was so determined to plague her, she would plague him back. He hid here, pretending to be someone he was not. She would not let him pretend with her.

He stopped whittling and looked up at her. "Did it ever occur to you that this is a dangerous game you play, lady?"

"It's not a game."

"Exactly," he said, and his voice was so hollow, she felt a rush of shivers take hold of her body. She pulled the thin blanket tighter around her.

He tossed down the piece of wood he'd been carving, leaving it a yet indecipherable lump.

"Rest while I am gone," he ordered. "I won't have you reopening your wound by needless moving about. You are here on my terms, not yours— and that means you will obey me. And do not think of running away from here. There is nowhere to go. You would be lost in a heartbeat. This forest is low and boggy, full of mists and unexpected dips and fearsome creatures that will eat you whole.''

With that, he left the hut. The wind rustled in the trees outside, and the fire sputtered pathetically within.

She wondered if he counted himself among the forest's fearsome creatures.

CHAPTER TEN

As a child, she had enjoyed being alone. She had sought out what isolation she could find, even commandeering the maid's antechamber for herself in the huge tower bedroom she shared with her three sisters.

But alone in Graeham's hut was a very different kind of alone than being alone in Castle Wulfere. At Castle Wulfere, she knew there were people just beyond the door. Many, many people. She could hear their raucous voices rising late at night from the great hall. She could look down from her tiny, slitted window to see guards marching out their watches on the wallwalks.

She could hear her sisters' whispers from the next room.

Here, she could hear only her heartbeat, fierce and heavy, in the tiny hut.

Graeham was nearby. He had to be. But he seemed determined to stay out of the hut as much as possible, leaving her alone. Avoiding her. She was both relieved and lonely.

He confused her. Just thinking about those intense falcon eyes made her stomach drop. She fought the peculiarness of the feeling, focusing her thoughts away from him with difficulty. Whatever had been between them was gone, long gone, dead as she thought he had been.

There had been no destiny between them, nothing that had been real. He had chosen his own destiny, and it had been a cruel, treacherous one. She couldn't feel anything for such a man.

She drew closer to the fire and stared into it, thinking of her home and her sisters instead, training her mind off Graeham and the bewilderment he instilled.

Was Gwyneth on the practice field, sneaking in among the squires the way she so often did, even now at fourteen? Damon had finally given Rorke, as his chief man-at-arms, permission to train her in the art of combat in an attempt to contain her persistent, unwomanly desires—but rather than contain her ambitions, it had fed them. She had approval only for private one-on-one lessons with a small, light blade, but that would never satisfy Gwyneth. She always wanted to be in the thick of the action, hefting weapons that would nearly send her reeling backward, the once-shorn hair Damon had ordered her to grow stuffed in a cap so she could blend in with the squires.

Damon had given the falconer orders to train Lizbet in falconry as well, and to the same end. Lizbet was more obsessed with birds than ever. She had her own cot in the corner of the mews and spent more nights there than in her bedchamber in the castle. When a young knight had visited in search of a betrothed, he'd found Gwyneth playing bat-and-ball in the mud, and Lizbet with feathers sticking out of her hair. Elayna had simply relied on her waspish tongue these past few years to keep her own suitors at bay.

Damon had not been amused by any of them.

And then there was Marigold—she had started out as the seamstresses' pet because she hid in their sewing room so often. She had since picked up their skills with needle and thread—and was fast becoming an expert dressmaker. Quiet, shy Marigold had already achieved a reputation among visiting ladies who clamored for her designs, which were artistic and unique. She often spent hours locked up with her sketch pad, creating her unusual patterns.

Elayna missed them all desperately, but she knew they were fine. Belle had become a mother to them, much more so than to Elayna. Elayna had been fourteen when Belle had come to Castle Wulfere, too old for a mother by then. She could remember feeling both jealous and relieved at Belle's arrival. Belle had taken so much better care of her family than Elayna had, only reinforcing Elayna's own feelings of failure. Belle never would have wanted her to feel that way, Elayna knew. But the feelings persisted just the same.

There had been a time when her family had needed her, when her father, and Damon, and even her sisters had been threatened. And Elayna had not done enough to save them.

She had not had the courage. It was one of the truths that made it easier to leave them. She was never quite sure she deserved her wonderful family.

Mayhap out there in the big, wide world she would find a way to believe in herself again.

Unwrapping herself from the blanket, she opened her satchel. It had occurred to her that he could simply steal her money—who was she to stop him? But it was still there. She examined the contents of the satchel, pulled out a spare tunic

and hose. She had only one pair of soft boots. He
had set them by the pallet. It hurt, just lifting her
arms to put the tunic on. She was too exhausted
to check the wound. She didn't want to look at it.
There would be a horrible scar. She didn't want
to think about it.

It was a good thing she'd decided to foray into
life as a boy now. She was less becoming as a woman
all the time. This didn't bother her as much as she
would have expected. She wasn't sure now why
she'd ever cared so much about hair ribbons and
gowns. Those accoutrements hadn't been *her*.
Beauty had been some sort of—what? Mask? Something to conceal and shroud her pain? If she looked
beautiful on the outside, then no one could guess
what was happening on the inside?

Her thoughts were confusing. She had never
thought of her life at Castle Wulfere this way
before. Somehow, getting away from it had crystal-
lized the falsity. She had been so very unhappy.
Even she had not realized *how* unhappy. With her
long hair and beauty creams and powders and
gowns gone, there was nothing to hide behind. It
was freeing and scary, especially considering she
was lost in a forest with the epitome of her pain—
Graeham. She would have to be very careful around
him. He was her weakness, and while truth was all
well and good to face within herself, it would be
dangerous to face with him.

He could still hurt her. She wasn't quite sure
how much truth she could handle on her own, and
especially how much she could handle in front of
Graeham. Secrets, lies. They were safe. Truth was
dangerous. And yet the yearning, stretching part
of herself wanted to face it, and she felt as con-
flicted as she felt confused.

Her truth, his truth . . . How much could she
face?

She tried to relax her thoughts. She needed to think about more practical matters, about how she would get to the city, to the booksellers district and the copyist shops. Graeham's hut was a place to recover, not a place to stay. The sooner she could get out of there, the better. Then she would be free of wondering about his truths, and free to face her own.

She frowned, staring back into the satchel. Something was missing.

Her erasing knives were gone.

A cold prickle swept up her back. He had not come right out and said she was a prisoner, but she was starting to feel like one. *You should have left when you had the chance.* Did that mean she couldn't leave now?

The erasing knives were hardly dangerous weapons, but still, they could be used in desperation.

He was not taking any chances that she would be that desperate. She swallowed thickly, looked around, wondered what he'd done with them. There was the huge chest. A heavy lock held it fast. Were her erasing knives in there? What else was in there? Answers to her questions? Secrets? Weapons, letters, clues? She had no way of finding out without the key, and she couldn't imagine getting hold of that item.

If Graeham slept, she hadn't noticed so far.

She turned back to the contents of the satchel, wondering what else Graeham had taken note of during his search of her satchel. There was the bound book of poetry that she loved. And there was her journal. Had he read it? She prayed not. It had been the place where she'd buried her heartache. It had been how she'd lived through losing him. She'd noted every season, every holiday, every birth and death, at Castle Wulfere. She'd written of visitors, suitors, her sisters, their servants.

It had been the only place she'd dared express her feelings about Graeham. She would have gone mad without it. The thought of him reading it—

She put her head down and forced her unquiet mind to clear. There was nothing she could do about it. Either he'd read it or he hadn't. She told herself she didn't care. She was still a good liar.

How long she slept, she didn't know. When she woke, it was with a start. She sat straight up, biting her lip to keep in the gasp of pain in her side from the too-swift movement, and realized that it had to be night. The journal slipped to the floor beside her. She hadn't even realized she'd fallen asleep holding it.

No light showed around the cracks of the door. She had slept the day away!

A rabbit, skinned and fat, and roasted over the low fire, so she knew Graeham must be close by. From somewhere outside, she heard a moan, just one, then more—low and hoarse and painful-sounding. For a moment, she thought it could be an animal, then she realized it was human.

She got up from the pallet, tossing the blanket over the stool, and crept to the door of the hut. She pushed the door slightly open.

It was even later than she'd realized. Moonlight ribboned down between openings in the tree canopy. The air outside was cold, and she shivered as the wind swirled in through the narrow gap of the door. A shadow fell down abruptly from a tree not far from the hut.

Not a shadow. Graeham.

She stared at him, unblinking. He looked like a dead man. He was hanging from his arms, she realized. From a branch. He made a sound, the low moaning she had heard, and she almost cried out in shock and relief. He was definitely alive.

His face was hidden to her, lost in the darkness. She could see his body, naked from the waist up, lit by a shaft of moonlight. Chausses were the only clothing covering him. Elayna had not grown up at Castle Wulfere, a place full of soldiers, and remained completely unaware of the mysteries of the male body. She'd helped tend men, both sick and wounded. But never had she seen a man like Graeham, a body so savagely etched. He was powerful by any standards, but it was not his muscles that transfixed her attention.

A terrible scar ravaged one side, cutting across rippling, straining sinew.

It wasn't a fresh scar. Even in this light, she could see it was whitened, toughened.

Just then, his stomach muscles sucked in violently and his legs kicked sharply. His entire body moved up into the shadows. A low groan emanated from him again. She understood, finally, what he was doing—forcing himself up and down slowly, torturously, training his muscles.

She could hardly stand to watch but couldn't seem to stop as he rose and lowered, rose and lowered, slowly, deliberately. It was beautiful and horrible at the same time. Her breath caught when he dropped carefully to the ground in a spill of moonlight.

His clenched fists and closed eyes held her stunned by the sheer emotion that he seemed to be so ruthlessly containing. She wanted to shrink away, or rush to his side. She wasn't sure which, or even why.

He moved, and she ducked back into the hut, tugging the door shut. Her heart rushed into her throat.

Instinctively, she knew he wouldn't want her to

see him like that. To see that he wasn't invulnerable. He felt pain—not just physical, but emotional. He was flesh and blood, like anyone else. He had a heart.

That stopped her thoughts cold. She had to remember that he was capable of anything. He was an outlaw, and she was, quite possibly, his captive.

On the pallet again, she hugged her knees to her chest and tried to get warm again—and to think. She had no idea how far it was to the road, how far he'd taken her after the boar attack. She'd spent the day of her escape hiding under a blanket. She knew the general direction of the road, but it had twisted and turned through the forest. Its precise direction from her current location would be only a guess. What choice did she have but to try? If she could make it to the inn, she could pay for passage . . . anywhere . . . and as quickly as possible, before her brother's men found her. They could circle back to the inn at some point, but that was just another chance she would have to take.

She would take his advice; she would rest. The sooner she recovered, the sooner she could continue her journey. Every time she slept, she woke feeling better. Soon, she would be well again.

Still cold, she pulled at the thin blanket, tossed over the stool where she'd watched him whittling earlier. As she pulled it toward her, something scraped along the floor with it, caught up in the blanket from near the stool. It was the chunk of wood he'd been whittling on earlier, only now it was finished. He'd been here, whittling, roasting this rabbit. *Watching over her?* She didn't know why she'd even come up with that thought. It was romantic and foolish and she thrust it away.

There was nothing romantic about Graeham.

She leaned forward and picked up the chunk of wood, turning it over in her hand, adjusting it in the light, realizing it was intricate and amazing and must have taken hours.

It was a tiny, perfect, fairy-tale castle.

She stared at it for a long beat, then realized something else. He'd left his small knife there, the one he had used for whittling.

CHAPTER
ELEVEN

He rubbed the soft cutting of hair between his fingers. He had taken a lock from the goosegirl of Voirelle, and it had become a ritual. After all, his life was made up of nothing but ritual. It had been time to start creating his own. God controlled the world with ritual, routine. So did he.

The few precious drops of his special tincture, designed to create weakness and sleep, came first. Then the punishment. Oh, how he loved the punishment. Then the aftermath—the disappearance of the body. The loss and confusion of those left behind. They needed him more than ever in those times. Then the return to his private lair. The opening of the pouches. The fingering of the locks of hair, one by one, all of them, going back to that of his beloved.

He hadn't planned to take a lock of her hair. It had happened quickly, without thinking. He'd been nearly caught. Hers was the one body he hadn't disposed of on his own. She'd been found. In her case, perhaps just as well. The discovery of her body—she had been barely alive but had died quickly—had created all sorts of interesting

098 *Suzanne McMinn*

*complications. He'd followed her that night, knowing full
well her destination. She had become a whore for the other
man, the other lover. She would give up everything for
this other man—or so she thought. He would be the one
to make her give up everything. He would be the one to
punish her.*

*She should have been his. How stupid of her not to
accept it. So he had made her accept it, made her accept
him. When she had resisted, he had brought forth the
vial he had prepared and forced her to drink from it.*

*Everything had been easy, everything had been as it
should be, after that. Until Damon of Wulfere arrived.*

*He had barely escaped with the lock and his life before
Damon burst upon the scene.*

*How fitting that the interloper had spent a year in
prison for the murder of his beloved. He had not planned
it, but he had enjoyed it. Then Wilfred of Penlogan had
taken his place. Of course, that had been no accident of
fortune. It had been then that he had realized his power.*

*He put the latest addition to his treasury of locks into
its pouch, then tucked it back into the secret compartment
from whence it had come, and considered his plans for
Elayna of Wulfere, when she was found. He knew she
would be.*

She was the one who would set him free.

Graeham cooked porridge over the hut's small
fire, mutely pushing a bowl of the hearty gruel at
her. She was starving for the porridge she'd
watched him sweeten with thick honey, but she
refused it when he pushed the bowl at her. She
didn't want to appear too strong.

Outside, thunder rumbled. She thought about
the knife under her pallet.

It was clear he wasn't seriously concerned that
she would escape. If he were, he wouldn't leave
her alone so much of the time. He took it for

granted that she was lost in this forest, that she had little hope of finding the road and that she was smart enough to figure that out.

Or did he depend upon his prayers to keep her there? When she'd woken, she'd witnessed him kneeling by the fire. At first, she'd thought he was simply tending to their meal, then she'd noticed his eyes were closed.

It had felt very intimate. His lips had moved in silent supplication. She hadn't been able to make out any meaning. His face had been hard, etched in that same pain she'd seen before. The length and fervor of his morning prayer had caught her off guard. Was he some kind of ascetic hermit now? Repaying his sins in holy seclusion? She didn't know what to make of him. He had a sword. She'd seen him practicing his knightly arts. A killer, a cleric, what was he?

He noticed her staring at him, and he frowned back at her.

"Eat."

"You've lost all ability to converse, haven't you?"

Never would she have thought she would miss the Graeham he had been. But this cold, pained, silent man was worse, much worse.

"I have no need to converse."

"Are you ever lonely?"

"I don't need anyone."

She wanted to accuse him of lying, but she wasn't sure of her conviction. She felt the same way—or at least she wanted to. She wanted to not need anyone.

"Is that why you live here alone?"

He looked away, didn't answer. She noticed how the lines around his eyes seemed deeper than before. He didn't look well. He should sleep more. Compassion struck her, followed by complete disgust with herself.

Graeham's father had been responsible for her brother's imprisonment, and nearly for his death. Graeham had fought to defend his father's crime. His response then had been dishonorable, treasonous. If he was fatigued now, it was because he was losing sleep keeping an eye on her, or keeping busy hiding her erasing knives. Or maybe it was his guilty conscience that kept him awake. Whatever it was, he didn't deserve her sympathy. He deserved her loathing.

But for a moment, he looked worn and guileless.

His gaze moved to meet hers again suddenly, and she felt odd, flustered, by it. The air felt different, hot, as if it scorched her skin with some invisible fire.

He moved abruptly, taking the porridge bowl. He lifted the spoon and held it up to her mouth. "Eat," he demanded again, but this time in a whisper.

She didn't want to take the food from him, but she had no will to resist him just then. She opened her mouth, swallowed the sweet spoonful.

He was very near.

She thought, for just a moment, a blinding, spinning moment, that he was going to—what? Kiss her? She pushed back in a jerky movement, and the pallet skidded beneath her.

Something shot out from beneath it. Something shiny. She breathed one of her new swear words and dived for the knife.

"It's not what you think," she said quickly, grabbing it, wondering what she was going to do with it now anyway. She didn't think she could bring herself to use it against him, stupid as that truth made her.

She tried to stand up but lost her balance on the slipping pallet and crashed into his arms.

"What do I think?" he growled close by her ear.

"I think you're getting worked up." She was breathing fast, and her thoughts were spinning just as quickly. "Over nothing."

"I beg to differ. You have a knife. My knife. Give it to me."

She considered cooperating and decided against it.

"You took my knives," she pointed out. "My erasing knives. Give them back, and I'll give yours back."

He scooped her up in his arms and rounded back to the pallet. She heaved and twisted to get free and managed to jab him in the chest, hard, with her elbow.

She got free, but by way of being unceremoniously dumped on the pallet. The knife flew out of her hand at the impact. He leaned over her, took it, and pocketed it somewhere within the folds of his tunic.

"I trust you are finished with being stupid," he said, then swore.

She didn't understand why until she realized there were black spots in front of her eyes. Her last thought was that she wouldn't be escaping today.

The fainting spell told her that she didn't have to pretend to be weak. She *was* weak. The brief strength she'd felt had been an illusion. Still, she intended to attempt escape as soon as possible.

He was outside when she came to. It took her several moments to realize that there was another voice, not just his.

It took a huge effort, but she got to her feet and made it to the door without collapsing. She damned this weakness. It was her side that was injured, not her feet, so she kept expecting to feel like her old self. It was the fever, she supposed, that had drained her so.

At the door, she pushed it just slightly, enough to see out.

There was a boy with Graeham. The boy couldn't be more than ten or twelve, she guessed. She blinked in shock at seeing someone else here, with Graeham, in this wild wood. She had accepted their complete isolation, never suspecting there could be those who knew his location, would come to him—for what?

She caught snatches of words.

"Bertrada . . . rain . . . willow tincture."

The boy was talking quickly. He looked winded. How far had he come?

Graeham said something, and the boy sat on an overturned log near the square of garden where plants still thrived in neat rows, the fall weather still warm. Herbs. The source of his collection of remedies he kept on the worktable in the hut.

So people came to him for these remedies, they were not just for his own use? Hermit, killer . . . healer?

She was stunned long enough to be taken by surprise when Graeham strode toward the hut. What was she doing? She had to get help; this was her chance. The boy had to have come from somewhere—perhaps from someone who would help her get to the city.

She ducked back as Graeham approached, let him pass through. His eyes would have to adjust to the relative dimness of the hut, and as he stood there, she whipped around the door, intending to slip past him, outside, to the boy—

"Not so fast." He grabbed her by the waist and pulled her back inside.

Fine. She could scream. She dragged in the breath to do it.

His hand clapped over her mouth.

"Don't even think about it." He held her tightly, her back pressed against his hard chest. The harsh movement had pulled at her wound, and pins of agony were shooting to every part of her mind. "Promise you won't scream, or I won't let go of your mouth."

She nodded. What choice did she have? She felt like she was going to black out or throw up. Her knees were like water. He was holding her up with his fierce grip.

"Who is that?" she gasped when he moved his hand. He didn't move his hand very far. He still held her in his steel grip. She could speak, but she couldn't move. "Why is he here? If I am such a bother to you, and clearly I am, why don't you let me go with him? Let me go—"

"No."

His curt refusal brought out her anger. "Why not? What is going on? Am I your hostage now, is that it? A prisoner? Why? What are you afraid of?"

He didn't answer her question. "It is you who has much to fear, lady."

"You are the one who is afraid! You are afraid I'll tell that young boy that you are a murderer? Is that it? You have a new life here—these people come to you for what, healing, prayers, protection?" Everything spun through her mind: the herbs, the morning supplication, the weapons and armor. What was going on here?

"You will not tell that boy anything," he grated in her ear. "You will not involve that boy out there in your stupidity, do you understand?" He whipped her around to face him. "I told you that I would not kill you, but let me assure you that if you do anything to put that boy in danger, I'll change my mind. Do we understand each other?"

She swallowed thickly. He gave her a slight shake,

and she realized he wanted her to move away from the door. He propelled her to the pallet and gave her a push. She sat down, knowing she couldn't fight him, not now.

He took a small container from the worktable and left. She heard him talking to the boy.

She lay down and let her jumbled thoughts settle however they willed. They settled on him, of course. She stared at the ceiling of the hut and tried to make sense of this strange new life of his. He lived alone, yet he was clearly a part of the greater community. There were people who relied on him. He had mentioned the inn, that knights had been searching for her there. He had ties there. Perhaps there was a village where the boy had come from. These people knew how to get through the dark, misty forest and find him when they needed him. They trusted him to cure their ills. He gardened and prayed and made medicines. He held women hostage and killed men. There was no sense to be made of him. She gave up.

When he returned, there was no conversation for a long time. He avoided her as much as one could avoid another person in such close quarters. He made her feel as if she had a loathsome disease he feared catching.

Eventually, she felt well enough to sit up and take out her journal. She was still angry, and she felt helpless. She hated being helpless most of all. She was daring him, and it was a dangerous dare. If he had read any of her journal, would he mention it now?

She took out blank parchment, unrolled it, and pressed it flat, then took out her pot of ink and unscrewed the cap. She tried to work up the courage to say something, to point out that this was her journal. To demand if he had read it.

The courage withered within her. She held the

quill in her hand for a long time without saying anything or writing anything either. She usually expressed whatever she was feeling, thinking, in this journal. She wrote of whatever was happening around her.

What was happening around her was Graeham. What she was experiencing, thinking, was bewilderment, anger, and hurt. She had no idea how to express what she felt. Her life had become incomprehensible.

She dipped her quill into the inkpot.

Do you know how much you hurt me? she wrote. It was the question she couldn't voice, she realized. The real question she yearned to voice. Not *Did you read my journal?* but *Do you know how much you hurt me?* It was why she couldn't ask the first question. The secret meaning of the first question was the second question. And she couldn't ask that question. Asking that question was asking to be hurt again.

And she couldn't bear to be hurt again.

She wiped off the quill with a piece of scrap cloth she always carried with her for that purpose. When the ink was dry, she untied the threads binding the journal and, using her small sewing needle, poked them through the new, almost blank page, adding it to the bulk of the journal. She put it away in her satchel. Graeham was busy at his worktable, as usual paying no attention to her.

"What are you doing?"

Her question didn't elicit an immediate response. She watched him as he packed a jar with some sort of herb, then covered it with oil. He set a lid on top, then took it outside. He couldn't have taken it far; he was back quickly.

"Why did you take it outside?" she persisted.

"A cold infusion requires sunlight," he explained without bothering to look at her. "It gets little enough of that outside in this mist, but it will get none of it in here.''

"An infusion of what?"

"St. John's wort."

She knew that St. John's wort was useful for many things, including burns. He didn't explain why he was out of the healing oil. She knew by examining her wound that he had sealed it by burning her. She didn't remember the process, and for that she was grateful.

"How did you end up here?" she asked instead. She didn't ask how he escaped Penlogan alive— supposedly burned in the fire that he'd set to destroy the hall of his father's castle. She could guess that his body had been misidentified some-how. He had been alive all this time, making this new life of his.

She would get to those other questions later, if at all. She wanted answers and didn't want answers. For now, she focused on his life in this forest. She had to figure out how to get out of there, so the more she knew of this place, the better.

He was cooking something in a pot over the fire. He stirred the concoction before he answered.

"Our lives are what God wills." He gave a dis-missive shrug as he moved away from the fire. He wasn't encouraging further conversation.

She was annoyed that he'd skirted her question.

"You believe in God?" she probed, thinking of how she'd seen him pray. Could a murderer be pious?

"You think I don't?"

He was busying himself now at the table where he kept the collection of herbs and ointments. He was grinding something in a small bowl with a pestle, then he came back to the fire and dumped the crushed herbs into the pot.

She didn't quite have the nerve to ask how a

murderer could believe in God. It was very hard sometimes to realize that he was a murderer. His demeanor, his bearing, was terrifying in many ways, and yet— There was something that bothered her about his eyes. Something haunted.

"I don't know what to think," she said honestly.

"Then don't think. Don't wonder. It doesn't matter."

She felt her stomach muscles clench. How could he be so cold? It was as if he didn't remember the feelings they'd once shared, the dreams they'd built.

"Is that what you do?" she demanded tensely. "You don't think, don't wonder?"

" 'Tis for the best," he agreed grimly, his eyes focused on the pot as he stirred it.

"You never wondered what happened after you left? To Penlogan? To my family? To me? All the people who'd once . . . *cared* about you." She'd almost said *loved*. She was getting angry now, and it made her feel better. She needed anger. "My father betrothed me to a man even older than himself. My father wasn't well. He was worried about all of us with Damon gone. He betrothed me to an old man. I was miserable. But you didn't know that, did you?" she flung at him bitterly. "Julian took over the castle when my father died. Damon was still gone, and Julian was hoping he'd never come back. He had a secret ring of bandits raiding the countryside, collecting treasure in heaps in the storerooms below Castle Wulfere. Marigold found it—and he terrorized her. Terrorized all of us."

She had his attention now. He stared at her.

"If Damon hadn't come back, I don't know what would have happened to us. Marigold didn't speak for months, she was so scared. Julian and his men tried to kill Damon and Belle. They would have killed us too. Or sent us away, separated us. But you didn't know any of that either, did you? I'm sure it was for the best.''

She was shocked herself at the fierceness of her words as they spilled out. She had been furious with him for not being there for her during that terrible time, and she was even more furious now, knowing that he had been alive all the while it had been happening.

"What happened?'' he asked, his voice low and upset.

She felt tears sting her eyes. Damn him, sympathy was worse than coldness. She swallowed hard to control the new sweep of emotion hitting her.

"Belle.'' She looked away, stared at the wall of the hut. "Belle came. Thank God Belle came. She figured out what was happening. Together, she and Damon caught Julian and the ring of men helping him. Marigold started speaking again and—'' She felt tired now. The anger had left her, and without it, she didn't know what to say.

"And you? What of you?''

He'd left the fire, come closer. His fingers gripped her chin and tugged her around to face him. His depthless gaze examined her.

"What about me?'' She shook off his touch.

He didn't back away. "You must have been brave. You must have held your sisters together until Damon and Belle came.''

"You don't know what I did. You didn't want to know. 'Twas for the best.'' She threw his words back at him.

"I know you.''

"You know nothing,'' she said, a brief surge of anger coming back. "I wasn't brave. I was scared. I was alone, and I was as scared as Marigold.''

He frowned. "You feel guilty—for not protecting your family? Against Julian, a grown man, a knight.

You, a girl, a child almost. You and your sisters lived through it, most of the time without Damon. You can't tell me you weren't brave."

She didn't want to talk about it anymore. She hadn't meant for this conversation to take place. The past made her feel guilty and flawed. He was wrong; she hadn't done enough.

"Forget it," she said. She lay down on the pallet as if she were going to sleep despite the fact that her heart was thumping hard and painful in her chest. She was tired but not sleepy. "You didn't want to know then, so you don't need to know now."

He left her alone, but she felt as if he stared at her for a long time.

She actually fell asleep, which surprised her. It was evening again when she woke. He was still tending some concoction by the fire, working with his herbs.

"What is that?" she asked, nodding at the pot on the fire as she sat up.

She was mindful of the conversation they'd had before she'd fallen asleep, and she avoided his eyes. She didn't want to know if he was still thinking about it too.

"Comfrey," he answered, his voice as careful and cool as her own.

She tried to think of all of comfrey's uses. Marigold knew her herbs backward and forward, but Elayna always got them confused. Comfrey, she recalled, speeded the healing of wounds.

"So you're an herbalist now," she said. "A healer." It still seemed so strange.

He shook his head, and there was something that almost looked like a smile that flicked at the edges of his mouth, then disappeared.

"I am no healer," he said. "There are those who come to me, and I help them. But I don't heal them. Only God heals."

Her mental portrait of him slipped and slid. Now he was the pious hermit again.

"So this is your life now," she said slowly. "Alone in the forest with your herbs, your prayers." She nodded at the heap of armor in the corner. "And what of that?"

He had turned back to his worktable. He ignored her reference to his armor. He had left his life as a knight behind, and yet he had not left his sword and his armor.

Did he still care about his old life, more than he feigned? *Stop,* she warned herself. Such thoughts could lead nowhere good.

"Our lives are what God wills," he said.

"We have the power to change our lives," she argued, thinking of her own choices.

"Is that what you were doing, changing your life?" His gaze sheared her now as he turned briefly to glance at her over his shoulder, and his voice grew bitter. "It hasn't worked out. Mayhap you wish you had trusted God's will."

"It's not God's will I don't trust."

He turned fully now and watched her across the small space.

"Then whose, lady? Your brother's?"

She trusted Damon. Was it Ranulf she didn't trust? She had always believed him to be an honorable man, and yet she had distrusted his sudden desire for her.

But even if he did seek to wed her simply for her dowry, that would make him no worse than any of the other suitors who had offered her for her hand, would it? And yet she had felt so terribly uncomfortable that night in the tower stairwell. . . .

Her reaction had been instinctive, not rational. She couldn't explain it, even now.

She had been careful not to tell Graeham the name of the man to whom she was to be wed. Things were bad enough.

She thought of her mother's teachings. Young women awaiting marriage were to be wholly dependent upon their elders' judgment. She had never been good at being told what was her fate.

" 'Tis my own will I'm not certain of," she admitted, because there was so much else she couldn't admit. "My own judgment. How does one know God's will when one sees it? I thought I knew once before, but I was wrong." She looked away from him because she was afraid of saying too much.

She didn't know if she was looking for an answer. She didn't expect him to give her one. How could he? She didn't understand her destiny; he certainly couldn't. He had clearly turned his back on his own, and on the one she had thought was hers. Their shared destiny.

"God's will has a way of slapping you in the face," he said, and turned back to his work with the herbs.

She didn't know what to say. She was tired again.

The next morning's routine was the same as that of the day before, only this time there was no knife to be discovered. He shared a breakfast of porridge with her that she was too hungry to refuse. He looked worse this morning. The lines around his eyes were deeper. Had he slept since she'd arrived? Surely he must have, sometime when she, too, had been asleep. His mouth was grim and he looked pale beneath his sun-dark skin. He consumed little of his own porridge, then left, sword at his side.

Guilt, she thought again. She reminded him of

his sinful past, and he couldn't sleep. It was why he didn't look at her.

She crept after him to the hut's door. Through the barely cracked opening, she watched him.

His broad back disappeared into the swirling fog.

There was no time to waste. He might be going to the road. He didn't take his horse, the one he kept in the lean-to barn behind the garden, but perhaps the road wasn't really that far. She had no idea what he was doing, but she had to be prepared in case it provided her a way to escape.

She went back for her satchel, then pushed open the door and soundlessly rushed across the soft, mossy ground. She followed him between the trees, staying just far enough behind to be able to duck behind the nearest tree trunk if he should happen to look back. For a moment, she looked back and thought of simply taking his horse. But where would she go? She had no idea which direction, and his horse was huge, a warhorse. She was not much of a horsewoman, and she had some doubt about her ability to control it. Most warhorses were keenly loyal to the knights who owned them.

She was better off finding her way out of this wood on foot. She just had to figure out which way to go. She followed him.

The foggy ground billowed up, covering her ankles, whirling around her knees, and she felt as if she walked through a dream, into—

What?

She didn't know. It was a strange sensation, and something about it made her wish she could turn back, but she had the terrible feeling that she was already lost.

She looked back again. The hut had disappeared, swallowed up by the fog and trees. Her breath came in quick gasps, her heart tapping hard against the

wall of her chest. She turned and sped after
Graeham.

The wood was full of noises. Her breathing, her
footsteps, but also twitterings of birds, rustlings of
leaves. And water, she realized with a sense of
shock. There was the sound of babbling water.

Gray light broke through the mist ahead. The
road? She watched him emerge into it through the
trees, and crept low, keeping her cover where the
brush was thick and low-hanging branches shielded
her from his view.

The place in which he had stopped was a haven
of cloud-mist light in the midst of the otherworldly
darkness. It wasn't the road at all. The land rose
up here, and the fog thinned and spun around it as
if bowing down to it. Straight through the middle, a
deep crevice of water bubbled over timeworn rocks,
glittering in the sunshine of the sweet, grassy glade.
It must, she thought, feed into the stream where
he drew their water and where he bathed. He'd
taken her there in the evening of the day before
and had invited her to bathe.

It had been a strange ordeal to bathe in full
knowledge that he was nearby, waiting for her. But
the clean water on her skin had felt good, and she
hadn't cared how inappropriate it all was. She was
living in his hut, for heaven's sake. She was past
propriety.

Not that he had given any indication, by word
or glance, that he had the least lascivious thought
about her or that he would take advantage of the
situation in any way.

She watched as he strode easily into the glade
now, his sword flaring in the bright day. He stared
downward, his feet relaxed, his stance open, as if
in prayer or supplication, then suddenly moved
left, parried. The weapon shone, blurring in the
swiftness of his movement as he brought it over

his head, pivoting. He passed forward, then pivoted again, this time kicking his right foot outward in a powerful thrust.

Again and again. Pivot, pass, heave.

She didn't breathe, just watched. She had come to find the way out of the forest. Instead, she found something as mystifying as the forest itself. What was he doing?

The sound of her heart beat loud in her ears. She knelt behind the cover of the low-hanging bent branch, unable to tear her gaze away. She'd known he had changed, that he was no longer the young, immature knight she had last seen, but the sight of him heaving the lethal weapon in the glade drove it home like nothing else.

This was what she saw in his eyes—the haunting pain, the ferocity, the deadliness—in tangible form before her.

This was not even a shadow of that untried, green knight, inexperienced and unsophisticated. This man was sheer power and mature might—and a daunting force of will that he seemed to struggle to conquer.

She thought of how she had seen him in the night, pulling himself up torturously on that branch. Why did he do these things? What invisible devil did he fight?

Or was the devil inside him, in his mind, his memories?

What had happened to him that day when Damon's men had arrived at Penlogan? *Were you there? You think you know so much, lady? Or do you just believe everything you hear?*

What had he meant when he'd thrown those accusations at her? She had left him alone, hadn't questioned him. She was, she realized, afraid to question him. Afraid to find out she was wrong, everyone was wrong.

Or afraid that she was right.

She pressed her hand to her mouth, so scared that she felt physically ill. She couldn't stop staring at him, struck by the haunted look in his eyes as he fought his unseen foe. Melancholy shaded his focused expression, making him appear inured to the pain she saw etched there, as if he were so used to it, he didn't recognize it as his own anymore.

Behind her came a sharp, snapping sound. Graeham stopped, his gaze piercing the dense thickness in which she hid. She waited in the darkness, rooted, glancing quickly around her.

To her left, she thought she saw a shadow of something—a boar? The lightning speed with which the attack had come once before flashed in her mind. She listened as hard as she could. There was a rustling.

Something was there. She didn't wait to see what. Emotion smothered her. Wild, irrational fear.

Without a second thought, she scrambled onto a low-hanging bough. It swayed beneath her, dropping down, and she grabbed onto the next branch above, and the next, climbing faster than she ever had in her life.

All those times she'd chased Gwyneth up trees in their mother's garden came back to her in blurred flashes of memory.

Rough bark dug into her palms. Her side throbbed. Her breath came fast and hard. She felt dizzy when she looked down, and foolish when she saw the tiny, beady face of a squirrel dashing away between the clusters of underbrush. A squirrel! She flattened her body against the thick trunk, her cheek pressed against its ungiving surface.

Idiot, she cursed herself. Would she see and hear boars everywhere now? The prospect irritated her sense of independence, as did the painful weakness that threatened to make her lose her grip on the tree. She was still not as recovered as she'd wanted to believe.

She opened her eyes, twisted sharply to peer down through the thick boughs into the glade. He was gone. She twisted back around, half losing her grasp on the trunk. Her hands scraped along the rough bark and she winced in pain at the same time that she looked down again. No sign of him. Perhaps he'd moved farther across the glade, where she couldn't see him through the thick leaves.

She waited, listening, trying to decide what to do. Go back to the hut, pretend nothing had happened?

Go on, hope they were near the road and that she could find it on her own?

Gripping the harsh trunk again, she began to climb down, stretching one foot at a time. Her hands slipped, scraped painfully as she grabbed on to the tree. She grimaced, annoyed with her own clumsiness.

The last thing she needed to do was fall. She searched cautiously with her foot for the next hold.

"Have a care, lady. I grow weary of rescuing you from your own foolishness."

She couldn't hold back the little scream of shock. She reared around, the face of Graeham below blurring as she realized too late that she'd let her hands slip again and that this time, there was no grabbing back on.

The sensation of falling was unreal. She felt the tug of her clothes as branches snagged, ripped at them, and the whoosh of air rushing up at her, then Graeham's arms around her, protecting her from the worst of the impact as she took both of them down.

Leaves flurried down in a snow of broken bits

of twigs. Then Graeham grunted, rolling her onto her back, off him.

He breathed hard, as if he were as winded as she. His enigmatic eyes glared down at her, his expression a scowl in his ruthlessly beautiful face. His hands came up from beneath her, where he'd braced her fall, to touch her cheek, then her shoulders, her side. His touch was rough, abrupt, but somehow gentle at the same time.

His hands were shaking, she realized, and that made her confused on top of embarrassed.

"Are you all right?" he demanded. "Your side. What were you thinking?"

He was angry, and she couldn't blame him if he accused her of being witless again. It hadn't been a smart thing to do. It had been a desperate thing to do.

"I was hoping to fall out of a tree and hurt myself again. What do you think I was thinking? I'm all right. Now let go of me."

He didn't let her go.

"Lady," he said, his breaths slowing, his voice thick and quietly dangerous, "you have a way of putting yourself in the wrong place—and at the very worst time. What the hell did you think you were doing?" he repeated. "You could have been hurt. You could have opened your wound. Anything could have happened."

He was still running his hands over her, examining her. He reminded her of the way Damon had looked when little Venetia had somehow managed to escape her nurse and crawl onto the parapet. Damon had been furious—and he'd yelled at little Venetia, making her cry. Instantly, Damon had kissed her and hugged her as if he would never stop. It had been his fear that had made him angry, and his love.

She didn't think Graeham loved her, but he

cared, she realized with a small shock. He actually cared if she was hurt or not, and he was angry because he was worried.

It added to her sense of confusion. The treacherous murderer had a soft side. He had acted for days as if he didn't care about her, but he did. Why did he hide it? What else was he hiding?

"What the hell are *you* doing here?" she retorted breathlessly, at a loss for more to say. She could feel the strength of his fingers as he moved his touch to her face, brushing threads of her wild hair from her cheeks, skimming her skin.

She couldn't think straight. She was in trouble, big trouble, and not just because he knew now that she'd followed him and that she was stronger than she'd feigned to be.

A frantic pulse leapt within her, warning her— But she was helpless to look away or even move. He was still scanning her, examining her with his darkened gaze.

The crushed brush beneath them, the summer-leaved trees above them, all combined to make her feel suspended, light, and unearthly.

"Why did you follow me?"

"I was bored," she returned without thinking.

"You're lying." His gaze on her was fierce, angry—at her or himself? "You shouldn't be here. Not in my hut, not in this wood. Not anywhere near me. I should have gotten rid of you in the beginning. I should have—"

In those impenetrable eyes of his she saw something more than pain then. She saw loneliness and need, and it chipped away at something inside, something that held her heart fast and safe. But not now.

"Why didn't you?" she asked, her voice wispy, her breath barely there.

"I want to be rid of you. I want it more than anything except—"

She couldn't bear it if he kept staring at her. She couldn't bear it if he stopped. She felt crazy inside. She wanted answers and she didn't want answers.

She wanted to run away, but there was no place to go, and he was holding her so very tightly in his arms.

Our lives are what God wills. That's what he'd said. She wasn't sure she believed it. She wanted to believe that her life could be what *she* willed. But either way, somehow she had found herself here, now, in this familiar stranger's arms.

"What do you want?" she cried, not at all knowing what she wanted.

You. She thought he said *you.* But she wasn't sure, because at that very instant, the storm that had been threatening on and off since the day before returned with a loud rumble.

And at the next instant, he was covering her mouth with his.

CHAPTER TWELVE

Her lips were succulent and sweet, and the fact that he didn't have any right to even this one taste of them didn't stop him. His hands were in her hair, his tongue stealing into her mouth, and there was no way he was going to stop.

She gasped against his mouth and he consumed it, capturing her doubt and his with an even deeper kiss.

He didn't want to kiss her, and she didn't want to kiss him either—he knew that. And yet she slipped her arms around his neck and clung to him anyway.

Her small, wonderful body felt so right. She was inexperienced, almost clumsy. She made a sound deep in her throat—surprise—that had his senses reeling, the reality of holding her, kissing her, discovering the secret flames inside her so much more than his imagination had prepared him for. And he had imagined, oh, how he had imagined.

It was why he'd made it his mission to stay away from her as much as possible in the interminable time since she'd been in his hut.

But she'd followed him, here of all places. The place where he trained, focused, meditated, gathered the mental fortitude to deal with what God had willed for his life.

How could she be here?

And now she was in his arms, and he couldn't let go no matter how much he wanted to. He wanted other things more—he wanted to feel her heart beating, breathe her breath. The hunger that had been born the day he'd found her in the woods had not abated, no matter how he'd sought to ignore it, neglect it, shame it from his mind.

He'd watched her and wanted her until it nearly drove him crazy. Late at night, when she slept and he couldn't, he had stared at her for hours and thought of how dangerous it was, this want. Kisses weren't enough. He wanted to lie with her, make love with her, sleep with her, consume and be consumed by her. Caught up in this dangerous wanting, he had underestimated her.

And so she was here.

He tortured her with ravenous kisses, moving from her mouth to her neck, to her ears, and she whimpered and clung and kissed him back. He felt the full arousal of his body press against the softness of hers, and she arched against him, against his hardness, and froze. With what bit of lucidity remained in his brain, he recognized the change in her.

"Stop," she gasped against his mouth, her voice trembly and thick and lost, as if she didn't know where she was.

He forced himself to tear away from her—honor and soul-deep desire destroying him. Blood pounded in his head and nether regions of his body. The taste and smell of her overwhelmed him. He felt lost too.

She took shallow gasps of air beneath him, and

he opened his eyes to stare straight into hers. There was something painful there that struck him so close to home, he felt emotion sting his eyes and he had to look away. The connection was so deep, so strong, as if they shared this pain as one rather than as two separate human beings.

He couldn't bear it. He squeezed his eyes shut, blocking the look of her from his mind, his heart. Inside his mind, he could still see her, feel her, smell her, taste her. His temples throbbed.

"Why did you do that?" Her voice was filled with perplexity, unsettled and strange.

He had to get away from her heat, her absorbing heat, so he could think straight. There was danger here—danger she didn't even realize. It was up to him to protect her. He was even more ashamed at that thought. Was this how he protected her?

He gave no excuses. "I beg your pardon. I don't know what came over me." He was lying. He knew exactly what had come over him. He shoved off her, rose and stomped across the mossy brush, then pivoted finally to look at her again. She'd sat up, yet still she looked small and hurt and he hated himself because he'd done something shameful. He'd taken advantage of her. He'd kissed her when he had no right. He'd touched her. He'd wanted her.

He'd let himself dream for a pulsebeat in time that he was just a man, she was just a woman, and that nothing else mattered except the desire between them.

And she had desired too. It hadn't just been him. But that fact was no consolation.

It only made everything worse.

She stood, still looking perplexed and off balance, and he wasn't sure if it was his immediate apology or the kiss that affected her so.

She touched her mouth. Did the taste of him

still linger there the way the taste of her lingered on his lips, taunting him? It was all he could do not to march straight back and take her into his arms again, convince her that it was as good and right as it had felt.

But it was not, and he knew that.

"What were you thinking when you did that?" she persisted, her voice low but stronger, clearer, accusatory. "You have scarcely looked at me for days, and now—"

"I wasn't thinking. That much must be obvious, lady. It was a mistake. Banish it from your mind. You need not fear it will happen again."

"I'm not afraid it will happen again. I want to know why it happened to begin with. I want to know why you're here." She took a deep breath, as if fighting within herself, then went on in a rush. "After all this time—why?"

Why what? Why he'd kissed her—or something else? He didn't want to know.

"Let it go, lady," he replied dangerously.

She was very close to him now.

"We have kissed before," she said quietly, her voice a whisper carried on the breeze.

She had made little direct reference to their former relationship. He had tried very hard to block it from his mind. It was a long time ago. It had meant nothing and everything, but it was over. She had believed the lies about him, as had the rest of the world he'd left behind.

She was part of that world.

He had spent days struggling not to think of it, losing sleep not thinking about it. His head pounded from not thinking about it.

"The past is dead."

"I thought you were dead."

"Did you care, lady?"

He wished he could take back that question. It sounded as if he cared about the answer.

"Yes." She held her head high. Her eyes were bright. "We were to be wed. You were to ask your father's permission. You were to come back, with my ring. Instead—"

She closed her eyes, lifted them back to him in boldness. More accusation. "You didn't come back. My brother's men came to you to offer you a deal that came from the king. But you wanted no part of their bargain. You murdered Damon's men in cold blood while they slept in your hall. You plotted your revenge, and there was no room in it for me."

Her last words were so quiet, so deadly, he felt as if a sword were thrust into his side all over again, as it had been on that night of which she spoke.

"You left me without a word, and you were alive all this time," she cried. "You saved my life, and now you hold me hostage—for what reason? You barely even speak to me. But you kiss me—kiss me!—and then tell me to banish it from my mind. I cannot, Graeham of Penlogan! I cannot. And if you can, then tell me how.

"Tell me the truth. Clearly, you have the secret to banishing the past, for you have walked away from it completely. Tell it to me. I have a right to know this much, to know why you are here, and why I am here with you, and why it feels as if you aren't going to let me go."

He saw the pain again, raw in her eyes, and he realized it was true that they shared it as one human being rather than two. But he couldn't let himself tell her that.

"You are here with me because you made a foolish decision," he said instead.

"How long?" She refused to back down. "How long will you keep me here?"

"If you are a prisoner, lady, it is by your own

making." He pushed away the guilt that came with his position—and yet still it hurtled back. "You chose this path, not I."

He avoided answering her question directly. He didn't have an answer. In the time since she'd recognized him, he'd turned the question over and over in his mind, and he'd come to no clear resolution.

She stared back at him, still breathing unevenly, her thick, beautiful hair—now so short, yet still beautiful—tangled with twigs and bits of brush, her mouth wet and shaky. Just kissed.

"Let me go. Help me."

"It's not that simple."

"Why? Because you're Graeham of Penlogan?"

"Because you're Elayna." Because she clouded his judgment, and he knew it. He was tempted to do so many things that were wrong—from kissing her again to letting her go simply to get her away from him.

He almost strode away from her again, but unexpectedly she reached out and gripped his arm.

"Will you not give me a forthright answer?" she demanded.

"I give you the only answers I can give you, lady."

"No, you don't," she argued. She seemed immune to the fact that twigs and bits of brush littered her hair. "You haven't told me why you won't take me out of the forest, to the inn, now that I'm recovered. I'm ready to travel now. I'm rested. You were the one who mentioned the inn in the first place. You were going to take me there—"

"That was then. Things have changed."

He didn't have to explain what had changed. They both knew. She had recognized him.

"You know I have money. I can pay for your time, your trouble. I will not reveal you. I do not even intend to return to Castle Wulfere. Where I

will go, no one would even know you. It won't
matter that I have seen you. It won't matter what
I know. It won't matter that you're alive."

She kept her hand on his arm.

How he wanted to believe her. But she was part
of the world that had betrayed him. How *could* he
believe her?

"I've told you I don't want your money." He
watched her carefully. "Where would you go? If
not to Castle Wulfere—where?" It bothered him
that she had run away, that she planned to keep
running away.

He'd tried to avoid questioning her, wondering
what she was doing, not wanting to know anything
about her. But he needed the answers.

When she spoke, her voice was urgent, and he
hated how easily he found himself falling into her
earnest eyes as she spoke.

"I set out on . . ." She frowned, seeming to
choose her words. "A sort of pilgrimage, actually—"

"To seek holy relics, miracles, healing, what?"

She looked frustrated but intent. "God's will. Or
my own human will. Destiny. I don't know. I don't
think I'm supposed to know. I have only just begun.
I know only that I could not stay at Castle Wulfere,
marry a man I could never love, without trying to
find—"

She stopped as thunder repeated its warning,
but he was focused only on her.

"You are on a pilgrimage to find your destiny?
Dressed as a boy?"

The whole thing bothered him. It was half crazy,
for one thing. And dangerous, for another. But
worse, it was impossibly optimistic. What was she
thinking?

"Yes, dressed as a boy," she insisted. "It's safer.
I didn't set out on this journey without a plan, you
know. I was going to the city, to Worcester, to the

booksellers district. I write. I'm an accomplished copyist, and I—"

"You have lost your wits, that's what you have done," he broke in, stunned at the sheer audacity of her plan. To think that she, a lady—

He stared at her, trying to see her as others might see her, with her shortened hair and boy's tunic. Her breasts weren't bound now, but even with them bound, how could any sane man not see that she was a woman? Her body was too lithe and delicate. Her hair too shiny and sweet. Her eyes too big and passionate. He could hardly breathe just looking at her.

Was he so intensely moved by her that he couldn't see her as others might?

Was she courageous or stupid? Mad or brilliant? He didn't know what to make of her. He was more bewildered by her than ever.

"God has already shown you what he wills for you," he said, only wanting their conversation to end. "Your brother has prepared a match for you. Accept it. You are his ward. You owe him obedience."

"I owe myself to find my own destiny!"

"Your destiny is where you left it, at Castle Wulfere."

"I don't accept that."

Her eyes blazed. His head pounded harder. It had been throbbing since the day before, and it only grew worse the longer he engaged in this discussion.

"Destiny is not for you to accept or reject," he dismissed. "It just is."

Did he actually want to send her back to Castle Wulfere, back into the arms of her betrothed? He told himself it was the right thing to do, her true destiny, but was it? Did he simply want to prove to himself that he didn't want her?

She wasn't finished. She stepped closer, poked him in the chest with her finger.

"Who are you to say what is my destiny? What do you know about destiny?"

"I know more than I want to know about destiny, lady," he said harshly.

"You turned your back on your destiny," she charged. "You hide here in this forest, with your pain and your secrets."

"I'm not hiding. I'm surviving. This is my life now."

"And what of the life you left? The people you left?"

"You left a life." He turned the conversation around at her. "You left your people, your family."

Her mouth tensed. Her eyes blazed. He'd struck a nerve, but she was ready. "I left them a note. You left without a word. And I intend to write them once I'm settled. They'll know that I am safe and alive. I'll see them again in time. It's nothing like what you've done. You didn't care what we thought. You didn't care that we grieved. You didn't care—"

"That's right," he ground out harshly. "I didn't care. So what makes you think I care now?"

He couldn't keep listening. He couldn't think about her grieving for him. He turned away from her determinedly to stride back to where he'd dropped his sword.

She spoke to his back, very close. She had followed him.

"You know, it's a lucky thing you're a hermit." Her words came out in a rush, as if she couldn't contain them. "If you spent any time around normal human beings, they'd probably kill you."

He turned toward her slowly, gripping the sword.

"Truer words than you know, lady," he said. "I told you I'm a nasty son of a bitch. Don't forget it."

"How can I forget? You keep reminding me. But what if I don't believe you? What if I think these are just more of your lies? Everything about you is a lie. You aren't going to hurt me. You said so yourself. You aren't going to stop me if I try to leave.

"What are you going to do? Tie me up? Chain me to a tree? You can't stop me. You can't—"

He came right up to her, and her words ended on a choked note as she stepped back until her back hit a tree trunk and she could go no farther.

"I can do anything I want to do, lady," he said in a deceptively soft voice, closing the last breath of ground between them. He placed his arms on either side of her, braced against the tree.

He wanted to touch her so badly, he shook. He was so close to her mouth, he could taste her already in his mind.

It was all he could do not to kiss her, not to take her into his arms and destroy them both.

"Is this what you want?" she whispered. "To kiss me again? Do it. I dare you. Kiss me. Or tell me the truth. Do something other than hide. I told you what I was doing here, where I was headed. What about you?"

He closed his eyes because he couldn't stand to look at her anymore, and dragged in a shuddering breath. She challenged things she didn't understand. He wanted to rail at her, but he couldn't. He couldn't do anything but hold in the pain the way he had for so long. He didn't want to answer her questions. He didn't want to answer his own.

It was easier not to think, not to feel. He'd made a new life. She had no right to criticize it.

He refused to feel anything for her, refused to let her make him feel.

The figure between his braced arms shifted, slipped down and away. It took precious, wasted seconds for him to comprehend that she was gone.

CHAPTER THIRTEEN

She didn't dare look back. Her mouth was dry. Her heartbeat thudded in her ears. It started raining.

The mist swirled around her, and she ran into it, praying for it to swallow her up, praying that somehow, some way, she would find the road on the other side of it.

Behind her, she heard her name shouted, repeated.

He was coming, and he was making no attempt to be quiet about it. She ran faster, tangles of dark branches materializing out of the thick whiteness, grabbing, scratching at her hands and face and legs.

"Lady!"

He sounded worried, and that almost stopped her, but she pushed the emotion that came with it aside along with the tangling branches. She had to keep her head about her. She had to think. She had no idea where she was, or in what direction she was headed. She had no idea which way it was to the road, or what she would do even if she reached it.

She simply knew she had to escape Graeham and the emotions that swirled as thickly as this fog. Why did she keep looking for that sweet boy she'd known in this demon-man he'd become? Why did she let him disappoint her, hurt her? What answers had she expected for her questions? She had gotten what she deserved for her stupidity. He was what he appeared, nothing more. He was what she had believed—a murderer, a traitor. She had sought something in him that didn't exist. She had sought a heart. It had been so stupid.

Rain blew down through the trees, and her feet slipped on the wet ground. She felt herself flung, weightless, then she landed hard on her injured side. The world went black and silent. It was his voice that broke through the numbing darkness. She was up again before she knew she was moving, forcing herself to keep going through her black-dotted vision.

A gnarled branch grabbed her hair, hurled her backward painfully. She choked back a cry. He was close. She could hear him.

She pulled her hair from the branch, tearing strands of it away from her scalp. She pushed herself back against an ancient tree trunk, her breath coming in shaking gasps. It was a huge tree, large enough to hide behind.

Tendrils of hair clung to her cheeks, the back of her neck. She was sweating and shivering. Her vision cleared, but she felt strange, almost disconnected from herself. Seconds flew by while she heard his voice coming ever nearer.

"Lady, come back! Don't be a fool!"

His voice was so close! Her hands trembled as she pulled the hair away from her face, cast her gaze about swiftly. The fog moved, lifted, sweeping in and out in ever-changing patterns. Rain kept coming down. Soon she would be soaked.

But she couldn't bring herself to give up. She didn't want to go back to that tiny hut—with him. He'd kissed her, confused her, threatened something deep inside her.

"I have no patience for this, lady." He sounded so very near. "It will get you nowhere. You can't make it out of this forest alone."

She heard more muffled curses. Then finally, she heard her name. Only this time it wasn't *lady*.

"Elayna," he said, and it was hoarse, almost a moan.

Her throat closed. She willed herself not to be moved by the sound of her name, by the emotion that seemed to come with it. She stood very, very still. *Let him search. Let him move past her. Let him miss her.*

She flattened herself as close as possible to the tree and waited.

To her right, she thought she saw a shadow in the mist, but then it was gone. Was he there? Had he seen her? She kept her back flat against the tree.

There was another movement to her left. Fog? The wind swaying a tree branch? Graeham?

She tried very hard not to think about boars. Maybe it was a squirrel again.

She was afraid to breathe. Her body was screaming to move, to flee in hysterics. She closed her eyes, pressing her cheek against the roughness of the bark, willing herself to be calm. She heard another sound—was it the snort of a boar, or the wind, or her imagination? She bit her lip to keep from whimpering.

He wasn't calling her name now. Or at least she couldn't hear him calling her name. Had he moved on? Had she lost him?

She opened her eyes and looked around. Nothing but fog and trees.

Rain beat down between the tops of the trees now. She was going to be soaked soon. Her side throbbed.

She wasn't sure what happened next. She was leaning against the tree for support, her knees about to give out from sheer fatigue, when a hand came out of nowhere and clapped firmly over her mouth.

"Enough." She heard his words as if they came from far away. His voice was low and unpleasant. "Will you not be satisfied until you get yourself killed?"

Pain shrieked down her still-healing side as he came around the tree, yanking her away from the trunk with his other arm, pulling her back up against his chest.

He let go of her mouth, and she could breathe again. She sank against him, cold, light-headed suddenly. He pulled her around to face him. "That's it," he demanded. "No more."

His breath came unevenly. He was hulking shadow and shape in the darkness of the wood, the light above and behind him distant. He was near and dark and she could almost hear her heart pounding.

"Don't force me to unpleasant measures, lady. I assure you that I will tie you, chain you, anything I have to do to keep you from killing yourself in these woods. You will obey me."

"How chivalric." She tried to push away from him, but he wouldn't let go of her arm. "I don't know if I can take any more of your protection."

"I don't know if I can take any more of protecting you," he said, and there was something like regret in his voice—or had she imagined it? "Say you will obey me," he instructed her. "Or I swear, I will do whatever I have to do to keep you—and myself— safe.''

She said nothing. She could feel the tension coiling tighter in the hand that held on to her.

"You really have no concept of what could happen to you,'' he went on harshly. "You're alone, vulnerable. You actually think you can make it out of this forest on your own? That you can make it anywhere on your own? There are thieves, errant soldiers, all manner of men waiting to prey on just such an innocent as you. If you think you will be safer away from me than with me, you're more witless than I thought.''

"I don't need your approval, or your permission—or your opinion of my wits.''

"Perhaps not, but you will obey me nonetheless. Whether you like it or not. Now say it. Say you will obey me.''

She gritted her teeth, everything inside her rebelling from the words.

At last, she nodded her head, a quick jerk, just once. She wouldn't say it aloud. It was surrender, and they both knew it.

But it would be only temporary.

Elayna sat up on the thin pallet by the fire in Graeham's hut, dressed in another tunic from her satchel, and wrapped in the blanket. Her wet tunic lay across the stool, drying. He'd left her alone to give her a chance to change clothes privately.

The return to the hut had been conducted in silence. She should have been exhausted now. Her side ached, and her body was physically fatigued— but she felt awake and nerveless, buzzing, edgy.

Rain continued to pour down outside. How much time had passed, she didn't know. The door blew inward suddenly, and he appeared in the opening. The forest behind him was stormlit—lightning flashed down, cracking eerie illumination before disappearing again, leaving pitch blackness in its wake.

Her heart thumped into her throat as he walked inside. He dumped a pile of wet wood against the hut's inner wall, then knelt by the fire to stir a pot that hung there, slightly crooked.

Taking a pewter cup, he ladled in a serving of something thin, some kind of vegetable soup, she realized. He passed it to her and poured a cup for himself. She sipped the watery mixture. It was surprisingly good—or she was simply very hungry. There was bread too—that he'd brought back with him from wherever he'd gone several nights before—the inn? She didn't know, could only guess. She sopped the last drops from the bottom of the cup with the end of the bread and looked up with the last bite in her mouth to find him watching her. His clothes were drenched too, but he made no move to take them off; rather, he let the fire dry them on his body.

He looked fatigued and not well. How long had he gone without sleeping?

When he spoke, she discovered he was thinking about her own well-being, not his.

"You could have died out there. You will not be so foolish again."

She watched him where he sat across the fire. He wasn't looking at her. He'd put down his own cup and had picked up a small knife and a bit of wood. He was whittling again.

"Or what?" she could not resist countering. "You'll do what? Clap me in irons? Stretch me on the rack? What?"

He refused to respond, used the knife and the bit of wood to ignore her.

"What are you going to do with me?" she persisted. "I deserve at least that answer. You can't keep me here forever as ... what? A prisoner? A hostage? Do you plan to ransom me?"

His face was shaded, but she could see that his gaze was speculative when he finally lifted it to her, the hand holding the knife going still. He seemed to be examining her intently, considering her words. Saints, was she giving him ideas?

He surprised her by laughing. It was a bitter, uncomfortable sound, as if he was a man who did not laugh much. Unexpectedly, she felt a sweep of sadness.

He had been a boy who laughed often.

"Should I ransom you? Would you fetch a high price, lady?"

"My brother would kill you if he knew what was happening. That would be a very high price indeed."

"And your betrothed, the man you ran from— would he kill for you?" He watched her, all traces of amusement gone from his hard, planed face now. "You made a fool of him. Will he want you back?"

"He is not my betrothed." She was beginning to regret this entire conversation. "There was no betrothal ceremony. It was not made formal."

"Would he want you back?"

"I don't know." Why did he persist in this question? "I don't care. I don't want him."

"Do you fear him?"

He watched her as if he cared to know her answer. As if he *cared*. She frowned at him. The look in his eyes bothered her. It was painful, those rare moments when he reminded her of the boy he had been. A boy with a heart.

She didn't know how to answer that question. She wasn't sure of the answer. "He's a good man, an honorable man." Was she trying to convince him or herself? "A man who doesn't *hide*," she added coolly.

His expression grew hard again. "Your tongue has grown sharp over the years, lady. He must be a very good man indeed, even a courageous man, to have wanted you in the first place."

She was tired of this discussion. "I can't believe I ever thought I loved you," she blurted out, then clamped her lips together and turned away from him. She lay down, her back to the fire and him. "I hate you," she whispered fiercely.

She didn't know if he heard her. She didn't care. He didn't answer. There was something on her cheek, and she reached up to wipe it off. She was shocked to realize it was a tear.

He paced the wallwalk, his cloak billowing out around him.

The waiting was the hardest. His appetite had increased, and yet over the years he had become more and more selective.

He was waiting for her now, the last one. Elayna of Wulfere. She would be found. He would be ready.

The village girl had been missed. She'd run away, a few hardy souls insisted. Like the others. She'd been stolen by the night-winged beast, the less stalwart among them whispered. Like the others.

His cloak flapped in the wind. He held out his arms, threw back his head, and laughed because he knew the truth. He was God. He was the beast. He could do anything because he had the power.

CHAPTER
FOURTEEN

She awoke to the sound of soft moans.

At first she thought she was home at Castle Wulf-ere. She thought Marigold, Lizbet, and Gwyneth were wrestling in the other room. They could be wild, which was what had led her to take the maid's anteroom for her own private use. There, just off the huge bedchamber the other girls shared, she read and wrote and sometimes shut herself up for days when suitors came to call or when she was fighting with Damon.

Marigold, Lizbet, and Gwyneth continued to share the larger chamber, mostly amicably but sometimes not. It was often hard to tell if Gwyneth and Lizbet were fighting or playing.

She started to tell them to be quiet because she was tired. She wanted more sleep.

Slowly, she realized the moans weren't coming from another room and they weren't at all girlish. They were deep and hoarse, and she opened her eyes, comprehending that she was in Graeham's hut in the middle of the misty woods, and she was still lost and trapped and very far from home.

The rain had stopped. It was dead silent except for the low sounds that came from him.

He lay near the fire. He'd taken off his belt and laid it carefully beside him. In sleep, his hand rested over his sheathed knife and pouch. His clothes had dried slightly on his body, but she could see that patches were still damp, especially the parts that weren't facing the fire and the sherte he wore beneath his overtunic.

The sounds he was making were not those of easy rest.

She shucked the blanket and crept across the floor. She reached her fingers out and skimmed his forehead, nearly recoiling. He was burning up!

She squeezed her eyes shut. She thought back to the past days, to his increasing fatigue, shadowed eyes. Saints, what was she going to do? He was sick!

It was her perfect chance to escape. She could take his horse, his knife, anything she needed and strike out through the woods. Another escape on foot frightened her even more than his horse did. If she escaped on horseback—

She opened her eyes and stared down at him. She felt as if her stomach dropped out of her body.

There was no way she could leave him.

His hard, planed face didn't look nearly so fearsome. He looked vulnerable in a way she'd never imagined. She'd seen one side of him in these past few days—pained, cold, harsh, relentless. But what she saw now was different. This look was unstudied, pure, ultimately human.

Without the haunted eyes, the tense jaw, he was the Graeham she remembered. The Graeham she didn't hate at all. The Graeham she—

The path of her thoughts would get her nowhere. She forcibly put a stop to them.

She took the blanket, draped it over him, and then gathered some of the wood stacked by the door of the hut. The fire sputtered and sizzled, but she poked the fresh wood and blew on the pitiful flame, determined, and nearly cried when it finally leapt to life.

The pop of the fire was the only sound in the hut.

He'd stopped making the soft moans, she realized, and she turned to look at him. He was making no sound at all now. She reminded herself that he was a strong man and this was just a fever—but she'd seen what fevers could do to strong men, and she wasn't comforted.

If she was going to help him, she couldn't be squeamish and stupid. She had to just get on with it. It was nothing. She'd helped the castle herbalist strip men to tend their wounds as part of her lady lessons, for pity's sake.

This was no different than any other time she'd tended any soldier or servant at Castle Wulfere.

She gulped in a deep breath, knelt over Graeham, and knew that she was wrong. This was different. She hadn't felt every pulse beat in her body when she'd tended other men.

Her hands hadn't shook; her heart hadn't pounded.

Don't be a half-wit, she demanded. She had to get hold of herself. Graeham's health depended on her. And she had her own future to think of too. She had to get him well, then she had to escape— before he could stop her. There was no time for nonsense.

She reached for the string that tied his sherte together at the neck. He was turned slightly to the side. She reached carefully behind his neck and pulled.

Her heart jumped into her throat when he suddenly reared up. He reached wildly, blindly, for his belt, for the knife.

He lurched into a sitting position. She reeled back, and for a horrifying pulsebeat, she was afraid he was going to kill her. His eyes were glazed, and he didn't seem to recognize her. Then he let go of the knife and pouch, but before there was time for relief, he took hold of her upper arms with both hands.

"Graeham!"

He blinked, seemed to focus in on her face.

"It's me." She dared to touch him again. "It's me."

"What—" He still gripped her arms fiercely, searching her face.

"You're sick. Lie back. Please." She encouraged him to yield with a light push on his chest.

He didn't let go of her, didn't yield.

"You're burning up," she said softly. "I'm trying to take care of you. You've got to get out of these damp clothes."

Something must have broken through, because he suddenly cooperated. The blanket pooling at his waist, he helped remove the outer tunic, and then let her loosen the ties at his neck to pull the sherte over his head.

"I can take care of myself," he grated when she tried to tuck the blanket around his alternately sweating and shivering body, but his objection came out sounding faint, slightly shaky.

"Lie down," she ordered him, and felt a stab of relief when he didn't seem to have the strength to contradict her further. "You're a terrible patient."

"Damn troublesome woman," he whispered hoarsely, but his eyes were closed again. He was asleep.

She felt helpless. She had his wet clothes off, but that wasn't going to do anything for this fever that had already taken hold. She had to do something to get it under control.

She went straight to his worktable. She wished for Marigold's herbal knowledge, then said a silent prayer and took stock of what was available. Not being certain, she decided upon a combination of herbs. She had assisted the apothecary in preparing sweating remedies to break fevers. She recognized elderflower, catnip, yarrow, hung in dried bunches above the table. She took some of each, pounded the leafy parts together in a bowl.

As soon as she put the crushed herbs in a pot, she realized she had no water. She took the water pitcher.

"I'll be right back," she promised. He gave no sign that he was aware of her departure.

Outside, the day was murky, layered of dream mist.

There was a sound, a low snort, and she realized it came from his horse. He kept the animal stabled in the makeshift half-barn to the rear of the hut. Through the muted light, she could see the horse had hay, and shelter beneath the overhanging eave. She thought of how she should have been taking her satchel—her parchments, her money, Graeham's dagger, and a bit of food to get her by— and be on her way by now.

She turned in the direction of the stream and ran. Her breath came in quick pants as she reached the bank, nearly slipping in her rush. She grabbed on to the root of an ancient tree to steady herself and dipped the pitcher into the cold water before hurrying—more carefully this time—back to the hut.

He was still asleep. She hurried to the fire and set the pot to boil before placing the pitcher with the remainder of its contents beside him. She tore off a clean end of cloth from the ruined tunic she'd worn the day she'd run away from Castle Wulfere. *A week ago?* It seemed like so much longer.

She knelt beside Graeham and dipped the cloth in the water. The low fire cast golden flicks of light over his chiseled body, and she focused on his face, avoiding thinking about the rest of his body.

Wringing out the cloth, she draped the material over his forehead. The cold cloth heated quickly on his scorching skin. His lashes trembled briefly, and his eyes opened.

"Are you all right?" she asked softly.

She was peering over him. He was sprawled on his back, and he struggled to recall what was happening. He was ill; she was tending him. He was passing in and out of some kind of liquid darkness that kept pulling him back down. He was determined to resist it. He couldn't afford weakness.

"Lay still," she chided.

He wasn't used to being taken care of. It was gut instinct to try to take care of himself, to show her he didn't need her. He didn't need anybody.

She pushed him down, but it wasn't necessary. Just as quickly as he rose on his elbow, a wave of sickening wooziness drove him back down. He wasn't proving anything to anyone.

Her hands were everywhere—along his temples, his jaw, his throat, his chest, running a cool cloth, touching him. All he could think was that she was touching him in all the wrong places. His fevered mind wanted other things. Other touches, other places . . .

He tried to focus on her. Why was she still here?

The question pounded in his mind as he swam in and out of the fevered liquid darkness. He didn't realize he'd said it out loud.

* * *

"Don't talk," Elayna said. "Rest. I'm taking care of you. You're too hot. I'm trying to cool you down."

He shivered even as sweat ran off his brow. He didn't seem to expect an answer.

She wasn't sure he realized what he'd asked. He was out of his head with the fever.

His eyelashes fluttered down as she took away the cloth, dipped and wrung it again, and brought it back to his face. Slowly, carefully, she skimmed his hot skin with it.

She moved from his forehead to his cheek, then the other cheek, and along his jaw. She bathed his neck and shoulders and chest, becoming familiar with every line and curve of his body as she pushed the blanket down. She lingered on the scar she'd caught a glimpse of before.

It was a wicked one. It ran down his side, straight and clean and deadly. It looked as if it should have killed him.

Why hadn't it? How had he escaped death, punishment for his treachery?

She looked up and saw that he had opened his eyes again. He was watching her. She felt a tingle of heat—not from his fevered skin but from inside herself. And she felt shame. How could she respond to him this way? He had murdered without mercy. But she responded to him anyway. She was weak, shameless in spite of her shame.

He didn't seem to blink and neither did she. It was a long while. She chewed her lip, thinking how strange their situation had become. He was her captor, and she was nursing him.

She broke the moment by moving to the fire. The tea was ready. She hoped she'd used the right quantities. Taking a pewter cup from the table, she

poured a measure, let it cool for a few moments
before turning back to him.

He still watched her.

"This is for your fever," she said. "I'm not good
with healing, but I did my best."

She pushed an arm beneath his and held the
cup up to his mouth. He drank it obediently.

When the contents were gone, she set the cup
down. Her arm was still around his back, supporting him, when he repeated his question.

"Why are you still here?"

Her nerves bounced. She forced a steadiness she
didn't feel.

She arranged some folded material beneath his
head.

"I don't want you to hurt yourself trying to chase
me down," she said dryly. "Now rest. Don't talk."

"Your pilgrimage waits for you. Your destiny waits
for you." His voice was a little slurred.

His words were further proof he was out of his
head. He'd already told her he didn't believe in
her idea of destiny as something she could find
for herself.

"I'm not leaving you. You're sick."

"Run away, lady."

"No," she said flatly. She wasn't planning to
elaborate.

His head nodded and his eyes closed. "Do you
ever do as you're told, lady?"

"No," she replied softly.

He mumbled something she couldn't catch, his
lips barely moving. He continued: "Not like other
ladies. I always liked that about you, not like other
ladies."

He almost sounded as if he were drunk, but of
course that was impossible.

"Loved that about you," he was mumbling now.
"Loved . . . you."

He didn't say anything else. He was out of his head with fever, she thought again. He didn't know what he was saying.

She draped the cloth across the top of the pitcher and she found another pot. There were vegetables, some onions, some cabbage, some roots. Enough for a thin soup, something warm. There was still bread, and she was hungry. It was the first time she'd been the one to cook, and the domesticity of it, there with Graeham, felt strange.

Afterward, she checked on Graeham. His skin was cooler, and he seemed to be resting more easily. She opened her satchel, pulled out her parchments, quills, and ink. This time, the words poured out. She chronicled every sound, every moment she could remember of the past week. When she stopped, her hand was aching and she felt drained.

There were no answers in the writing of it, only more questions.

She spent some time cleaning the hut and generally poking around. She didn't feel the least bit guilty about it, but her curiosity remained unsatisfied. There was nothing her inspection revealed that she didn't already know. He appeared to spend his time on his herb collection and his carving. There were bowls and other useful objects. She found no more intricately created castles.

The chest was still locked. A brief investigation—covert and careful—revealed the key in his pouch. It was late, well past dark, when she took it out and stared at it. She approached the chest immediately.

He suddenly began to moan again and to thrash about. She ran back to him. The blanket went flying, and she barely managed to reach it and jerk back a corner of it before it was caught in the fire.

She touched his forehead. His skin was burning up again. She dropped the key in her pocket and started to take up the cooling cloth again, but his voice stopped her.

"Nay!"

His voice was anguished, hoarse, and it took her a pounding beat to realize he wasn't talking to her.

"What are you doing?"

She stared at him, shocked.

"This is madness! Have mercy on these men, they've done nothing— Oh, God. They're burning, can't you hear their cries?"

He sat straight up, his eyes open suddenly, glazed. He grabbed her tunic at the neckline, bunching the material into his fist. *"God have mercy—"*

She could tell he couldn't see her. What did he see? What was he talking about?

"—on your soul."

He collapsed back, and he shook so violently, she could hear his teeth chattering.

"Graeham! Wake up!" Elayna's heart pounded, horrified at the anguish on his face. "Graeham, please," she whispered, daring to shake his shoulders again. "Graeham!"

She took the cloth again, and the water, and worked to cool his skin. There was more of the sweating tea, but she wasn't sure he could take it now.

Her mind was reeling with the words that had burst out of him. They couldn't be things he'd wanted her to hear. He was out of his mind—or was he *in* his mind, in the past?

She swallowed thickly. What men had he been talking about? He'd been begging for mercy for them, not himself.

What men?

The men had arrived at dusk, Damon's men, with orders from the king, led by Ranulf. Graeham had let down the drawbridge, opened the gates, served them good food and ale, gave them a warm place in his hall. He had made promises, agreements. He would relinquish Penlogan-by-the-sea freely, in accordance with the king's will and his father's crime. He would return to Castle Wulfere with the men to await Damon's return. He would serve among Damon's men until such time as the king settled upon his future. But he had never planned to abide by any of it. He had drugged the men he'd so freely let in his hall. And he'd slit their throats, every last one of them. Then he'd set fire to the hall, its wooden interior and floors quickly turning into a hell. Pitch, they said. He'd soaked the floor in pitch. But he had not escaped. He'd perished with them, destroyed by his own hand, his final crime.

His body had been buried! He had died!

But he had not. He was here, in front of her, in spite of the story she had been told.

And for the first time Elayna let herself truly consider that it might not be the only part of the story that was a lie.

Her heart was in her throat. What if it was *all* a lie?

CHAPTER
FIFTEEN

Graeham awakened slowly. His body felt as if he'd been through a battle and been beaten— he was enervated, achy. He lay there for a while, uncertain how much time had passed.

He was alone, and that realization worked its way to the surface of his consciousness as the events of the past days clarified and he opened his eyes.

Elayna.

Jumbled images, voices, memories, came together. Rescuing her, tending her, living with her for too many difficult days, kissing her, chasing her, then—what? He'd been sick.

He'd been sick, and she'd taken care of him. He'd told her to leave— Had she?

Other images tore through, images of the past, images of horror. They were mixed somehow with the past week and more with Elayna, but they were nightmarish, blurred, and he couldn't make sense of how they fit in.

He focused on his surroundings. There was her

satchel. It remained. She wouldn't have left without her belongings.

But why hadn't she gone?

It would have been a relief if she'd taken the opportunity to run away.

As he looked around, he noticed that things seemed different. The bare earth floor had been swept. She'd scattered straw around the room save the hearth area, and she had strewn herbs. The hut smelled fresh, clean. Even his worktable had been tidied. A pot of some sort of soup simmered on the fire.

The door opened, and he turned his head toward the muted light. She looked radiant. Her hair was damp. She smelled like dew and hope. He wanted to snarl at her for no reason at all.

There were evergreen boughs and tiny, delicate-stemmed late-season flowers in her arms. He focused on them.

"What is all of that?"

She smiled. *Smiled.*

"Good morning," she said. "It's such a beautiful morning, and I thought these would cheer up the place."

He frowned. What was she up to? He felt suspicious of her mood.

"How are you feeling?" She put the flowers and evergreen boughs on his worktable and placed her hand on his forehead.

"I'm fine." He jerked away from her touch and sat up. He leaned back against the wall of the hut, wincing at the tingling in his body. That had been some fever, based on the aftereffects.

"Good, the fever's gone." She fixed a bowl of soup for him. "Time to eat. You didn't eat at all yesterday. You woke up burning with fever, and it raged off and on all day. I was worried about you." She nodded at the bowl. "You need your strength."

The better to chase after her the next time she ran away?
The question of why she was still there continued
to plague him.

"I don't want soup," he said. "I want an enormous piece of meat."

"Then eat your soup so you can hunt," she
replied lightly. "Besides, this is probably all your
body can take right now." She held the bowl,
crouching near him, and he realized she intended
to feed him.

"I can feed myself," he said, and took the bowl
out of her hands. He drank the soup in one long
pull, burning his throat in the process, then shoved
the bowl straight back at her. "Happy?"

Her damned candleglow eyes met his for a long
time. She didn't say anything, just took the bowl
away.

He wanted to tell her he didn't need anyone to
take care of him, hadn't in more than four long
years, and he wasn't going to start now. But the
words stuck in his throat.

The truth was, he *had* needed her. He'd been
sick, and every time he'd opened his eyes, she'd
been there, but the thought only fouled his mood
further.

"What did you do to my house?"

"I cleaned it. Do you expect me to live in a
pigsty?"

She turned away, busying herself with cleaning
up the hearth. He watched her, occasionally catching glimpses of her watching him.

He didn't say anything, just watched her sneaking glances at him as she worked.

Her look was . . . wary. Not wary in the way she
had been before, as if she were looking for some
way to escape or wondering if he would hurt her.

This wary was different.

* * *

The day passed in tedious increments, and his mood didn't improve. He forced himself to endure the hours of rest in order to recover his strength. The quicker he was back to his usual self, the better.

Elayna sat across from him, writing on those parchments of hers. She seemed capable of losing herself in them for long periods of time. He had done his damnedest to ignore her, but he kept finding his gaze drawn back to her, watching the way she tucked her bottom lip beneath her teeth as she wrote, and thinking how absolutely lovely she had become, wondering how it would feel to touch those waving, drying tendrils that framed her face, to breathe in her stream-sweet scent. . . .

These observations did nothing for his temperament, especially when she would look up at him in that wary-watchful way again.

Eventually, he lay back, closed one eye, still keeping the other on Elayna. She stopped writing finally, and then puttered around the fire, tidying up for all the world as if she were a wife. It was too cozy.

What was she up to?

She'd had plenty of opportunity to escape, but she hadn't. Was she waiting for him to sleep again, and lulling him into a false sense of security in the meantime? Why hadn't she run already, when she'd had the chance?

She came over to him when she finished her puttering, knelt down, and reached a hand for his forehead. He tried to ward her off, but she was determined.

"Your fever could return," she said.

He glowered up at her with enough heat to torch the hut, for all the good it did him. "I'm fine."

She ignored him. Against his skin, her fingers

felt feathery and cool. She soothed his forehead with the heel of her hand, her fingers brushing lightly along his hairline.

Her touch rippled a pleasant chill down his arms. He experienced a treacherous throb in his groin. The physical craving was strong, urgent. His body wanted what it had been denied for so long— but he wanted not just any woman, he wanted *this* woman.

He had to be crazy to even be thinking it. The only positive light he could put on it was that if he was desiring her, he was definitely on the mend in a hurry.

"I think my fever has been adequately checked." He pushed her hand away. "I'm fine. If I'm not fine, I'll take care of myself, as I'm well accustomed to doing."

He went on the offensive, searching for some badly needed perspective.

"What is your game, lady? Not so long ago, you were willing to risk anything to run away from me. Yesterday, it would have been easy. You could have taken my horse, anything you wanted, and run. I *told* you to run. So why didn't you?"

She'd moved back to her pallet and sat cross-legged now, her damnable boy's tunic's folds tucked around her. He noticed again the sway of soft hair caressing her jaw. She was so feminine, so beautiful, even now. Especially now.

"What kind of person do you think I am, Graeham?" Her forehead creased angrily. Finally, he'd gotten a rise out of her. "You saved my life. I couldn't leave you when you needed me. You had a fever. You should rest instead of asking questions. You had a very bad night."

Something niggled at the back of his mind. Bits and pieces came back, the pieces that didn't fit. Dreams. Or nightmares, to be more exact.

He guessed the nightmares had come as a result of Elayna and the past week's events. He had made it his mission not to think of the past, but she had brought it all back simply by being there. These were memories he didn't bear willingly. He had changed his name, his home, his entire life, but there were some things that would never change. He was Graeham of Penlogan-by-the-sea, whether he accepted the name anymore or not. He would have been lord of Penlogan now if his father hadn't been betrayed and murdered.

If the same hadn't nearly happened to him.

He could, in dark moments, still smell the sick stench of burning flesh, feel the choking horror, the cold, the confusion. He had been powerless to stop it, to save them or himself from forces he hadn't understood—then or now.

He had turned his back on everything of the world that had betrayed him and his father. He wanted no part of it.

But there were moments when it still wanted him, when it still tormented him. Moments like last night, and like now, when all he had to do was look at Elayna and know that he couldn't deny that he had lost something, that it hadn't been all bad.

Fragments of memory clarified, and he thought— Had he said aught in his fevered state?

His heart raced. He couldn't bear to sit in the small space with her any longer—with her eyes of regret, sadness, confusion, pity. He got up, ignoring her surprised protest, and stormed out of the hut.

He felt a sense of panic that he hadn't expected, and it almost robbed him of air. Merciful saints, what had he revealed?

His mind reeled with the possibility that she knew anything, any part of what had truly happened that day at Penlogan. He had left her behind all those years ago. He'd had no choice. Forgetting her, giving up on what they had shared, had been as difficult as giving up Penlogan and his very name. But she was part of the world that had turned its back on him, and to have contacted her in any way would have been to endanger her as much as himself.

She had believed what they said about him; he had always known that, but seeing it in her face, in her eyes, in her voice since her arrival in the forest had made it that much more painful.

But even more painful would be the truth, that he had loved her, that he hadn't wanted to leave her.

You plotted your revenge, and there was no room in it for me.

Those words had been the sword in his side all over again. He hadn't wanted to hurt her ever. But he'd had no choice.

He sucked in the fresh autumn air until a measure of calmness returned to him. He was safe. She couldn't know everything. No one did. In truth, even he didn't know everything, so he could hardly reveal it, no matter how fevered his state.

Graeham let out a deep breath and looked heavenward through the trees, forcing the tension out of his body. He was feeling better, he realized. There was no cause for alarm.

He was more convinced than ever that he had to get rid of Elayna. He was no longer holding her captive, that much was obvious. She could have gone. He'd *wished* her gone—despite the risks. So what held her here?

And could he forget her . . . again?

Elayna put away her writing things. She had recorded everything that had happened last night, everything she had thought and wondered about the horror she had heard in Graeham's voice. He wasn't himself today. Not that she was certain of what Graeham's temper should be on any given day.

She was only fooling herself if she thought she knew anything about him—in the past, or the present. He was an enigma, and maybe he always had been. He certainly hadn't been what she had believed him to be then. He had disappeared, hadn't he? The perfect young knight she had fallen in love with wouldn't have done that to her. Had she ever truly known him? Had he ever been perfect? Did she want him to be perfect?

There was something about the painful, secret man he'd become that drew her more. Tugged at the wounds inside her, as if somehow they could heal each other.

She couldn't stop thinking of the horror that had been in his voice the night before. It hadn't been horror he was inflicting on others. It had been horror inflicted on him and on men he sought to protect.

The thoughts went round and round in her head, and she doubted there was any sense in asking Graeham for explanations. He had been noticeably short in the area of answers. He'd stomped out a few moments earlier as if just being in the same room with her was too much.

She could leave anytime. He'd made that clear. And yet, something was stopping her. Not yet. Not until . . . She drew up her legs, crossing her arms over her knees, and then froze. *The key*

CHAPTER SIXTEEN

She didn't know what she expected to find. An extensive search of the hut the day before had revealed nothing she hadn't already figured out. Graeham spent his time practicing his knightly arts and perfecting his herbal lore.

Still, she was surprised when she unlocked the chest. First, she found books. There were several herbals, and she realized he must have learned what he knew about healing from them. There was one other book, a modest volume with no decoration. When she opened it, she discovered a book of hours containing services and prayers for personal devotion. Parts of it were in Latin, parts in English. It appeared well used.

You believe in God?

You think I don't?

She was ashamed as she recalled the conversation. She'd judged him easily, but the truth was complicated and still far from known. She was as confused as ever. Graeham of Penlogan, a young, compelling knight, a lord in waiting, was now what—a religious hermit? Was he atoning for his sins? Had the world cast him out, or had he cast out the world?

She stacked the books outside the chest and looked at what had been beneath them. There were weapons such as she would have expected to find to accompany the plate body defenses she'd already seen. There was a jeweled dagger, a war hammer, a crossbow and quiver. She also found her missing erasing knives. She piled the weapons on the floor, setting her knives aside, and was surprised at what she saw next. What at first looked to be a pile of material turned out to be clothing. She took out the first piece and realized it was a jupon, laced down the back, ornamented with the heraldic symbols of the lord of Penlogan—a tower and a lily in a pattern of green, white, and blue. A gash tore through one side of it, and it was steeped with a dark brownish stain. *Blood?*

Beneath the jupon there were other items of clothing that appeared to go with the first, and a sword-belt. Its engraved pattern consisted of embossed metal with insets of red enamel. Each enameled inset was emblazoned with a tower out of which sprang a dragon. An embroidered silk pouch was attached.

She pulled the string that tied the pouch, tilted it up, and poured the contents into her palm. It held only one item: a garnet ring. Red fire. Dragon fire.

Keep it, hold on to it, know it is my heart.

She'd been thirteen years old when Graeham had given her this ring and she had said those words to him, telling him to keep it until the time when their fathers approved the match.

He had kept it for more than four years. There were few things he had brought with him from

Penlogan—his armor, his sword, the clothes on his back. *Her ring.*

Elayna's throat tightened and her heart wobbled. She could hardly believe she was thinking anything so hopelessly sentimental. It was wishful thinking gone mad. It was dangerous to her peace of mind and her future. She shouldn't attach romantic fantasies to lost causes, and a hermit or whatever he was locked in a secret forest was a lost cause if she'd ever seen one. Graeham was a childish dream she had outgrown. Nothing could ever come of this bizarre interlude for more reasons than she could count. There was no way he could still love her. He was cold, heartless, unemotional.

But even as she thought it, she knew it wasn't true. What *was* true? Lies, truth—they were impossibly mixed together. She was hurt, still stupidly hurt, and she had a right to know the truth. This ring would have been hers.

He came in quietly, and she didn't realize he was there till he spoke. She stood, purposeful, and tipped her chin at him. He was massive—all muscle and sinew, hard eyes and harder mouth. He'd been gone for a while, and she could see from his damp hair that he had been to the stream to bathe, mayhap to cool off his temper, though he didn't look very cool now.

"What's going on here, lady?"

"That," she said quite coolly in complete defiance of her pounding pulse, "is what I would like to know."

"From where I'm standing, it looks like you've been going through my things." Graeham didn't like what he saw. She'd managed to get hold of the key to his chest, no doubt sometime while he'd been ill. Now she'd searched it.

She had stood when he walked in, but she hadn't moved away from the chest. Her fingers were curled around something. She wore a dark green tunic, one of several she'd brought with her.

As usual, she looked nothing like a boy.

"Give me the key," he demanded, approaching her.

She didn't make a move to cooperate.

"I've already seen everything," she said. "The books, the sword-belt, the weapons, the clothing—the clothing you wore the night Penlogan burned."

He heard her hesitancy beneath the calm outward appearance. He honed in on her face, her lips. There was a vulnerability in her expression even as there was also a challenge. What was going on?

I've already seen everything.

"I found the ring." She uncurled her fingers. Red dragon fire shone from her palm.

"It's a ring." He shrugged with painful deliberateness. "Nothing more, nothing less." He wanted to lash out at her. The stricken look in her eyes seared him. Stricken, and yet hopeful, damn her.

Guilt was always crushing, and he held it in abeyance with one strategy: He blocked it.

But she was right there. She wouldn't be blocked.

"It's not just any ring. It's *my* ring."

"Then take it. Put the rest of the things back and go away. Go away, lady. You have my blessing. You are free. Take my horse. Ride it northeast, and you will find the road. You will be quite near the inn. Leave my horse at the edge of the wood. It will return on its own. It is well trained. It knows the way."

He walked to the fire, presented her with his back. It was done. He didn't care what happened as long as she left him alone. He had been alone for over four years. He liked it that way. He liked his life. It was his, and it was painful, but it was safe—from the past, from the hellish temptation of her.

"Tell me what happened."

"It's my business, lady, not yours."

"Oh, please," she said, approaching him, her tone exasperated, "we're not going to play this same tired game. I'm not going anywhere, so you might as well start talking. You held me captive—well, now I'm holding you captive. I'm not giving up this time. I'm not going away. I want to know what happened."

He stared into the flames. She wouldn't give up. That's what was wrong with her. Something inside him was taut, stretched to breaking, and he was afraid of what would happen if she didn't stop.

"You don't know what you're asking."

"I know exactly what I'm asking! Maybe it's you who doesn't know." She took hold of his arm, and he turned his head. "I'm asking why you left me. Don't you see? This wasn't just your life that was destroyed. It was my life, my heart too."

"I didn't choose this life, lady."

Her eyes sparked. "Don't call me lady! Call me Elayna. Can't you even do that?"

"No," he said.

"Why?" she demanded, softer but still insistent.

She gripped his arm, willing him to look at her. He had no choice, and as he did, he felt something cracking open inside him. He held it together with every bit of his might.

"*Why did you keep this ring?*" she asked.

"It was in my pouch that night. I left with little more than the clothes on my back. You can see that for yourself." She had been through the chest; she knew.

"You kept it all these years."

"Do not read meaning where there is none."

"Then you tell me the meaning! Tell me what happened that night—to the men, to Penlogan, to you. To me. Last night, you cried out in your fever. You begged for their lives. You begged for mercy—for them."

"I was not in my right mind last night." His fists clenched and unclenched at his sides.

"Did you kill those soldiers?"

He stood mute, unmoving.

"Did you set fire to Penlogan? Did you burn them, yet half alive? Did you destroy Penlogan rather than let the king award it to someone else?"

"That is what they say, lady, and do you not believe what they say?" he rasped.

She whirled away from him, grabbed the satchel from the floor, and tore back through the pages of parchments. It was her journal. He didn't even want to look at it, much less know what she was doing with it now.

He turned his head, tightened his jaw. He was aware of her settling on the pallet, her papers in her lap. The fever had long left him, but his head was pounding again. She started reading.

"Graeham welcomed them in—a score of Damon's men, led by Ranulf and Kenric, with Father Almund at his side. Graeham gave them meat and drink, all that he had. But it was a trick, a terrible trick. He had sent away most of the castlefolk, leaving only the pages to serve their masters. The men were weakened suddenly, overcome by some kind of mad potion that must have been secreted in the ale, when hell erupted around them. The hall was afire, pitch and oil poured into the rushes.

"The bodies that weren't burned too badly for recognition were found with their throats slit—as if burning them wasn't enough. Then he killed himself, fell on his own sword."

She stopped reading, stared up at him. "*That* is what they say. And I believed them. I believed all of it. I didn't understand how it could be true, how the wonderful knight I knew could have turned into such an evil beast. And yet— It was true. It had to be true. There was nothing else to believe. There was nothing else but— What? What happened?''

He gazed down at her without expression. "Destiny.''

"Who saved you?''

"God.''

"Damn you, Graeham of Penlogan, answer me straight!'' She stood, throwing her parchments down at her sides as she did.

A corner of one parchment caught in the fire. Elayna shrieked and made a dive for the page.

"Watch out!'' He gripped her shoulders, pulled her back. The burning parchment fell near the hearth, and he swiftly stamped the flame out. Other parchments scattered around the stool at her feet, but none of them had burned.

She started picking up the strewn pages of her journal. He could see her eyes were wet.

"I'm sorry,'' he said quietly. He started to help her gather her parchments. "That was my fault. If you hadn't been upset with me—''

The words on the first sheet, carefully lettered in her rounded, bold script, stopped him cold.

He rode in on a white horse. How romantic, Lizbet said. What does she know. If he had been there for her, she would have stuck a feather up her nose. Gwyneth had blackened her teeth just in case he was there to see her. But he was not. He was there for me. He was gentle and rich, and Damon said he made a fine offer. He would make a fine husband. But he was not Graeham.

Graeham picked up the next one. His hand shook. They were dated but out of order from having fallen.

The entries spanned the years since he'd left.

He stayed a week and never ran out of amusing tales. He was tall, with red hair and a thin face, and he was very rich—but I liked his stories much more than his money. I actually spoke to him. Twice. Even Gwyneth and Lizbet liked him after they were sure he was not interested in them. Damon said he made a fine offer. But he was not Graeham.

There were more, and they all ended the same way. *He was not Graeham.*

She hadn't stopped wanting him, loving him. Not for years. Maybe not even now.

He was ashamed that the first thing he felt was exhilaration. It was a useless, impossible reaction made worse by the next page he picked up.

This one was recent. It was from here, the hut. She had been keeping her journal since she'd arrived. He'd watched her write. The top of the page he picked up had one large, scrawled question.

Do you know how much you hurt me?

Guilt was a powerful emotion. He had learned to control it, to tolerate the knowledge that men had died while he had lived, and that he had left a beautiful, sweet girl behind. He had had no choice. But that knowledge didn't take the pain away, only allowed him to bury it for a time, where he didn't have to think about it or know that just like his pain, her pain hadn't stopped with that day.

She had gone on hurting.

The guilt told him he should have done something about it.

He set the parchments aside and looked up at her. She was watching him silently, and suddenly she looked ridiculously young, her cheeks flushed, her eyes bright with emotion.

She looked like the girl he'd pledged his love to that day on the battlements. He murmured her name, hoarse, and his palms cupped her cheeks. The heat of the fire swam over him, and then the heat *was* her. He made another sound, this one deep in his throat, and then somehow, impossibly, he was making a terrible mistake. He was kissing her.

CHAPTER SEVENTEEN

He swept his tongue inside her mouth, his heart pounding crazily. Graeham felt her fingers in his hair as she kissed him back just as fiercely, just as hungrily. She pressed herself against him even as he tried to pull her closer and he knew, even in her naiveté, that she wanted more than kisses. So did he.

All he had to do was ask, and she would be his the way she had been before, the way perhaps she had been all along. It would take almost nothing for her to be caught up in the past. She was sentimental and hopeful and everything that he wasn't.

He could bury himself in her sweetness, lose himself in the forbidden. And tomorrow she would wake up with her lost innocence and a ghost—for that was all he was. A ghost.

The light would fade from her eyes when she realized he had nothing to offer her. *He wasn't Graeham.* She'd written that about all her suitors. But the truth was, he wasn't Graeham either. Not the Graeham she wanted him to be when she kissed him this way.

And he never could be, and he had to make her see that.

He found the strength to gently push her away. "We can't do this," he rasped.

Elayna's sweet, dark gaze clung to him. He recalled the sensation of her lips pressed to his, her mouth opening to him, and the wanting inside him was almost unbearable.

Yet he had to think of what was right, not just for himself. He had to think of what was right for her.

"We have to do this," she argued. "And you can push me away, but it won't make me *go* away. You haven't answered my questions yet."

"You won't like the answers."

"I'm not afraid of them." Her voice was calm, her eyes certain. "Or you."

Graeham was struck by the irony of the situation. Elayna was the only person he had, forsooth, betrayed, and yet while he'd lost everything else he'd ever had, he hadn't lost her trust.

His chest felt tight.

Her hand was on his arm. They were both still on the floor by the fire. She said nothing, simply waited, her expression expectant and open. She was offering him something he hadn't experienced in a long time. *Closeness, intimacy* . . . It was frighteningly appealing.

"Maybe," he said slowly, " 'tis I who am afraid of you."

She swallowed, baby-bird wings fluttering in her stomach.

"Why?" she asked, and waited.

"Because you ask impossible questions. You push and pull and don't let go."

"I can't help it! I'm worried sick about you. You

live here in this forest with nothing but secrets and lies. You help others— Who is helping you? You bury yourself here with your herbs and your prayers and your sword practice. What is it all for? It makes no sense. I can't help worrying about you, and I won't pretend to be sorry."

"How can you care after all this time, after what I've done—left you, held you captive—"

She crossed the space separating them. "Of course I care." She touched his arm.

He closed his eyes as if her touch were painful.

"It was wrong for me to keep you here," he said. He opened his eyes, faced her with his intense, haunted gaze. "It was wrong, and it was selfish. None of this is your fault. I hurt you—then and now. There's no excuse for it, and you shouldn't care. If you want to know what happened, you have the right. I want you to know that I do know how much I hurt you. And I'm sorry."

She felt tears burn her eyes. "Then tell me," she whispered. "I'm ready."

He turned away from her and began to pace. When he began to speak, it was in a low, disembodied voice, as if the tale he told had occurred to someone else, not him.

"My father's squire had arrived from France just ahead of Ranulf." His voice was low, barely audible. His mouth twisted bitterly as he looked somewhere across the fire into nothingness. "My father was dead, executed for the rape and murder of Angelette, the daughter of the lord of Saville. Her body had been found outside a tavern in an alley, where she had gone secretly to meet her fiancé, Rorke of Valmond."

Rorke was Damon's close friend and comrade throughout the king's campaigns in France and now served as Damon's chief man-at-arms at Wulfere. She thought of Rorke's haunting pain even as she watched similar emotions move across Graeham's face.

"Rorke had been injured in a tournament, unable to meet Angelette as they had planned," Graeham went on.

"Damon went in his place," Elayna filled in.

"A fateful decision." Graeham stopped to look at Elayna now, and she saw the pure torture of his gaze directly. She wanted to look away, but she could not.

She had been wrong; she wasn't sure she was ready to hear this, she realized. It was too painful—for him, for her. Damon still hurt at the mention of Angelette. And Rorke . . . Angelette was never mentioned in front of Rorke at all.

So many people had been hurt, she thought. And for so long. And that was why she had to hear it no matter the cost.

"Damon found her," he said. "There was no place to take her—the tavern was full of whores and drunks. Château Blanchefleur, her father's castle, was on the rise above the village, not far, but it was too late. She died in his arms by the time he reached the gates, and her father seized Damon."

"He was in prison for a year." So far, Graeham had been repeating a story Elayna well knew. It had been awful. Without Belle's love, Elayna didn't know if Damon would have healed.

Even with Belle's love, it had taken a long time.

"He was lucky," Graeham said.

The bitterness of his voice stunned her, but she knew what he meant. Damon had lived. His father had been executed.

"Rorke never gave up on him," she said softly. "Ranulf too, and Kenric. They worked hard for his freedom. They were convinced he was innocent."

"They gave my father up for Damon's freedom."

"But your father *wasn't* innocent. They found proof, a witness—"

"They found a lie."

She swallowed thickly. They were coming, the things she wouldn't like to hear. This, she knew, was where the story she had known and Graeham's story would begin to diverge.

"I don't understand," she said. She went back to the story she knew. "Your father confessed. He had been in love with Angelette for months. He had approached her, and she had rebuffed him. Seeing her with Rorke had driven him mad with jealousy. He had discovered her secret plans and had made certain he was there first, in that alley where she was to have met Rorke.

"Angelette and Rorke were going to run away together to be wed. Her father would never let her marry an English knight. Your father couldn't bear to let another man have her—he forced himself on her, and when she resisted, he killed her."

The words were terrible, but there was no avoiding them. Everything started there. Whatever had happened at Penlogan that awful day more than four years ago, it had begun in that tavern alley in the village below Blanchefleur.

"He never touched her," Graeham said. "He wasn't there."

She wanted to believe him, if only because it was so clear that he believed it. But she needed more information.

"He was executed because he confessed," she pointed out. "The lord of Saville had tortured Damon for a year to get a confession from him, and he wouldn't give it. Your father confessed right away—"

"My father was an old man," he said harshly. "He was in poor health. He knew what Damon had been through. He knew he wouldn't withstand it. He asked Thomas to beg my forgiveness for his cowardice, and he died.

"Damon believed *he* had been betrayed, that my father let him all but die in that French dungeon for his crime, but it was a lie. Damon was betrayed, but not by my father. Whoever betrayed Damon went on to do the same thing to my father. When the hue and cry would not let up over Damon's innocence, the murderer of Angelette set up my father to take Damon's place."

"My God." Elayna sat frozen, transfixed by Graeham's terrible story.

"My father spent that night asleep in his bed with none but his squire to vouch for him. No one listened to him, not when they had a respected warden of the village to say the opposite, that he saw my father with Angelette that night.

"He said he saw my father put his hands around her neck and strangle her—and that it was because he had interrupted the crime that Angelette had lived long enough for Damon to arrive. But he was so in fear of the lord of Saville that he didn't report what he had seen. He knew that, like Damon, the wrath of the lord of Saville might come down upon his head simply for having been there."

"Are you saying that the village warden lied?" Elayna asked in bewilderment.

She struggled to take in all the ramifications of what he was telling her. If Wilfred was innocent— then who? And—

"Why?" she whispered.

"Either the warden lied or my father lied." Graeham's words were flat, unemotional. He was staring into the fire, and the pattern of flames lit his face, delineated each line of tension.

"And you believe it was the warden."

He glanced at her. "He was my father. He was an honorable man." His mouth settled in a hard line. "And there was Thomas, if you can't accept that. Thomas was with my father that night, *all* of that night. He was nowhere near Angelette."

"Why would the warden lie all that time later? He didn't know that the lord of Saville would soon be dead." Elayna thought of all she knew about that last day at Blanchefleur.

Damon himself had killed Angelette's father in a final battle for his life. The lord of Saville had promised to free Damon but had gone back on his word, determined to torture Damon one last time, to find out if Damon had known all along that the true culprit was Wilfred of Penlogan and had actually protected Wilfred out of loyalty to his foster lord. But what Saville had not known was that his guards, ordered away in haste, had already released the bonds holding Damon's arms.

What had ensued had been a fight to the death, and Damon had won. He'd escaped Blanchefleur and returned home to Castle Wulfere. Wilfred of Penlogan had already been dead.

"The warden would have still feared the lord of Saville's wrath," she insisted. "Speaking against your father put his own life in jeopardy."

"I don't know," Graeham admitted. "Maybe he was paid. Maybe he was promised protection. Or maybe he was simply wrong."

Elayna didn't like what she was thinking now, not at all. Now she knew why he'd said she wouldn't like what she would hear. Not because it was all so awful, which it was, but because it would hit too close to home. If someone had been behind a false accusation of Wilfred—

"Damon would never have wanted to gain his release by any means that were dishonorable," she said sharply. "Certainly not by any means that would accuse—falsely—your father, who was his foster lord. Damon loved your father!"

"And my father loved Damon," Graeham said in a dangerous voice. "My father would not have allowed Damon to sit in that dungeon for his crime for a year, and yet Damon accepted that as fact."

"Only after your father confessed," Elayna said. Her mind reeled. "Who else? Ranulf? Rorke? Kenric? The king? Who would want to place your father in that dungeon over Damon?"

"Someone who wanted the questions to stop." Graeham's face hardened even more. "Or someone who had something to gain."

Elayna blinked. "Everyone gained except Rorke. Rorke would never want anyone but the true murderer to be punished. Rorke loved Angelette, and the only gain he would care about is justice. He lives naught but a half-life even now, tortured by guilt that he wasn't there to save Angelette that night. He believed your father was her killer.

"So did Damon—I know he did," she continued quickly. "So did all of them. I saw them when they came back from France! For all they gained, they were in pain. Damon gained his life, but he couldn't forget how he had been tortured, and how your father had betrayed him. Kenric gained his brother's release, but he, too, was tormented by how he let Damon down because he was not with Damon that night. Ranulf gained—"

She gasped. "Ranulf gained Penlogan, but at what cost? Wilfred was Ranulf's foster lord too! He lives with guilt of possessing a castle of a man he loved and was responsible for seeing executed. None of them would have wanted to gain anything this way. Your father confessed!" she said again, almost desperately.

She couldn't believe that her brother, or any of the men around him—even Ranulf, would have taken part in something so evil, but then, what did happen? Graeham was here, alive—

And it was Ranulf who had witnessed his presumed suicide, Ranulf alone who had returned to tell the tale. *Ranulf.*

She lifted shocked eyes to Graeham.

"Three men survived that night," she breathed. "Ranulf, Kenric, and Father Almund. Kenric and Father Almund had succumbed to whatever evil had been in that ale. Ranulf pulled them to safety. He was burned himself!" She frowned, feeling so sick inside. "He saw you die. He saw you die at your own hand!"

He was silent, and from outside the hut she could hear the light rustle of the night breeze coming up.

"But I'm alive, aren't I?" he said. "And I'm innocent—as was my father. He knew nothing of Angelette's death. He was hunting, and Saville's men came upon him with no warning. He was seized and taken to Blanchefleur, and the next thing he knew he was facing the torture chamber.

"He had a choice to make, and he made it. Thomas fled, fearing for his own life, for he had been loyal to my father and he had been with him the night Angelette was murdered. He tried to make it back to Penlogan as fast as he could, but he didn't make it back fast enough."

"Go on," she said softly. She wanted yet didn't want to hear more.

Now the story had returned to English soil. Now the murder of Angelette had come to Penlogan. She knew the next part of the story would be even worse.

CHAPTER EIGHTEEN

He was silent for a very long time.

"Thomas knew Damon's men carried the king's orders along with the news about my father," Graeham began again slowly. "He wanted to get to me first. He wanted to be the one to tell me that my father was dead and why—not Father Almund or Kenric, and especially not Ranulf. Thomas carried a secret letter for me . . . from my father. He wanted me to find out what happened in my father's own words."

He paced away from her again. She wanted to go after him, wanted to comfort him but wasn't sure she would be welcomed. When he turned back, he stared across the space separating them, and she saw more than those few strides between them. There was something intangible, a distance created by more than space. There was torment in his eyes, and then he controlled it, and a cold, hard mask slipped into place.

She watched him, wondering if he expected to

keep his feelings locked away forever behind that hard mask, hidden in this forest hut.

Had he allowed himself to grieve at all for his father? Or had he distanced himself from those feelings the way he had distanced himself from everything and everyone else?

"What happened to the letter?" she asked.

His eyes were bleak. "Thomas was still afraid that he would be seized," he continued, his voice so low, it was barely audible, "afraid that he would be held to blame for Angelette's death and Damon's false imprisonment. Damon's men were already at the gate. There was no time to examine the letter. He was frantic, and I was . . ." He closed his eyes a moment, controlled his pain again, shoved it down to wherever he kept such unallowable emotion. He paced briefly, stopped in front of the fire. "I was in shock. I had just found out my father was dead, executed as a criminal."

He was near enough that she could touch his arm, and she dared. He didn't move, didn't acknowledge the gesture, but she saw something flicker on his face, a slight tightening of his jaw. Control. He was a master at control.

The moment passed. He walked away, turned. Now he glanced at her.

"There are tunnels beneath Penlogan," he explained. "As you know, the castle overlooks the sea. The cliff upon which it's built is rife with caves. The cliff wall is sheer, and few know that one of those natural caves opens into a man-made tunnel. My grandfather discovered this cave during a reconstruction phase. Much of old Penlogan was still timber, and he was fortifying a new stone tower surrounding an old wooden structure, and new family quarters—an entire new wing. They were excavating new dungeons to be stationed beneath it, and suddenly they found themselves tapping in to the base of a cave. He repositioned the dungeons and had an architect brought in to make secret plans for tunnels that would connect the cave to certain chambers inside Penlogan.

"My grandfather had enemies," Graeham explained. "He liked the idea of having a secret exit from Penlogan should it ever be attacked. Within the thick walls of Penlogan lie a warren of secret tunnels, and in the cave there are boats, ropes, ladders, everything that would be required to launch an escape to the sea far below."

"I don't understand." Elayna was amazed to discover the existence of this maze of tunnels—she'd been to Penlogan several times during her life and had never heard of the tunnels—but she was perplexed. What did the tunnels have to do with the mystery of that night at Penlogan?

"I told Thomas to hide in the tunnels. There was no time—Damon's men, with the king's orders—were already at the gate. I could either hold them off and create a siege situation that would endanger the lives of everyone in the castle, or I could let them in, hear them out, seemingly acquiesce while I made plans. Thomas disappeared into the tunnel behind the tapestry in my father's chamber. There was a panic in the castle, and I sent word through my men to send as many of the servants home to the village as could be spared. With a skeleton staff, I greeted Ranulf with a feast."

The fire was between them now, and she watched the shadows play on his ungiving features. He was wearing a plain tunic, woodsman attire, and yet he was as formidable as the knight he was truly born.

She could imagine him, in her mind's eye, facing a line of armed men at the gate of Penlogan, coolly letting them into the great hall of the castle, feasting them with meat and ale. He had been still young, but he had had a courage and composure

that men much older would envy. Those virtures
had been combined with compassion and wisdom.
He had cared more for his people at that moment
than himself, had put them first, ensured their
safety by preventing a siege. He would have made
a good and just lord of Penlogan.

How could he possibly be the same man who
then turned around and caused not only the death
of Damon's men but also the loss of countless people of Penlogan by burning the castle down around
them? How could she ever have believed that of
him? She was ashamed and still hopelessly confused.

But why had he turned his back on them all
these years? If his father was innocent—

"What happened next?" She was impatient for
answers.

He took a deep breath.

"I don't know."

She hadn't expected that answer.

A frown knitted her brow. "What do you mean,
you don't know? You were there—"

"I was there, but it's not that simple." He let
out a long breath, paced again. "I could have gone
into the tunnels with Thomas. We could have been
gone before they even broke down the main gate
and found their way around the main tower, much
less found the tunnels—if they ever found them.
But these were Damon's men. Damon and Ranulf
had spent years, half raised by my father as his
foster sons. They were like brothers to me."

"You trusted them," she whispered.

"These were Damon's men!" he said again
roughly. "Yes, I trusted them. Even then, I couldn't
believe Ranulf could have been involved in what
happened to my father. I couldn't believe Damon
or Kenric could have been involved either. I
planned to hear them out, and then I planned to

go to the king on my father's behalf. I would start
an investigation of my own. I still believed in justice
and honor, in everything that was the world in
which I'd been raised."

Bitterness seeped into his tone.

"But there was no justice or honor in that night,"
he said.

Elayna held her breath.

"Father Almund was the first one to show the
signs of something wrong. He had come back from
France with Damon's men, to be with me when I
learned the news. He sat with me on the dais. He
leaned over to me during the feast and told me
that he believed my father was innocent. He was
fearful for my safety, he said, but there was no time
to plan.

"I remember the rushlights seemed brighter, the
hall huge and swaying. I remember Father Almund
falling onto the floor. I felt as if the world were
spinning in one direction and the castle in another.
I passed out—for how long, I don't know. That
night is only flashes of memory to me now. Painful,
nightmare flashes. What I remember next was wak-
ing, realizing the castle was burning. There was a
smell—pitch, I thought—but I have no idea where
it came from, how it got there.

"Despite the new stone outer walls, the hall was
raised to a second story with a timber floor, as well
as being connected to the rest of the old part of
the castle by wooden outbuildings. There was a lot
of smoke, and my vision was blurry to begin with
because I was suffering the effects of whatever
cursed potion had been in the ale, but I started
toward the men I could see. The stairs were made
of stone, and if we could get to them, we would
be saved. There was a figure, through the smoke
and fire, and I called out, begging for help to get
the men out. They weren't moving. I knew they'd

had more ale than I. The figure came closer, bent over one of the men, and it was then I saw that he was not saving their lives."

Elayna swallowed tightly. "What was he doing?" she breathed.

He looked straight at her. "He was cutting their throats while they lay incapable of fighting back."

Time stretched between them.

Graeham went on: "I couldn't believe what I was seeing. I was half blinded, and I thought I had to be wrong, but then as I stumbled madly from one man to another, they were dead, all with their throats slit. I went after him, but he was ready for me—and he wasn't weakened from the tampered ale as I was. I remember his eyes, blazing as bright as the flames, reaching out from—a face I couldn't see. All I can remember is shock, and then pain as he drove his sword through my side and left me for dead."

Elayna forgot to breathe. She could barely think. The story was horrifying. "Who?" she whispered. "Ranulf?" It was still so hard for her to believe.

He shook his head. "Even I don't know for sure—how can I hope to convince someone else? In my mind, I see his eyes, that's all. And I see them too often. Sometimes, every time I close my own. I learned to live with less sleep, just to avoid those eyes."

"Why didn't he kill you, just slit your throat?"

"He would have slit my throat," he explained, "but if he had, it would have destroyed the plot I came to understand only later. I was to be set up as the murderer of Damon's men. I was to be set up to have burned down Penlogan rather than turn it over to another knight. All those people died—not just the soldiers, but the people of Penlogan—and it was laid at my door."

Elayna stared at him for a horrible moment. "But why? You had already been stripped of Penlogan."

"To solidify Ranulf's hold on Penlogan? I don't know."

He let the sizzle and low pop of the fire fill the air while she thought of all he'd said.

"How did you get out?"

"The tunnel. The boat. Thomas had heard the chaos, and he had wavered, uncertain of what was going on and what he should do. By the time he emerged, the hall was engulfed. He found me bleeding to death, unconscious, and dragged me out even as the floor was collapsing. It was too late for anyone else. He barely made it, he told me, before the entire floor dropped out. He took off one of my rings, the one that held the seal of Penlogan, and pushed it onto the finger of a dead soldier—hoping that if the body burned, it would be assumed to be mine. The soldier burned; I was dead."

Elayna pressed a hand to her mouth, realizing only then that her fingers trembled. She was so caught up in his story, it was as if she were there. She wanted to *do* something, and she felt very scared. It reminded her of how she'd felt when so much terror had been created at Castle Wulfere by their cousin, Julian.

And how she had not done anything then.

"They buried that body as yours," she said shakily. She had never visited the grave. She hadn't been able to bear the thought. She had never been to Penlogan since Graeham's presumed death. Ranulf had immediately embarked on a restoration and expansion. Penlogan had been under construction nonstop since that time, construction only recently completed. "And the letter—"

"We were lucky to make it out with our lives," he said by way of answer. "Thomas stopped in

Cradawg. It was the home of his wet nurse, so he had been raised there as a babe. His family had oft stopped at the inn on journeys and had always taken time to visit the old wet nurse. He couldn't take me back to his family's manor in Leonvale. He didn't know what to do with me, and God knows he had done enough, so he left me here. He went home—and he visited me at first. But it wasn't long before he was taken by the great plague, and my last link to the past was gone." His gaze revealed a stark grief, then he controlled it. "He was loyal to my father, and without him, I would be dead. The same is true of the people of Cradawg. They took me in, saved my life.

"You asked me once where we are—we are in the forest near Cradawg. I work at the inn there, mostly to repay the kindness of the innkeeper, without whom I would be dead. He protected me at one time, and I return the favor when I can. I began to study herbs, an interest I'd had as a boy. I use what talents I have to help those who helped me. It's my life now, and it's good. They come to me—Jordie is usually their runner—for their aches and pains. Bertrada with her painful joints when it rains, Amalise with her sore tooth, Marcus with his cuts and scrapes. They are strangers and friends at once. They respect my privacy, and I respect their pride. They repay me with breads and chickens and pies, and they never ask questions. I believe it is what was meant to be."

She was shocked. "How can you say that?"

His eyes held a grim resolve. "My father was murdered. Damon's men were murdered, and they would have murdered me. They believed they did."

"But you lived."

He was shaking his head. "I am not the Graeham whom you knew. I am another man now, Gray of the Wood. I am of these people now, and my life is here. This is what God willed for me."

"How can you not go back and demand to know what happened? That was your father, your people, your castle. Your life!" She couldn't understand. "The letter—"

"I can't change the past, lady!" he said harshly. "The letter is long gone, left in my father's desk— for Ranulf to find when he took it as his own."

She noticed how he called her lady now. Did he use that term to distance her? It made her angry.

"You *can* change the future," she snapped, angry at more than him—at the world that had perpetrated these horrors upon him—but she had only him to lash out at. "For one thing, you can call me by name. Stop using my title to separate yourself from me."

She wasn't dancing around the subject anymore. Let him deny that he was using the term *lady* to do anything but distance himself from her.

"You have to go back," she urged him. "It's your home, your right. Letter or no letter. Go to Damon—"

"No!" he interrupted. "I cannot. Don't you understand? This is what you don't want to face. Ranulf committed these crimes—but was it Ranulf alone? What about your brother? What of Kenric? And who else? There is no one left for me to trust. You don't want to accept that—"

"I won't accept that! Damon would never do that—"

"Someone did it," he said flatly, roughly. "*Someone* did it, lady. And they probably didn't do it alone. How could they? There were numerous men involved in the search and interrogations that led to the village warden, not just Ranulf. There was more than one man involved the night Penlogan burned. How could Ranulf have done it all alone?

Damon wasn't there, but his men were. Kenric was there."

"Stop!" She couldn't bear it, these suspicions. She felt sick and scared.

"Don't you see? There would only be more of this if I returned." He shook his head. "And as for distance—what else can I demand but distance, lady? There's no use in my getting close to anyone. I'm a walking dead man. My very existence threatens the crime against my father and the crime against all the souls who died that night at Penlogan. I can do nothing but harm by going back.

"I can cause more deaths—for what? To see justice done? There is no justice for my father, for those soldiers, for the people of Penlogan. They are already dead. I won't be the cause of more deaths by trying to reclaim something I don't even want anymore. My father died for greed, ambition, power. I care naught for any of it. That is a world that turned its back on my father and on me."

"And you have turned your back on it," she breathed, understanding but not liking what she understood. He had created a new world for himself in this forest of Cradawg. A world where he did good, saved lives, cured ills, where he had control.

She swallowed thickly, uncertain how to tell him why that was wrong.

"The past—" she started to say.

"—doesn't matter," he said flatly. "I am what I am now—a hermit, a healer, a ghost. To return could mean only more death—most certainly mine and perhaps others'. Here I save lives. I give back to those who gave to me. It's my life."

"What kind of life? A hidden, secret life?"

"*My* life," he said emphatically. "There is nothing but death in the other direction."

In the space of silence that followed, she was aware of the floor's earthen hardness, the smell of the simmering soup, the herb- and flower-scented straw.

She gazed into his harshly beautiful features and haunted eyes and tossed aside any useless sense of pride as her full heart burst.

"There's me," she whispered. "There's me."

CHAPTER NINETEEN

He reached up and cupped her face, staring down at her with his amazing, haunted eyes. She wondered if he understood the truth, that she'd never stopped loving him. She had only just then realized it herself.

She almost hoped he understood, because she didn't know if she had the courage to admit it. She didn't know if she could face finding out that he didn't feel the same way. Was she strong enough to lose him again?

"You don't think you're in love with me, do you?" he asked softly, his voice almost distant and yet as close as the blood pounding in her ears. He was only a breath away from kissing her again. "Because that would be very, very foolish."

"No," she lied, because she couldn't be the one to say it. He had left her; that fact still hurt. When he had given up that old life, he had given up her.

But she had given him up, too, when she had believed the fantastical stories of his treachery.

Guilt surrounded her heart, tightening it.

"I'm sorry," she said suddenly, and she felt the warm tracks of tears on her cheeks. She couldn't hold them back. "I should not have believed that—"

He made a strangled sound in his throat.

"No," he grated, moving his hands to grip her shoulders, gently shaking her. "Don't ever apologize to me for that. You were thirteen years old. You were so young. Too young."

"So were you," she whispered roughly. She touched his face. "I can hardly believe what you've been through, but I do. I believe you. But it's not enough. I want to know the truth. I want to know—"

"No," he said, and his voice was very harsh, his grip very tight. "No. You will not do anything about these things. There is no blame for you. I left you without a word—any blame belongs to me. But it is too late for these regrets. This is the only reason I told you this story. I had to make you understand why—"

"Why what?"

"I had to make you understand," he said, his voice tight and controlled, "why there can be nothing between us. Why my keeping this ring can't mean anything to either of us."

He swung away from her, releasing her so abruptly, she nearly fell.

"But it *does* mean something." She went after him. She still clasped the ring in one hand, and she opened her fist, held the ring in front of his eyes. He shut his eyes against it, but she wouldn't let that end the matter.

She didn't know how to reach him. She acted without thinking, not waiting for courage.

"I thought you were dead, and still you were the man I held every other man against—and found them wanting. I haven't stopped thinking about you in all these years, and now—"

She twisted the ring in her fingers, and slowly, she slipped it onto her third finger and stared at it in wonderment before lifting her eyes to his.

"I would have been wearing this ring all this time if things had been different," she whispered. "And they *are* different, I know that. But still, I find myself watching you, thinking about you, dreaming about you. I wonder what would have happened if things had been different, and I wonder if we can do something about it now. Most of all, I wonder what your lips would look like, feel like, taste like, and I wonder if you will kiss me again."

She had surprised herself, but it didn't matter. She wasn't ashamed. Tears flowed down her face, but she didn't care. All that mattered was that he believed her.

"No," he groaned. His eyes opened slowly, and he started to push her away, but she grabbed his arms and held on to their fierce strength. "I can't kiss you again," he said in an agonized voice. "I'm afraid if I do—"

"What?" she urged him. "What?"

"I'm afraid I won't stop."

"I don't want you to stop." She was afraid too—of what lay between them, the past, and the present, and most especially, the future. But she longed for it anyway, and every bone in her body leaned toward him. The longing was stronger than the fear.

She was breathing rapidly—from fear or anticipation or both. She had to do something. He was so strong, so controlled. Somehow she had to break through. This was Graeham, and it was a miracle, she realized, that they had found each other again. It was a miracle worth fighting for. All the stretching, needing, yearning that had been building in her recently seemed to find a purpose now.

She had been hurting for so long, and it had

taken her this long to recover. Only in the past few months had she felt like herself again, like she could open up to something new, to a future.

She'd known, instinctively, that her future couldn't be a betrothal to a man she didn't love.

Destiny had led her here. Searching, following her one passion, her one talent, had brought her to this wild wood and this dark, aching man. It was meant to be.

Her writing—it had been a way to keep him alive in her heart, she realized. Finding work as a copyist had been a wrong turn in that passion.

She had misread her own fortune.

Marilette had been right.

He was your first love, and he will be your last.

You will lose him before you find him. Great love comes with great tragedy.

"Elayna," he said, and all the raw need he felt in return for her was apparent—not only by the fact that he had finally said her name, but because of the way he said it.

Desperately.

"Kiss me," she dared him wildly, "and don't stop, because if you do, I think I might die."

Graeham's jaw clenched tightly. He was without words, part amazed, part ravenous. She was his weakness, his want, and she was offering herself to him. It wasn't a possibility anymore; it was reality. There was no way to detach and pull away from her. No way to control what was happening.

All of his intense feelings—the wanting, the guilt, the desire, the pain—whirled together inside him in a great maelstrom of emotion.

"I've wanted to be your lover," she whispered huskily. "Forever. I've wanted you forever. That's how it feels."

He was beyond lost. He pulled her into his arms, close, and kissed her. There was no choice.

Sweet God, he'd wanted her for so long too.

Tonight he would do the thing he'd been born to do—love this woman. Tomorrow seemed far away.

He kissed her with all the passion that had been locked up inside him for the years they had been apart. She kissed him back with like fervor, and he relished it. He kissed her face, her neck, all the while her fingers running through his hair, down his back, as if she couldn't get enough of him.

Then her mouth was on his throat, her tongue tasting him, making blood pound through him.

Graeham clutched at her greedily, guiding her precious lips back to his so he could claim them again in an even deeper kiss.

She made a sound, a low whimper that seemed to go straight to the core of him.

"Say it again," she moaned against his mouth.

"What?" he pulled back enough to ask.

"My name," she whispered. "Say my name."

He felt emotion sting his eyes. Not until now did he realize he had hurt her by his refusal to use her name. Perhaps not until then had she even realized it. But he felt ashamed just the same. He had protected himself, but that was no excuse for hurting her.

"Elayna," he said softly. "Elayna." Her name was so lovely to him, so perfect, and then he kissed the wet tracks on her cheeks, replacing the pain with tenderness. "I'm so sorry—"

"No," she cried. "No. You were right. No apologies. It's too late for regrets. Just kiss me and don't stop."

He kissed her again, and she kissed him back, pressing her body against him until nothing else existed. There was no past, no future.

He broke the kiss only to scoop her into his arms and cradle her to his chest before placing her gently down upon the pallet. He moved in beside her, his pulse surging at the wonderment of her body alongside his.

His hands stroked her through the material of her tunic, pulling her closer to him, and she seemed to melt against him. He kissed her eyelids, the corners of her eyes, her nose, her jaw, everywhere he hadn't kissed her before. He wanted to taste every inch of her, and he was only getting started.

He caressed her through her clothes, but that was not enough for her, and she began to pull at the confining garment.

He stopped her by catching her wrists in both hands. "Not yet," he said. "Let me."

Elayna smiled at him, her look beguiling and stunning. Again, he realized how much she had changed, matured. She was a woman now, and his need for her was unbelievably complex. It wasn't mere sensual pleasure. It was so much more, but he couldn't let himself examine it. He was already out of control.

This life of his was a sort of armor, a protection against vulnerability, against emotion. He was a part of Cradawg and yet separate from it.

His life was one of fulfillment and emptiness at the same time. He hadn't known that until then, until he'd held Elayna and kissed her and watched her open herself to him.

She was giving him a taste of another life, the one he'd left behind, and he had the terrible foreboding that now that he'd had this taste, he would miss it. But he couldn't turn back.

Like her, he would die now if he stopped.

* * *

Elayna's heart was storming in her ears. Feelings of sweet helplessness fluttered up and down her body. He was gazing at her with a strange, wild energy that made her stomach drop away. That energy in his eyes was need, pure need.

"Go ahead," she said shakily.

"I'm getting there," he said with a low chuckle.

He kissed her again with heated lingering, and then slowly, deliberately, his eyes never leaving hers, he tugged at the ties of her tunic. But instead of taking it immediately off, as she wanted, he merely loosened its ties, pushing it back to expose the rounded swells of her breasts.

She resisted the sudden shyness that made her want to cover herself. Amid her new boldness there was old modesty. He sat back, not rushing her, watching her with his hooded eyes.

"Are you sure you know what you're doing, what *we're* doing, if we don't stop?" he asked seriously.

She nodded. She knew. She wasn't going to turn back. They were going to make love without benefit of holy wedlock. They were betrothed—or they had been, long ago—but even that wasn't what gave her the peace to go on. The sureness was in her heart, not on a piece of paper.

"I'm sure," she said quietly.

Firelight flickered in the background, framing him in golden silhouette. He leaned forward and placed a single tender kiss upon her collarbone.

"You said you were getting there," she whispered huskily, "but you're getting there very slowly."

She felt heavy everywhere. It was a lovely sensation, the feel of his mouth on her skin, his roughness skimming her softness.

Her eyes were closed; they were heavy too.

"I'm in no hurry," he said. "I need to taste you

here." He kissed her mouth again. "And here."
He teased his lips along the line of her throat.
"And here." He kissed the swells of her breasts.

She loved everything he was doing to her.

"Elayna," he said, his voice deep and rough.

He was stroking the underside of her breasts
through the material of her tunic. Her nipples
hardened in reaction.

She freed her arms from her sleeves, and he
helped her rise in order to allow him to pull the
tunic over her head. Chill air met her bared skin,
and he stood over her to unbuckle his belt, his
eyes smoldering with a hunger that took her breath
away as he shed his garments one by one.

Her heart thudded in anticipation as he came
back to her. She felt her mouth go dry with want.
They were both completely unclothed, and the
contact of his body—skin to skin—was startling.

"Don't be afraid," he said, his gaze dark and
deep.

"No," she said, smiling. She touched his face
with her hand. "I'm not afraid. I trust you. I was
just thinking—"

"What?"

"I was just thinking that I was afraid I would
forget to breathe. You do that to me."

"Want me to stop?"

It was her turn to laugh. "I can breathe later.
Don't stop."

He was gazing down at her, his eyes somber in the
lowering firelight that flickered from the middle of
the cozy, now sweet-scented hut. Still, he was giving
her time to be sure. She loved him all the more
for his consideration, his restraint. He put her first,
and she was coming to see that he had always put
her first. He had left her to save her.

But this is what would save her now—this night,
with him, living what she'd lost.

Threading her fingers through his hair, she whispered, "I can't wait anymore."

He clenched his eyes shut briefly, and she was acutely aware of him sliding his hand over one bare breast, cupping it. As he opened his eyes again, their gazes held as he scraped a finger over her nipple, forcing a moan from her. She felt an echoing tug somewhere deep inside, a tug of shock and pleasure.

She tipped her middle upward instinctively, bringing her hips toward his, thrilling to the low sound he made in his throat.

His hand slid down, over her hip, lingering, and she looked down and saw that he had stopped on her wound. Her injury had healed to an uneven red welt, long and narrow.

It was ugly, and she was self-conscious as she lifted her eyes back up to his. What she saw there dispelled the momentary disquiet. He was concerned for her but as hungry as ever.

"You're beautiful," he said. "So perfect."

She felt her heart melting all over again.

"Does it yet hurt?" he asked.

She shook her head, reached down, and guided his hand to move on, to explore— She didn't know what she was doing, but the yearning deep in her womanly center drove her. She didn't know what she'd expected, but the jolt of enjoyment that his first touch brought took her by surprise.

He surprised her again by taking her breast into his mouth even as he continued to awaken that most hidden part of her body with tender touches. Sensations careened through her, and when he took her mouth again, it was like gasping in air to her.

He was air to her.

Her tongue tangled with his in a wild dance, and she clung to his huge shoulders, giving touch for touch, kiss for kiss, heat for heat. Her hands splayed over his back, ran over his shoulders, down his sides. She nipped at him with her teeth, tasted him with her tongue. She felt his scars—several small ones and especially the long, horrible one in his side.

Then he was pressed against her, leaving only enough room for his hand to continue to work its magic. She could feel his core, hot and rigid, against her belly.

Her entire body convulsed as he probed the secret cleft of her womanhood with his hand. He brushed his warm lips to the side of her throat while his fingers delved ever deeper, breaching the soft curls that protected her womanly center.

The flick of his fingertip against an inner nub she hadn't even realized existed made her gasp with sheer delight.

She whimpered, then she moaned, and she was way past surprise when he slipped his rigid core inside, pressing, filling, withdrawing, and then pressing deeper the next time. She expected pain, and bit her lip but could not prevent a cry at the sharp, tearing shock.

He froze, and her eyes, shut in sweet abandon only a moment before, now flew open to find his locked on hers in regret.

"I'm sorry," he said. "It's the way it's supposed to be." His voice faded away, and she fisted her fingers in his thick, rich hair as he held on to her tightly, their bodies fused and still for a timeless beat, both of them breathing hard.

Slowly, the aching burn of the pain began to change, to transform into something else. Aching pleasure.

"Don't stop," she whispered.

"Oh, sweet Elayna, I'm not stopping."

He began to move inside her again—and she moved against him in response. Her movement was instinctive but in rhythm with his movements so that they created something tender and deliberate and magical.

The ache inside her now was one that demanded satisfaction. It quivered, built, spilled over.

She wrapped her legs around his back, pulling him closer, burying him deeper. He moaned and rocked back and forth. Her own breathing became little cries.

Graeham leaned down and kissed her, and she kissed him back, and she felt as if together they rocked to the stars. They left the forest, England, and shot away to where the only real thing was this power they created together.

As the pleasure became as intense as pain, she clutched at his iron-muscled arms. He moved faster, harder, as the first tremor washed over her. Alive, she thought wildly. She'd never felt so alive. It was almost too good, too incredible.

He waited until she could breathe again, and he drove into her again, touching her now with his hand, too, caressing and grinding against her velvet folds. She fell into a thousand splintering bits of flame as the second tremor hit. She was vaguely aware of him tensing inside her. Her cry became his own as they went over the edge of bliss together.

Graeham collapsed over her, spent, leaning to one side so he didn't crush her. The scent of him, musk and mint, was exciting and comforting at once. His head was turned to her neck, and he laid gentle kisses there while she marveled at the joy they'd shared.

When she looked at him again, he was watching

her with a solemnness that struck a chord inside her. He was her lover now, this outlaw of the forest. Her lover, and her love.

She fell asleep in his arms and dreamed of the future, and he was there.

CHAPTER
TWENTY

Graeham stared into the smoldering fire, sleepless, afraid to sleep, afraid to dream. Afraid even to think.

He'd spent years making sure he needed no one, and in less than a fortnight, Elayna had brought down every wall he'd constructed. He'd tried to ignore her, frighten her, get rid of her.

But in the end, all he'd done was need her.

Dear God, what had he done?

There was no way they could be together in any permanent sense. Was he doomed to disappoint her, hurt her, endanger her?

The scent of the herbs on his worktable, the flower blossoms she'd strewn in the rushes, the woodsmoke of the fire, all surrounded him, too real, reminding him where he was and what his life had become. He shifted to cover both of them with the thin blanket, protecting them against the growing chill as the fire lowered. He pulled her closer, wrapping her in his arms, wrapping her in the dream that was already being snatched away by cold reality.

How could he go back to his life as Gray of the Wood? And how could he not?

He had to live with these tormenting questions—but what worried him most was that so did she. She was too young and beautiful and full of life to share the darkness into which he could well be doomed if he tried to change anything now.

Could he change anything now? He had never believed it was possible, never believed it was worth it. But she had made him believe in everything again—in the world that had betrayed him, in love, in life, and even in himself. She had revived his dead heart, breathed life into his soul.

She had given him a taste of what it would be like to be whole again.

He looked down at the woman in his arms, and emotion came upon him so fierce as to nearly blind him. He wanted to keep her safe forever, but he hadn't even been able to keep her safe for one night . . . from him.

There had to be a way, and he would find it. But first, he had to make her safe.

The hut was dark when she woke, but she knew it was morning by the misty light that showed through the cracks around the door. The fire had been stoked again, fresh wood placed upon it. A pot of something bubbled and popped over the flames. She knew it would be honeyed oatmeal, Graeham's standard morning fare.

Her plain green tunic was across the hut on the floor. His clothes were gone—as was he. He had gone out somewhere, perhaps for his morning ablutions. She remembered the night before with a dizzying combination of panic and thrill. It was all very vivid.

His arms, his eyes, his voice, his heat. She held

the memories close to her heart, smiled as she pushed back the blanket that was wrapped around her, and scampered across the floor, the chill air raising gooseflesh all over her body, to pull on the tunic.

Slow down, she warned herself. She was beginning to toy with a fantasy that was as fantastic as any story she might write. She was imagining that Graeham was somehow a less complicated man and that somehow they could go back to the way things had been all those years earlier.

She stood in the middle of the hut and twisted the ring she still wore on her finger. She was too wise to believe things could ever be that simple.

So what was she doing?

Light shafted into the hut as he returned.

She saw only his silhouette at first. She remembered the first time she'd seen him come into the hut, when she'd been injured and half aware of what was going on. He had seemed so huge then, so frightening and so powerful. He was still all of those things but so much more. He was tender, too, and she wished he would slide his arm around her waist, pull her softly to him, blow sweet kisses along her neck, and sweep her back onto the pallet. He could slip those amazing hands down her body, over her breasts, into the dip of her waist, and lower.

He could make love to her all over again, and she wouldn't stop him.

But as he shut the door behind him and stepped into the light of the fire, she knew from his masked, unreadable eyes that he wasn't going to do any of those things. He was distancing himself from her, and it hurt already.

"Are you—" He let the question hang half asked for a moment. "Are you feeling all right this morn?"

"I'm fine." She didn't know what else to say. Fine was so inadequate. She was tremulous, breathless, yearning, and scared. She was far from *fine.*

But she wasn't quite sure why he was asking or if she wanted to know.

"I was concerned that sometimes— The first time— I have herbs that might help, for soreness and—" He frowned and looked uncomfortable.

She understood what he was asking now, but she was uncomfortable about it too. "I'm fine," she repeated.

He walked around her, set something on the worktable, a fistful of herbs he'd brought back with him. He turned back to her.

"I'm sorry—" he began.

"We agreed there would be no apologies," she interrupted, a feeling of desperation seizing her. *Why was he apologizing now?*

"This is different." He turned toward her, his back to the worktable. "There are things I have to say. Things I have to make you understand."

She was shaking her head, but he didn't stop.

"I need to say certain things to you. I need to tell you that I'm sorry—"

"But I am not," she said fiercely.

A muscle in his jaw throbbed, but he went on. "I want to say that I'm grateful—"

"Oh, God, don't thank me," she choked out. His gratitude was even worse than his regret. "What are you going to do next, offer me coin?" She looked at the rush-strewn floor, the massive chest where he kept his books and mementoes, the worktable where he stored his herb concoctions, anywhere but at him. She felt bitter hurt clutch her heart.

"Elayna."

He closed the space and gripped her forearms

through the light material of the tunic. She refused to look at him.

"I don't thank you to insult you. What happened between us was an honor and a privilege to me. It was beautiful," he insisted in his rough-gentle voice.

He let go of one of her arms to take hold of her chin and tenderly force her to face him. His haunted eyes seared her.

"*You* are beautiful," he said. "You are like a drop of sunshine in a dark, misty world. You are rare and precious and good, full of hope and light and life. You remind me that there *is* hope and light and life—and I'm grateful for that too. You remind me that I can feel. But none of that changes what is just as true and real. You are not part of this world, and I am not part of yours."

"I am part of yours. I'm here."

"Look around you, lady," he said. He let go of her completely now to sweep an arm around the hut. "You cannot live your life here. Don't try to tell me you can. It won't work. You have been here less than a fortnight. You have no idea what it's like to live in a forest hut day in, day out, year after year, through winter snow and summer heat. There are few comforts and no luxuries. In time, you will resent that, and me."

He was calling her lady again.

"You don't know it won't work." He was right. Forest-dwelling in this hut would be hard. She hadn't thought it through, but she knew that she would be prepared to try rather than give up on what they had. Why wasn't he? "I'm willing to take the chance. How can you make decisions for me? I think what we have—what we *could* have—is worth it."

"What we could have is a dream, lady. A dream of the past." His expression was implacable. "This is reality. A poor woodcutter's hut in a tangled forest. You were meant for more. Go to your copyist shops in the city, if that's what you will. You were right—you can make your own destiny. You have a dream, your writing. Live it."

She clenched her eyes shut a moment in frustration, then lifted them to him again. "I have another dream, and I've already been waiting more than four years to see it come true. The copyist shops—" She tried to think how to put into words what she had come to understand about herself. "I wrote to forget, to remember, to dream. I ran away rather than confront Damon with the truth about my own feelings. It was a mistake. I can't live my dreams as someone else—and neither can you."

She put her hand on his arm and searched his eyes for hope. "Come back with me. Talk to Damon. We will go to Penlogan, find the truth. Together."

"No."

"You were born to rule Penlogan. It's yours. If you would only go back—"

"You think it's that simple, lady?" he scoffed harshly. "If they knew I was alive, I could be dead before I could scarcely breathe the sea air of Penlogan—or Wulfere, for that matter."

"But you didn't do it!"

"Are you so sure?"

He challenged her with his eyes, and they were so cold at that moment that she almost believed he could have done the wicked deed, but she knew what he was doing. He was distancing himself. He was trying to turn her away.

"I believe what you told me last night."

"Then you know we have no future, not now."

She stared at him for a long while. *Not now.* What was he planning? Suddenly, she saw something in his eyes, something that made her think—

"Then when? Are you saying that we could have a future at some point later?"

"I'm not saying anything."

She lifted her hand to her mouth to hold in a gasp. "You're going back. Without me. You don't want to endanger me—"

"I'm going on with my life. You must go on with yours."

He wasn't answering her directly. He was planning to go back! Her heart took up a hard beat. If he had changed his mind, if he intended to go back, it had to mean that he cared about her more than he wanted to admit.

The thought was dangerous, and she put it away. She couldn't let emotion take hold of her now. He was making no promises, and there was a reason for that. No matter how he felt about her, he wasn't ready to love and be loved. She had to remember that and be careful of her own heart. And even as she warned herself, she knew it was too late. She was in too deep already.

She focused on the task at hand. She had to persuade him to let her help him.

"I can speak to Damon for you. I can—"

"You can do nothing to help me."

"Yes, I can," she said. She had held a secret back from him, but he had to know now. "The man to whom my brother bade me wed, the man of honor for whom I felt no love, no desire, no destiny, is Ranulf. I was to wed Ranulf."

She saw shock in his eyes and then dawning horror. She went on before he could stop her.

"I will go back, agree to be betrothed. I'll ask to be sent to Penlogan to better acquaint myself with him in contemplation of marriage. I could search for the tunnels—"

"No!" he roared. He grabbed her arms again,

and this time when he shook her, it was not gentle. "You will do no such thing!"

"You're worth it," she said quietly, blinking back sudden tears.

He let her go, whirled, raking a hand through his hair, and when he turned back to her, the look on his face frightened her more than anything.

"You don't know me," he said cruelly. "I'm not worth it—not what you think I'm worth anyway. You see the boy I was, not the man I have become. I'm a man of solitude and darkness and nightmares. I'm not the young, cocky, innocent knight whom you loved. You are risking your life for someone who doesn't exist anymore."

"No," she said. "No." She walked to him, placed her palm on his face, stared into his eyes. He was still doing it, trying to turn her away. She was unswayed. "You are good and honorable—not in the past but now. You saved my life, and that works both ways. It's my turn to save your life. I'm not walking away from you. I'm not going to let fear stop me, not this time."

Determination settled over her. She straightened her shoulders as she dropped her hand to her side.

He looked like he wanted to shake her. "Is this about me or about your family, Marigold and your sisters? Are you trying to make up for the past? You didn't save your sisters, so— What? You think you can save me? Well, you can't," he said without waiting for her to answer his question.

"Want to wager on that?" she said, her voice brittle. Maybe he was right. Maybe there was a part of her that was trying to make up for the past— the mistakes she'd made with her sisters as well as the mistakes she'd made with him. And maybe it would be easier if she let herself believe that was all she wanted, redemption. This course was dangerous enough; no need to add the extra risk of hoping to win his love. He cared for her, she knew that. But he was also deeply scarred, and to think that one night of lovemaking could wipe it all away would be foolish. She would start small, with one bit of trust, then another. "I can do this, and I will do it. With you or without you."

He glared at her. "I won't let you do this."

"You can't stop me," she said quietly. "This is my brother we're talking about. My family. They could be in danger. Do you think I can ride away to Worcester, join the copyist shops there, and forget that my brother's best friend is a murderer? I'm involved in this as much as you are. This isn't your fight alone anymore." She sat down. "It's mine now too."

CHAPTER TWENTY-ONE

Castle Wulfere felt different, but Elayna knew it was she who had changed, not her home or her family. It had still been daylight when Graeham had left her at the foot of the bridge that crossed over into Fulbury. That was where they'd separated.

He was taking more of a chance than she. Once inside Castle Wulfere, she knew she would be safe, protected, loved.

On the other hand, once he was inside, Graeham would stop being Gray of the Wood, a free man. He would become Graeham of Penlogan, a fugitive.

She had been desperately afraid that he would turn around and disappear before entering through the gates. Had he agreed only to the plan to place her back in the safety of her family's arms? Would he trust her, trust Damon, enough to take the risks that would follow?

Their plan had called for him to wait behind beyond the village. He had selected a cottar's hut near the woods and had approached the villein. He'd paid him good coin to keep his horse, promising him more when he returned. He would approach the castle on foot sometime after she did, and during the chaos of her return, he'd slip inside the castle. The gates were left open for the villagers to come back and forth throughout the day. Many of the castle servants lived in the village, and while the gates were watched, each individual villein wasn't stopped.

Graeham, in his woodsman attire, would go unnoticed through the gates. The next step of their plan was not so simple. He had to walk into the keep, find his way into the tower and the family quarters. He had to find his way to her.

She had waited, too sick with nerves to eat much of the food Fayette had brought her. The night had been interminable. She'd bathed in the round tub they'd brought to her chamber, but she'd refused the maid's assistance, not wanting her to see the still-healing wound in her side. Damon was upset enough without finding out she'd nearly died. Afterward, she'd waited for her sisters to fall asleep, then waited for Fayette to fall asleep on her pallet at the foot of her sisters' bed.

At the door, Elayna waited, listened. Would he find a chance to slip past the guard Damon had posted in the corridor to keep her from running away yet again?

Graeham had made no bones about the impossibility of their relationship. Her safety was all that mattered to him. If their plan didn't work, he'd disappear again—without her. If he wasn't dead.

She'd fallen stupidly, hopelessly, in love with him all over again—had she ever been *out* of love with him?—but it was starkly clear that he was in fierce control of his own feelings.

She couldn't say the same about herself, but she was ready to face the consequences—of all her actions, all her mistakes. The stretching, growing, yearning inside her was courage, she realized. Courage she hadn't known she had till then.

Graeham about been right; it was too late for regrets. She had been a little more than a child herself when Julian had threatened her sisters. It hadn't been her fault that he had nearly destroyed their family. She had been frightened too. And it wasn't her fault that Graeham had been betrayed and vilified, that she had believed what she'd been told.

What mattered was what she did now. She'd insisted he look to the future; it was time she did too. But first, they had to clear up the past.

Damon had been too angry to talk to her the night before. He wouldn't be less angry when he finally did come to her. She could only pray that he would hear her out.

She had answered no questions for her sisters or Belle. Her sisters had stared at her, round-eyed— Gwyneth especially. Elayna's hair had caused a stir. The guards hadn't recognized her at the gate for a stunned moment. The expressions on the gate-keepers' faces would have made her laugh if she hadn't been so nervous.

Finally, when she had almost given up, Graeham had come. She didn't know what was going to happen next. She had the terrible feeling he was ready to die.

They had spent so many nights together in that hut in Cradawg, but the night they spent together secretly in her small tower chamber was the best and the worst all at once.

He hadn't wanted to make love to her at first. She knew he saw it as a mistake that they'd ever made love at all. She refused to view it that way. It was a miracle, not a mistake.

He was afraid she would become pregnant. She was afraid she wouldn't, though she didn't tell him.

If he died, she wanted a piece of him to carry into the future.

"This plan is dangerous for you," he said as they stood in her small, dark chamber, the door shut against the world. Tomorrow, everything would change again.

But there was still tonight.

"I don't like that," he went on. "If this plan didn't involve your brother, I wouldn't be here. Maybe if I'm lucky, he can talk some sense into you."

"He's never succeeded before," she said lightly because the subject was too heavy.

"I'm not letting anything happen to you."

"It's more dangerous for you," she countered. "I will be under guard the whole time. The only risk to me is if we don't prove your innocence. I'll lose everything—I'll lose you." She held his gaze, daring him to look away.

"I can't make any promises," he said softly, coming closer. "I made a promise to you once, and I broke it."

"That was then," she said. "This is now."

"That's what I'm afraid of."

For once, she saw that he wasn't trying to hide his feelings from her. Or from himself. She saw it in his eyes first, the way his gaze dropped. It was wordless, but it was real. In the candlespill-light and quiet, only their breaths and their pulsebeats were audible.

He leaned toward her just a little. His hand tilted her chin up, and there in the darkness he kissed her gently on the mouth. He was pressed against her. She could feel his hard body, sense the control he was trying too hard to maintain. Through the thin nightrail, she fancied she could feel his heart beating. Her boys' tunics had been confiscated by Damon. Her copyist-to-be life had her entire family in shock, she knew. It was just one of the many reasons Damon had not been ready to talk to her yet, not sure how to deal with her.

For the first time now in all these years, she stood before Graeham in the trappings of her womanhood. Lace and soft chemise and perfume, her hair held back with tiny silver clips.

He broke the kiss and held her face in his hands, staring deep into her eyes. "I still can't believe you thought anyone would take you for a boy."

"I would have gotten better with practice," she defended. "You should see Gwyneth. When she dresses as a boy, you would never know the difference. You should have seen her looking at my hair! I know that's part of why Damon is so angry. He's probably afraid of the repercussions, that Gwyneth will rebel against all the lady lessons Belle has spent years instilling."

"Damon has plenty of good reasons to be angry," Graeham said. "You ran away—"

"I've run away before," she said. "But you're right, I worried him. And I'm sorry. It was the wrong thing to do. I didn't want to let him down, and yet I did. I'm going to tell him the truth, how I feel about—about Julian and my sisters. About him and Belle. I'm going to clear the air. You were right—it wasn't my fault. But until I tell him, I don't think I will ever feel right. He needs to know that I'm sorry."

"Elayna." Graeham put his arms around her, and she didn't want him ever to let go. He had no idea the solace his arms brought her. He pulled back and looked down at her. "Your family is lucky to have you."

He didn't say that *he* was lucky to have her. Even now—or maybe especially now—he wouldn't admit she belonged to him. It was obvious, yet he refused to accept it. And she knew there was nothing she could do about it. She could only keep praying.

She felt as if her heart were bursting out of her chest. She loved him so much, completely, forever. A seed of hope filled her. Anything was possible, or at least it seemed so for one night.

"Make love to me, Graeham," she whispered.

"Oh, God, Elayna." He tried to turn away from her, but she wouldn't let him go. "We can't—" he began, but she stopped his words with a kiss.

When she let go, he was breathing hard because they had both forgotten that they needed to breathe.

"I want to make love to you more than anything," he said roughly. "But nothing has changed. If anything, things are more impossible. Now I can't even offer you a poor life in a woodsman's hut. Now I can offer you nothing at all. I could die tomorrow if your brother so wills it."

"He won't."

"You believe that. And there is a part of me that is beginning to believe it too," he said. "You make me want to believe—in the future, in life, in love and hope and honor. You make me want to believe the world that betrayed me is not all bad. But we could both be wrong."

"We aren't," she whispered thickly.

She watched his eyes, praying he wouldn't turn away from her. He'd come this far, and so had she.

"I can't give you—"

"You can give me tonight," she said. "All I want is another night with you."

He touched her face, the corners of his hard mouth turning up in a sad smile. "Do you think I am strong enough to hear you say that and not make love to you?"

"I think you're strong enough to do anything you want to do," she said.

"I'm not strong enough to let you go," he said. "If I were that strong, I never would have taken you back to my hut in the first place."

She felt dampness fill her eyes, and lost herself in the intensity of his own dark depths. He touched her lips to hers, and she fell, tumbling headlong, into the inevitability of what would happen next.

This time his kiss was not gentle. It was rough and full of need. And—oh, God—she surrendered to it, to hope and miracles and him.

He swept her into his arms and back onto the soft, downy bed that took up most of the space in the small room. She was aware of everything—his male scent, the sputtering candlelight, the lavender rushes, the comforting surround of stone walls and the warm heat of the small hearth. It was familiar and alien at once now that Graeham was there. It was home and heaven. He seemed to fill the entire space so that she breathed, smelled, tasted, touched only him.

His lips were hot and demanding on hers, his tongue and teeth devouring her. Then the fierce kiss broke, and he moved away briefly to blow out the candle and pull the heavy bedcurtains, shutting them deeper into their private world. In it, they fumbled with each other's clothing, undoing ties and buttons, pulling and pushing until at last they were free of any confinement, two bodies, two souls, with nothing between them but the fear that this night would not last forever.

The only way to make it last was to savor each instant, slow and pure and desperate.

She recognized now this feeling sweeping over her, the touch of him leaving trails of fire all over her body. She recognized the solid feel of him and the power sheathed within him. Her body wept for him, straining, trembling. He parted her thighs with his leg and she opened to him, breathing his name like a plea.

She gazed up at him, woman and innocence, his name a breathy moan on his lips, and he felt the last of his restraint fall away. Any noble resolution to protect her from him evaporated in the face of her willing surrender.

He loved her. He could not tell her so, but he did love her. He loved her more than life itself, and if he died for this chance to have a future with her, then it was worth it.

"Graeham?"

This time, she said his name with a question. She was waiting, worried.

He dropped his head down and kissed her again, wanting her so badly, his hands shook. Had he ever thought he could resist her? How often would he fool himself in regard to this dear, sweet woman-dream he had loved as long as he could recall, even before that fateful tournament week? He had loved her since the first time he'd laid eyes on her, when they were both nothing but children, taunting each other, chasing each other, playing tricks and games.

Now she was everything to him. And for a blessed breath in time, he actually believed that their plan would work, that it was meant to be, that it was God's will after all.

The warmth of her skin against his was a delicious torment that became intolerable as she arched against him, inviting him to know her as they had once before. He leaned back to the side of her, braced on one elbow, and ran a finger down the center of her chest. His hand rose and fell with her breaths, then slid lower to the soft curve of her belly and then the silken curls at the apex of her thighs.

His eyes had adjusted to the darkness, and within it he could see her watching him with intense concentration.

"I want this to last all night," he said, his fingers fluttering against her sweet woman's center, rubbing, tantalizing, driving them both crazy. "I want to look at you and touch you and taste you."

"I want to pretend tonight will never end," she whispered back.

He streaked his mouth over her neck, her shoulders, across her breasts, all the while keeping up the delicate torment between her legs. She writhed and sobbed in his ears, her arms tightly clinging to his neck. It was different than before, this slow, sensual storm they created. It was not enough for him to feel pleasure. He had to know that he had given it all to her, and first.

Her skin was hot and slick, his pace maddeningly deliberate. She couldn't catch her breath, and he breathed for her, claiming long, demanding kisses. In between, she made helpless sounds in her throat that drove him almost as wild as he was driving her.

Her passion was nearly his undoing. He could not let her touch him. When she reached for him, he pushed her hand away. He would explode if she touched him. He wanted to sink right into her, but he wouldn't allow himself, or her, that easy release.

Each determined stroke of his fingers brought her closer to the sheer edge, and when she reached it, he felt her fingernails dig into his shoulders. She clawed at him, wet and hot and needy.

Her eyes were clenched shut, her body quivering.

"Look at me, Elayna," he demanded. "Look at me."

She opened her eyes, and he'd never experienced anything so perfect as her ultimate surrender. His moved his hand again, torturing her at the core of her heat one more time, and she gasped, startled. He swallowed the storm inside her with a hard kiss on her mouth. His arms tightened around her, and he knew his control was spent.

"More," she breathed raggedly when he released her mouth. "Please. Now. Come to me. Come inside me. Come—"

She didn't have to ask twice. He gave in to the powerful tempest they created together. His breath and heart almost stopped at the paradise of being inside her again, sheathed in everything that made his life worth living.

No longer clawing at him, she pulled him close, pulling him deeper as he thrust into her at the same time. She held on, moving with him. Her eyes were open, her steady gaze full of wonder and emotion. He tried to set a slow, deep rhythm, but it was she who speeded it up, and he had little will left to resist her.

The whole world was spinning around this joining of their bodies, harder, faster, her legs wrapping around him, his heart and soul wrapping around her. She buried her face against his shoulder, her smooth teeth biting his shoulder. He felt her heart and soul reaching to his, needing him deep, deep, deep, the way he needed her.

She shuddered beneath him, reaching release once more, and he was lost to it, helpless, urgent. She was crying again, and the poignancy of her capitulation struck him hard. He wanted to comfort her, keep her, protect her, make all the promises he'd forbidden himself to make.

But he couldn't. So he buried himself in her sweet heat and let her shatter him one last time. It seemed like so much later that they fell apart, aching, gasping. He kissed all her tears away, saying nothing, only kissing her, holding her.

They curled together and said nothing. In exhaustion, they slept.

There was a knock at her chamber door. Elayna blinked against the dim light that framed the bed-curtains. It was morning. The night had not lasted forever after all.

"Who is it?" she called, her heart in her throat. She sat up, throwing her legs over the side of the bed and pushing back the bedcurtains slightly at the same time.

"Fayette." There was a hesitance. "Yer brother is asking for ye."

Graeham had come instantly awake. He was already reaching for his clothes. The night was over. The ache between her legs told her it had not been a dream though. It had been real.

"Where are my sisters?"

"In the hall. Breaking their fast. Yer brother will be here soon, he said, milady. Would ye have me help ye to dress or—"

"No," Elayna said quickly. She went to the door and spoke softly. "Leave me to dress alone. Ask Damon to give me a candlemark. Please."

"Yes, milady."

Elayna looked back at Graeham. His face was grim as death. She felt nerves jitter up her spine. Her stomach felt sick.

"You don't have to go through with this," she said suddenly. "You can sneak away. You can go back to Cradawg, to your life."

He was shaking his head before she finished. "No."

"I'm afraid for you—"

"Don't be." He closed the distance between them.

"I can't—"

He touched his fingers to her lips. She felt the heat that spun from him to her, the awareness.

"Whatever happens will be God's will," he said.

"You said it was God's will for you to be in Cradawg," she pointed out. Her heart thumped heavily.

"It was. But you were right too. We have a part in our destiny, and I can no longer deny mine. I choose this path." He stopped, studied her face, and touched her cheek, then dropped his hand again. "Go. Trust your brother. I'm ready to go home."

CHAPTER
TWENTY-TWO

Fayette had left a tray with bread and cheese and ale in the outer chamber for Elayna to break her fast. She was starving. She hadn't eaten well the night before, but she was too nervous to eat now. Graeham didn't partake of it either.

She had dressed so as to least rouse her brother's wrath. She wore a loose-fitting embroidered blue gown and had covered her shorn hair with a veil held in place by a gold fillet. Her look was very feminine. Graeham had watched her prepare. His hooded eyes had told her nothing, but she knew full well that his control was back in place. She felt a strange sense of calm settle over her too. There would be no turning back.

Alone, she waited for Damon in the outer chamber. It was the large, airy tower room where her sisters slept. Her small antechamber connected by a narrow door. The large chamber felt empty without her sisters. She missed them and she wished desperately to tell them everything that had happened to her. She wanted to share her joy, her love for

Graeham, with them. But she couldn't. Their safety
was too important.

What she was about to ask of Damon was terrible
enough.

There was a knock at the door, and she called
out to him to enter. Damon walked in, saying nothing at first. His expression was a hard mask. He
was angry with her, and deservedly so. She had
much to explain, and she didn't know how he
would react.

She had found it all hard to believe herself. How
much more difficult would it be for Damon?

His dark tunic fit snug against his massive shoulders. She stood by the fire, waiting, as he came
toward her. He stopped beside her and stared into
the fire. She looked up at his profile. Here he
posed with the scarred side of his face toward her.
The scar was white against the sun-browned skin.
He had suffered much in France, and he wore the
scar like a badge of that horror.

He had been frightening to her when he'd
returned from France, nothing like the merry
brother she had recalled from earlier childhood.
The torture of the lord of Saville in the dungeon
of Blanchefleur, and the betrayal by Wilfred of
Penlogan, had changed him. Now she had to tell
him it was not Wilfred who had betrayed him. How
little that would ease his pain by the time she had
finished. It was Ranulf who had brought forward
the witness who had testified against Wilfred. There
was no getting around that fact and others. Had
Ranulf bribed the warden who had pointed the
finger at Wilfred?

Had Ranulf killed Angelette himself? Or did he
protect whoever killed Angelette? Why would he
protect someone else? Was he the one who murdered those men at Penlogan, and was he the one
who drove the sword into Graeham's side? If it

wasn't Ranulf, he had to know who had. It was Ranulf who had claimed to see Graeham kill himself. Whatever the truth was, Ranulf was involved, and deep.

She could be placing Damon in danger once she told him what she knew. But there was no choice. Damon could be in danger already. She couldn't let her brother continue to count as his ally a man who could well be his worst enemy.

They all needed the truth.

"You slept well?" Damon asked without looking at her.

His voice was not gentle.

"Yes, thank you."

She didn't know how to begin.

"I'm sorry," she said, and she meant it with all her heart. Though she knew now that somehow it was all meant to be—because if she hadn't run away, she wouldn't have found Graeham—but she still knew that she had hurt her brother. "I'm sorry that I worried you. I'm sorry that I didn't trust you enough to believe that you would listen to how I would feel about being wedded to Ranulf. I shouldn't have run away, but—"

"There are no buts," he broke in harshly, shifting now to slice her with his gaze. "You could have been killed. Anything could have happened to you out there, alone, unprotected. Anything."

There was a roughness to his voice now. Emotion. Despite his hard appearance, what few understood about her brother was that he was a sentimental man, kind and loving. He hid it under a disciplined surface, but Belle had coaxed his secret heart to life.

He would never again be the merry brother who had left for France so many years before, but he was not the frightening, cold shell of a stranger who had returned either. He was something in between, something wrought of pain and now restored by his wife's pure love.

She wondered if she could be as strong as Belle, strong enough to heal Graeham the way Belle had healed Damon.

"Something did happen," she said quietly, holding her brother's gaze. "Something . . . miraculous."

Damon watched her, his look haunted and questioning. "What happened? Were you hurt? Attacked?"

She knew her brother would hunt down and destroy any man who hurt her, and his protective love made her want to cry, but she blinked back the emotions. She had too much to explain to let tears take hold. She had to be strong.

"No," she said. "No, I'm all right. I wasn't hurt— Well, I was injured," she clarified. "I was gored by a wild boar and I—"

Damon's eyes widened and he opened his mouth to speak, but she cut him off.

"I'm fine. I'm really fine," she promised him. "I was rescued by—I was rescued by a stranger who took care of me. He saved me."

Damon watched her as if he didn't quite believe she was all right.

"Who saved you? If there is someone to whom we owe our thanks—"

"Yes," she said. "We owe him. But—"

She stopped, considering carefully her next words. She turned away from Damon's piercing gaze, walked across the room, away from the warmth of the hearth, toward the cool glass of the tall, narrow windows set deep in the thick stone.

"There is something I have to tell you first," she said, "before I can explain anything else."

"I'm listening," Damon said.

"I know you're angry with me for running away. I know that I worried you."

She pivoted to meet his gaze. He hadn't moved from his position before the hearth. His eyes never left her.

"There is no excuse for it," she told him. "But I want to make you understand nonetheless. It's not your fault that I ran away, and I know that you blame yourself, have always blamed yourself for our troubles—mine and Gwyneth's and Lizbet's and Marigold's. I know that because I've blamed myself too."

He would have spoken, but she didn't let him.

"I know that when you returned from France and found Papa dead and us alone and so changed," she went on, "you blamed yourself for leaving us so long—even though part of that time you were in prison and couldn't even save yourself, much less us."

She turned away again. "It was Belle who saved us all, wasn't it?"

"Yes," he said. His voice was closer and she realized he'd moved toward her. She shifted to watch him close the space between them. He stopped an arm's breadth from her. "But you have nothing to blame yourself about, Elayna. You kept our sisters together, cared for them, after our father died. It was a heavy burden for someone so young."

"I could have done more," she said, and her voice nearly broke. She took a deep breath to steady herself. "I was absorbed in my own problems."

"You were fourteen."

"I was selfish," she corrected him. "I knew something was wrong with Marigold. I knew Julian had threatened her. I wasn't brave enough or strong enough to tell you. I was too angry to even talk to you most of the time, angry that you were holding me to the betrothal that Papa had agreed to when he was sick and hardly knew what he was doing."

"It was a matter of honor," Damon said grimly. "There was no backing out. The king had approved the match, wanted the marriage as well. You know—"

"I knew that I wasn't in love with him! I knew that I was in love with someone else and that my heart was breaking! That was what I knew."

She hadn't meant to blurt it out like that, but she had kept this secret for too long. It wouldn't be tamed now.

Damon's expression revealed shock. "What are you talking about?" he demanded.

"I never told you," she said, her tone careful now.

She was feeling scared suddenly. She knew Graeham was waiting for her in the antechamber, giving her this time to speak to Damon alone, to explain. How good a job she did could determine his future.

"I couldn't tell you," she continued. "I didn't want to hurt you."

"How could your being in love hurt me?"

"I was in love with the son of your enemy."

A silence stretched over the chamber. No sounds penetrated the thick stone walls. There was only their breaths and the spit of the fire.

"I don't understand. Explain." Damon hadn't moved; his gaze pinned her.

"I was in love with Graeham of Penlogan."

Confusion and pain passed through Damon's eyes.

"How—"

"There was a tournament, the last one Papa hosted before he became so sick and reclusive. Graeham was there. I was thirteen. He was newly knighted. I was a girl but a woman too. I was growing up, and for the first time, he noticed. We weren't children at play anymore. We fell in love," she told him, the words coming out all in a rush.

Damon was shaking his head as if he didn't believe her. "You were too young—"

"No," she said firmly. "I was not too young. Less than a year later, Papa had me betrothed to Lord Harrimore. I was not too young for him, was I? I was not too young for Graeham. Graeham was much closer to my age than Lord Harrimore. I loved Graeham, and he loved me. But Papa was ill, and Graeham planned to write to his father in France. He wanted his father's permission before he approached Papa. It made sense, and we kept our feelings secret. He left at the end of the tournament week with a ring and a promise. He would return and put the ring on my finger—as soon as he heard from his father. Neither of us expected any resistance."

The ring was on her finger now. She reached instinctively for it, rubbing the garnet dragon fire as if for strength.

"There wouldn't have been any resistance," Damon conceded. "Then."

Elayna nodded. "Everything changed," she whispered.

He waited. She could read nothing in his eyes. When he was hurting, he was unreadable. She had been afraid of this, of hurting him.

"He died," she said. "And I was in so much shock. It hurt so much. I felt as if—"

She swallowed tightly, knowing Graeham was in the next room. She had already explained her feelings to Graeham, but it still hurt to say them again, now, to Damon.

"I felt as if he had loved revenge more than he loved me," she told him. "I felt betrayed. And when Papa signed that betrothal agreement with Lord Harrimore, he was so sick that I couldn't bring myself to tell him how much pain I was in. The news had only just come of your imprisonment, and then Wilfred's perfidy—and Graeham's. It was all too much. When you came back, Papa was dead. How could I tell you that I couldn't marry Lord Harrimore because I was in love with your enemy's son? In love with the man who had murdered a band of your men in his castle? I felt as if I was betraying you by grieving for Graeham."

"Oh, God, Elayna." Damon reached for her, folded her into his arms.

"I was angry with everyone," she said against his shoulder.

He shifted back to look down at her. "I wish I'd known."

"I should have told you," she said. She moved away from him, walked back toward the hearth. "I was mired in my own pain, and I let my family fall apart around me."

She whirled, knowing she had to face him as she said this. It was the only way to finally let the guilt go. "I knew something was wrong at Castle Wulfere, and I did nothing. I was young, and I was in pain, and I did nothing. I know it wasn't my fault—I was scared of Julian too. But I felt guilty about that for a long time. I blamed myself when you were nearly killed by Julian too.

"It was Belle who saved us," she pointed out softly, "when I had been here all along, too absorbed in my own problems to stop what was happening."

"You couldn't have stopped what was happening," Damon insisted, coming near her. He stood beside her, touched her chin, and drew her face up to meet his gaze. "You couldn't have done anything. You were a girl. Julian was a grown man. And Belle was a grown woman."

"I'm a grown woman now," she said. Damon

dropped his hold on her jaw, but still watched her closely. She felt butterflies flit in her stomach. There was more she had to tell him. "I ran away before you came home, several times, to protest the betrothal to Lord Harrimore. When you came, I promised you that I wouldn't run away, at least not until you brought Lord Harrimore here for me to meet. You promised you would consider my input. Lord Harrimore died and that was the end of that, and ever since then you've held your word, considered my input on every suitor."

"You've found them all wanting," Damon said dryly. "But Ranulf—"

"I don't love Ranulf," she interrupted. "I could never love him. He is like an uncle to me, or another brother. But never a man I could love as a husband."

"Then why did you not simply tell me that? Why run away? Dressed as a boy, no less! I would expect that of Gwyneth, but you—"

He stopped, shook his head as if he had no words to describe his shock. She couldn't help smiling slightly, briefly. She had shocked herself too.

"It seemed like a good idea at the time," she said. "I have but one talent, my writing. And I've become quite a good copyist in the practice of my writing. I figured if I had to support myself in the world, it was my one skill. But they don't accept women into the copyist shops. I had thought about it for a while. I knew I could never marry. Not Ranulf, or any man, because—"

She took a deep breath, blew it out slowly before continuing. "Because I had never stopped grieving for Graeham. It all became so clear when Ranulf made his proposal to me. I would never marry. I had never stopped loving Graeham. I didn't know how to tell you. You had been so hurt in the past, and I didn't want to hurt you now. I still don't want to hurt you, but—"

"What has changed?" Damon demanded. "What happened to you when you ran away? You said it was something miraculous."

She nodded. "It was. I—" She swallowed thickly. "I fell in love."

Damon frowned. "With whom? With the stranger who saved you? Where were you? You didn't make it to the city, to the copyist shops, did you? Where have you been all this time?"

"No, I didn't make it to the city, to the copyist shops," she said, answering the easiest question first.

"Where were you?" Damon demanded more fiercely this time. He was impatient with her now.

"I was in a forest, a thick, misty, wild forest. Not far, actually. I didn't make it very far. No more than a half day's ride, less even on a swift horse. I was in the back of a minstrels' cart."

He nodded. "I suspected you had hidden away with the minstrels who had been here then. We tried to track them, but they disappeared."

"I had done it before," she said. "It was easy. Then they found me, and they threw me out. They recognized me, even in the boy's tunic and with my hair clipped short. They knew I was your sister, and they feared you. They wouldn't take me even so far as to the next inn. They wanted nothing to do with me."

"They left you along the road," Damon said, and she could see the hard line of his mouth tensing with fury at their treatment of her.

"They didn't hurt me," she said. She didn't tell him about the money Drogwyn had stolen. It didn't matter now. There were more pressing issues. She doubted those minstrels would ever darken the gate of Castle Wulfere again, knowing she could be there, that she could recognize them and knew their perfidy. They were petty thieves. She was after a murderer. "I could have walked to the inn. I knew there was one nearby. I'm sure they knew, too, that I could walk there. They had passed it not long before they discovered that I was in the cart."

"Then what happened?"

Damon's jaw remained tight. She knew Drogwyn and his troupe would face Damon's wrath if he ever came across them.

"It started to rain. I ran into the forest—" She left out the explanation that Drogwyn had chased her there. No sense giving Damon any more reason to fret than he already had. Drogwyn robbing her was one thing, his threat of rape another. That would give Damon nightmares. "For shelter," she said briefly. "I tripped and fell, and the next thing I knew, a boar charged me."

"Elayna—" Concern tore through her brother's eyes. It was the epitome of his fears for her, she knew. He had worried she would not only be attacked in some way but that she would die. And he would have blamed himself, she realized. Dark guilt swept her even as she knew in her heart that it had all been necessary. She had run away, been thrown out by the minstrels, gored by that wild boar, all so that she would find Graeham.

"But I'm fine." She repeated her earlier assurance. "I was injured, but a stranger came. He took me back to his hut. He saved my life."

"Who saved your life?" Damon demanded. "Tell me his name. He should have a reward."

There was a soft creak that she knew. It was the door of the antechamber. There was no time to explain. There was no more time to make amends. She had to trust Damon and Graeham, and especially herself.

"He said his name was Gray," she said. "Gray of the Wood. But that wasn't his real name."

Damon had heard the sound too. He started to turn.

She knew what he would see. She put her hand on his arm as she turned too.

Graeham stood in the doorway, his muscular frame filling it. He looked like a woodsman, a stranger, her lover, her knight.

Damon reached immediately for the sword at his belt.

"What's going on?" Damon demanded in a hard, ungiving voice. Always, he was ready to defend his family, his home, and Elayna knew he would not hesitate to run a sword straight through this stranger he had found in his sister's chamber.

She kept her hand secure on his arm. "This is the man who saved me. This," she went on, her voice husky, her eyes swerving to meet Graeham's with love and hope, "is the man I love. This is Graeham of Penlogan. He's alive."

CHAPTER
TWENTY-THREE

Graeham was unarmed. He didn't move, simply waited. He was starkly handsome, and Elayna knew she would never forget this moment. No one had ever trusted her this much. She was determined to deserve his gift.

"Damon," he said into the stillness.

Damon stared at him. "Graeham of Penlogan is dead by his own hand," he said harshly. "What trick is this?"

"It's not a trick," Elayna said, her heart beating hard against the wall of her chest. She still held her hand fast on her brother's arm. "It's unbelievable. It's a miracle. Graeham is alive."

Damon pushed her hand away and took slow, deliberate steps toward Graeham. Graeham held his ground, keeping his weaponless hands at his sides.

She watched her brother shaking his head. "Graeham died more than four years ago," Damon repeated. "He killed himself after betraying and murdering an entire band of my men and burning

Penlogan." He stopped several paces from Graeham, examining the other man's face across the short distance separating them.

"It's not true," Elayna said quickly. "You have to understand that it's not true."

She could see Damon was having a difficult time believing what he was seeing. Graeham had changed, but Damon knew him well. It was only a matter of time till he accepted it. What was important was that he understood the truth when he did, that Graeham was no killer.

Damon still glared at Graeham. "Where did he come from?" he asked Elayna. "How did he get in here?"

"He walked through the gates," she said simply. "He brought me back yesterday. He paid a cottar to tend his horse." She didn't want to point out that Graeham had sneaked past the guards in the corridor outside her chamber, but that would be obvious to Damon once he'd had time to think about it. They would be in for a tongue-lashing. Graeham, on his silent forest-feet, would have had no trouble easing past them, she knew.

"He spent the night here?" Damon looked as if he might drop his sword and throttle Graeham with his bare hands.

"In my small room," Elayna clarified. "Not in the outer chamber. The girls never knew he was here, so there's no need to worry for them. He could hardly announce himself at the gate and request an audience with you, could he? He'd be in the dungeon!"

"Damn right he'd be in the dungeon!" Damon declared. "That is where he belongs now!"

"He didn't hurt me," she argued. "He's done nothing wrong. *We* have done nothing wrong."

"That's for me to decide," Damon said angrily.

"I'm a grown woman," Elayna reminded him.

"I've lived with him for nearly a fortnight in a hut in the forest."

"You are not making this better," Damon ground out. "Who are you?" he demanded of Graeham with a fury that would have had a lesser man crumbling in his boots. "And this time I want the truth. No lies! I have no more patience."

"My name these past four years and more has been Gray of the Wood," Graeham stated quietly, his spine straight. He gave no recognition to the clear threat of the sword in Damon's hand. "But I was born Graeham of Penlogan, son of Wilfred."

His words fell into an aching stretch of time, one beat, then another.

"He didn't kill those men," Elayna said. "He didn't burn Penlogan."

"Have you gone mad, Elayna?" Damon demanded without looking back at her. He wasn't taking his eyes off Graeham. He stared at the other man grimly, acceptance seeping into his expression. "I can't believe it. But it's true, isn't it? You're Graeham. You've changed, but— I can see it in your face, your eyes, your build. You're Graeham of Penlogan." Damon's voice faltered for a moment, as if he were overcome with unexpected emotion, then just as quickly he was in control again. "You've been hiding all this time, all these years? Living under a false name? In this thick, misty wild forest of which Elayna spoke. You took her in—what did you do to her? Did you hurt her?"

He closed the space between them suddenly, pressing the blade of his short sword against Graeham's neck.

"He didn't hurt me! He saved my life!" Elayna cried.

"I found her," Graeham said, his voice steady, his eyes blazing into Damon's. "She was hurt, gored by a wild boar. There was an inn nearby. I should

have taken her there. But it was raining, and I—"
He closed his eyes briefly, then opened them again.
He looked past Damon now to Elayna. "He has to
know the truth, the whole truth." He looked back
at Damon. "I couldn't bring myself to let her go.
I held her captive. I told myself it was because I
was afraid she would reveal me, but the truth was
that I couldn't bear to let her go."

Elayna felt tears spring to her eyes, but she
blinked them back. She couldn't let emotion sway
her when her brother was holding a blade to Graeham's throat.

"He never hurt me," she said. "He took care of
me, and when he did tell me to go, I wouldn't
leave. Neither of us could let the other go. We
found each other. It was a miracle, Damon. Please,
he has a story to tell. Listen to it. If not for him,
for me. He is my betrothed," she pointed out.
"Never have I renounced that vow—and I won't.
You know that means we are as good as wed. It was
one thing when we thought he was dead, but now
he is alive! Would you kill the man I'm pledged
to marry without hearing him out?"

Damon blew out a frustrated breath, stepped
back roughly from Graeham. Elayna ran to Graeham's side. Her brother glared at both of them.

"You're mad, both of you, and I don't know what
to believe," he said.

"Believe that I love him," Elayna said softly. She
took Graeham's hand, and he squeezed hers. It
was the only sign of emotion. His hard face yielded
none. He was so like Damon—disciplined on the
outside but soft inside—and she loved them both
so dearly.

"He's a fugitive," Damon said. "My men died,
that is a fact. Penlogan burned."

"But Graeham didn't die by his own hand, did
he? So all the facts we were told aren't true," Elayna

pointed out. "Maybe none of them are true." She let go of Graeham to move to her brother. Damon still held his sword ready. "I've heard his story. I believe him."

"You have been bewitched," Damon grated out. "This man is a criminal, a killer. Like his father." The words seemed to come ripped from his chest. Elayna knew how much Wilfred's presumed perfidy had hurt Damon.

She shook her head. "No." She stared into her brother's eyes, willing him to open his heart to her words. "He's honorable, as was his father. He has been betrayed, just as you were. Just as Wilfred was."

Damon froze. "What are you talking about?"

"Wilfred didn't kill Angelette," she said. "Thomas, his squire, brought the news to Graeham, and Wilfred's last words. He was innocent, and he wanted Graeham to know."

"Where is this squire?" Damon demanded. "Why didn't he come forward?"

Graeham shook his head. "He was afraid for his own life, and he died shortly after returning home. Not long after he saved my life."

Damon's look was wary, measuring. "I'm listening," he said.

"Ranulf and your men were at the gate," Graeham began. "The castle was in chaos. Thomas told me my father's dying words. My father was innocent, but Saville's torture had quickly broken him. He had sent Thomas to beg my forgiveness and to convince me of his innocence—as if I would need convincing. But I knew others would. He had made a confession. I intended to investigate, to find the truth. There was a letter in my father's hand, carried back by Thomas, but there was no time to examine it. I went out to greet the soldiers. Then—"

His quiet gaze held Damon's. "Then all hell broke loose."

"Graeham lost his father, his home, his castle." Elayna placed her hand on Damon's arm again. "He loved his father's name. He would never despoil it. He loved his home. He would never have burned Penlogan! Wilfred would never have murdered Angelette or betrayed you. This has hurt you all this time because it was so impossible to believe, to accept, that your foster father would do this to you. Impossible because it was a lie."

"Then who did?" Damon asked harshly. "Ranulf was my foster brother, fostered together with me and Rorke under the guidance of Wilfred. Are you saying Ranulf killed Angelette?"

"I don't know who killed Angelette," Graeham explained. "But I know it wasn't my father. And I know that it was Ranulf who suddenly came up with the warden who gave the false testimony that got my father executed. And I know that it was Ranulf who came to seize my castle, and Ranulf who said I drove a sword into my own heart and died."

Damon's eyes chilled, pain and horror mixing as words he didn't want to believe sank in.

"What of this letter? Where is it?" Damon asked.

Graeham shook his head. "Gone, as far as I know. We escaped that night with our lives and nothing more. I have no proof. I have only the truth in my heart. I felt betrayed, angry, for a long time, so destroyed inside by the world I'd once loved that I turned my back on it. Everyone believed the worst, and I saw no point in trying to change their minds."

He glanced at Elayna again. "But she made me see that I was wrong." He looked back at Damon. "If there's a chance that I can find the truth now, I have to take it."

Damon was still in shock. "Are you saying that

Ranulf burned Penlogan? Murdered the men helping him seize it? Surely you can see that makes
little sense!"

Elayna knew her brother had been betrayed so
many times that he resisted accepting yet another
loss.

"I can't make sense of it," she said. "But it's true.
I know what my heart tells me. I know Graeham is
innocent." She seized upon the one piece of proof
they had. "He didn't fall on his own sword to kill
himself, did he? If Ranulf lied about that, what else
is he lying about?"

Graeham met Damon's eyes evenly. "I've run
long enough," he said. "I'm ready to go home—
and I'm asking for your help."

Elayna held his hand tightly. "*We're* asking for
your help."

The canopied cart rolled over the smooth road.
Elayna sat huddled in her velvet cloak. It was lined
with fur, but she was cold, even protected from the
elements as they were inside the covered cart.

She tucked her finger around an edge of the
canopy material and looked out at Graeham, riding
with the men. It had been two days since their
conversation with Damon. Two long days. Damon
had sequestered Graeham in a chamber at the top
of the tower, with guards posted outside under
strict orders to maintain his custody, guards who
were told nothing of his identity. Damon had listened and absorbed the story Graeham had told.
He'd sent for Rorke. Aside from Belle, Rorke was
the only one who knew the true reason for their
present journey: to find the truth about the mystery
that stretched from Penlogan to Blanchefleur, the
truth about the rape and murder of Angelette, and
the betrayal of Damon and Wilfred and Graeham.

There was no certainty yet that Damon believed in Graeham's innocence. But his story was convincing enough, and her brother's love for her strong enough, that Damon was ready to find out. Her brother was in pain, torn between loyalty to his friend, Ranulf, and loyalty to the man he'd loved as his foster father. He had to know which one of them had betrayed him.

If it was Wilfred, and Graeham, who had indeed committed the crimes rather than Ranulf, Damon had made it clear that he would see to Graeham's punishment himself.

Elayna shivered, remembering her brother's cold eyes as he'd made that promise. She prayed that the truth would be found, that their plan would work.

Tomorrow was Allhallows. Festivities would be gearing up at Penlogan just as they were at Castle Wulfere. When Ranulf had learned of Elayna's return and willingness to go through with the interrupted betrothal to him, he had sent word by return courier, along with a gift of an engraved silver bracelet for Elayna, that he would welcome her to join him for the holiday at Penlogan-by-the-sea. They had set out immediately, the entire family.

It would have seemed odd to leave her sisters at home. Damon had brought along a larger-than-usual band of soldiers. He would protect his family during their stay at Penlogan-by-the-sea, against whatever tumult resulted from what they were about to do.

Watching Graeham now, riding close among Damon's men as one of the soldiers, his hooded cloak hiding his face from even the men beside him, her heart ached to be with him, to ride with him, to hold him again.

It was close to unbearable to be so near and yet

so far, to know that he could be riding straight into his death.

"How does it feel?"

Elayna blinked, turned her head, and dropped her hand from the canopy to look back at her sister. Gwyneth watched her with careful eyes.

"How does what feel?" Elayna asked.

"Your hair." Gwyneth reached past the veil that hid Elayna's short hair and rubbed the blunt ends between her fingers. "I've forgotten how it feels to wear it short."

"It feels . . . free," Elayna said. "You should have told me it was so fun to be a boy."

Gwyneth smiled. She was prettier than she realized. She was ever boyish, even with her hair long, as Damon insisted. She'd stopped cutting it because Damon had promised her that if she kept it long, he would let her practice her swordsmanship with the squires. Practicing the knightly arts she loved—but would never be allowed to perform in battle—was a reward high enough to gain Gwyneth's recalcitrant obedience.

"You look pretty even with your hair short," Gwyneth said.

"You're pretty too, Gwyneth," Elayna said. Gwyneth's eyes clouded. In the last few years, Elayna had sensed a new struggle in her wildest sister. Gwyneth had spent so long behaving like a boy that she had no idea how to be a girl. Lately, Elayna had suspected that boyish Gwyneth was changing.

They were all changing, she thought, looking at her other sisters. Marigold sat with her face poked in her sketchpad. She rarely stopped sketching long enough to do anything else. Even now she didn't speak much. She grew more serious as she grew older, and she was shockingly brilliant. It was hard sometimes to believe she was a child at all, only nine years of age.

Lizbet was pouting, having been forced to leave a tiercel at a crucial point in its training. But she pouted quietly. Her training in falconry had resulted in a patience that had matured her beyond her years. At twelve, she was already attracting many suitors. Men who visited the castle often thought Lizbet was older than Gwyneth, whose wildness managed to send most noble suitors running.

Elayna worried for her sisters. What would happen after this was all over? She prayed she would be wed to Graeham, but she wondered what that would mean for her sisters. Their own marriages would become an issue once she was settled.

They were quiet most of the trip, and she wondered if they were thinking the same thing. She had parried their questions about her time spent away from home, and there was an awkwardness between them. They had held firm as sisters, bonded against being forced into marriage.

Now Elayna was giving in, and they knew full well she didn't love Ranulf.

Beneath the surface was an anger and a sense of betrayal. She knew they would understand and be happy for her if she could tell them the truth, that she really was in love—and not with Ranulf. But she couldn't tell them anything. And so the trip passed mostly in silence.

She had brought her journal, but she struggled with the thought of writing in it. There were secrets too important to put down in writing, though she imagined writing the story of her adventure in the forest and the mystery that had torn them apart and then brought them together. Perhaps she would, someday, when it was all over. Graeham would never ask her to give up her dreams, she knew. She wondered again at the miracle that had allowed them to find each other again and knew that had to be more than accidenal. It had been God's hand.

Somehow, it had to work out. Their love was meant to be. *Destiny*.

Still, the knot in her stomach held fast. She was afraid.

"Do you think they collect soul cakes on Allhallows in Wildevale?" Lizbet asked after a time.

Wildevale was the tiny fishing village that hugged up to the foot of Penlogan Castle. There were farmers' huts and a few craftsmen, but for the most part the village had made its living by the sea, under the protection of the lords of Penlogan.

She wondered if it would be safe to send her sisters out at night for the traditional collecting of treats, if Damon would let them leave the more controlled environment of the great hall. "Perhaps it would be best to confine our celebration within the walls of the castle. This is not home, you know."

" 'Tis to be *your* home," Gwyneth pointed out.

Elayna made no rely.

"You'll have to play nutcrack," Lizbet put in. She looked at Elayna without smiling. Elayna had seen nutcracking practiced often at Castle Wulfere between members of the castle staff. Lovers intending to be wed would approach the fire, toss in two nuts. If the nuts burst loudly, it was a promise of eternal love.

If they only burned, then the love would soon die.

"If he loves me, pop and fly; if he hates me, lie and die." Gwyneth repeated the rhyme that went with the game.

Elayna shivered again and hugged her cloak around her. *How was she going to go through with this? How would she stand by Ranulf and pretend to love him?*

She yearned to confide everything in her sisters,

and it was almost painful to keep her secrets. But they weren't hers alone. They were Graeham's too.

The journey passed in agonizing increments.

She was surprised when she fell asleep, as nervous as she was. She woke to the sound of men calling out and realized they were at their destination. She pushed open the curtain again to see Penlogan towering above them.

They had arrived.

He felt like a stranger as he saw Penlogan. The feeling could be at least partially accounted for by the fact that he was older, wiser, harder. But there was no doubt that real changes had occurred to his home even as they arrived, before they even swept through the huge stone gates.

Wildevale looked as if it had been decimated by a war. The majority of the huts hung open, empty, shutters flapping in the autumn wind, thatched roofs gone.

"The plague hit this area hard," Damon reminded Graeham.

The pestilence that had wiped out a third of the population of England had left its black mark on Wildevale. Hidden away in the forest outside Cradawg at the time of the plague, this was Graeham's first real look at the aftereffects of the terrible, mysterious sickness on his demesne.

Once inside the castle walls, he saw more changes, but they were of a different sort. There was evidence of new construction everywhere. The loss of population had not stopped Ranulf from increasing the size and strength of the fortress he had—in Graeham's estimation—stolen.

The increase in the castle's size was no doubt approved by the king, who believed Ranulf a hero, as did everyone else.

An unsubstantiated accusation would never hold against a man as powerful as Ranulf. Graeham needed a confession.

He pulled his hood close around his face as they were welcomed into the keep. He kept carefully toward the rear of the group of soldiers as they put up their horses and were greeted with warm cider and snacks of fresh apples and sugared breads in the restored hall.

Flashes of the night he'd nearly died here, the night it had burned around him like a hell on earth, nearly sent him reeling.

He stood with his back to the hall, his cold hands outstretched to the hearth. Whatever he did, he could not be seen, recognized.

"Welcome, welcome," he heard Ranulf boom, his voice coming from the far end of the hall, where a stone staircase connected the hall to a separate wing of family quarters.

Voices roses and fell in buoyant chatter.

He picked out words here and there.

"—betrothal—"

"—honored—"

"Elayna—regrets—changeable—a woman—what can you expect?"

The men laughed. Damon was playing his part, making light of his sister's escape and return, smoothing everything over. Making sure Ranulf suspected nothing.

"They will be blessed," came another voice, thin and frail as always. It tore open another hole in Graeham's heart. Father Almund.

Graeham hadn't seen him since that night at Penlogan. That last memory of Father Almund collapsing had haunted him. He hadn't been able to bring himself to ask if the priest had survived. He hadn't wanted to know that he was dead. And yet he was alive, just as Graeham was. Graeham's only regret was that he could say nothing to express his feelings, at least not then.

The last person he could let see his face was Father Almund. He couldn't put the priest in danger. Father Almund had half raised him from childhood. He would recognize Graeham faster than anyone.

Most of the castle staff that he had observed so far, and the soldiers serving here, seemed to be new. He suspected there were few left from his father's day at Penlogan.

"Nothing worth having is won easily," Father Almund went on in his pacific way. "Especially a woman."

"Of course, of course, of course," Ranulf was saying. "I agree completely. What is the joy of winning if there is no risk of losing? I've won the lady's heart and hand, and I'm thrilled that she has come back to us, back to me, safe and beautiful and ready to be betrothed."

Graeham dared a glance over his shoulder. Elayna smiled faintly, looking pale and ill. Someone had taken her cloak. She wore a figure-fitting gown of gold samite, embroidered with white thread. She looked like a bride already.

She took his breath away, and he wanted to kill Ranulf just for touching her.

He had no choice but to watch the other man bend over her hand and kiss it. Ranulf was tall, thin almost to the point of being gaunt—but he was strong, all wiry muscle and hard deliberation. Graeham didn't underestimate the older man's strength. He was a powerful foe on more than one level.

Elayna lowered her eyes as Ranulf kissed her hand, but Ranulf lifted his to her. Graeham watched, recognizing the avaricious gleam in the other man's gaze. He had no doubt Elayna was right; Ranulf wanted her for her money. There was no love in his eyes.

That should have made him feel better, but he realized it made him feel worse. If Ranulf didn't love Elayna, he would be willing to hurt her if necessary. This course they had embarked upon was perilous.

Graeham had no doubt that Ranulf was capable of anything.

"My lady," Ranulf said, straightening. As he did, he drew her toward a trestle prepared for their arrival.

A large bowl rested atop the brightly white tablecloth. Crowdie, Graeham recognized. It was a whipped sweet cream combined with spiced apple sauce. Traditionally, six objects were dropped in it: two marbles, two coins, and two rings.

Ranulf handed Elayna a spoon for dipping.

"Find a ring, my sweet lady," he said, "and you are soon to be wed."

A cheer went up from the men of Penlogan, Ranulf's men, and his servants that were in the hall, as if on cue. Graeham saw Ranulf nod at them in approval. The men seemed to lose interest immediately. Most of them had been dicing by the fire near Graeham, and they went back to their entertainment.

How loyal were they to Ranulf? Would they die for him? Would Damon, Rorke, and their men have to fight for Penlogan even after they secured Ranulf's confession? *If* they secured Ranulf's confession.

The man Graeham was the most concerned about stood near Ranulf now. Kenric. Ranulf's brother. He had served in Damon's band for many years. Graeham had caught up with the people he'd once known by asking Damon exhaustive questions during the past two days he'd spent at Castle Wulfere. Damon and Rorke had been his only visitors to his tower seclusion.

Kenric had been a foster brother to Graeham. They had both become knights under the tutelage of Hugh de Galtres. Kenric had gone on to serve Damon. Graeham knew now that Kenric had returned two years ago to serve with his brother's men at Penlogan.

The last person Graeham wanted to hurt was Kenric. But he couldn't forget that Kenric had been with Ranulf and Damon's men that fateful night Penlogan burned. Kenric had been one of the few who lived.

He couldn't trust Kenric.

"Find a marble," Gwyneth piped up, "and you'll be single forever."

Graeham watched the sisters' eyes meet. He sensed a tension between them and hated knowing he was the cause of it.

Elayna had to be suffering, not being able to confide in her sisters. He knew how close they had always been.

"Find a coin," someone else put in, Graeham couldn't see who, "and be wealthy all of your days."

"My lady is already wealthy," Ranulf said, brushing away the last comment. His eyes glowed again. "After all, she has love."

Graeham saw Belle and Damon stiffen, their eyes meeting. Belle glanced across the hall then, and for a moment, her clear blue eyes held his. She nodded.

He hadn't spoken to Damon's wife yet, but he felt at that moment that she was pulling for him, for him and Elayna and their love.

He nodded back, and she glanced away.

The crowd of family, castle staff, and soldiers watched Elayna dip the spoon into the crowdie. She lifted it, tipped the spoon, and the sweet liquid dripped out. The spoon was empty. No ring, no marble, no coin.

"Nothing—a life of uncertainty," Elayna said quietly, pronouncing the final foretelling. He could see that she was careful not to glance Graeham's way.

"Ah, but you must try again, my lady." Ranulf placed his hand over Elayna's and guided her by easy force back to the bowl, dipping, swirling, and finally coming up again. He tilted the spoon, his hand still over hers, just slightly, letting the liquid seep out while still retaining the prize.

"A ring!" he shouted.

Graeham looked away. He couldn't watch anymore.

"Naught in the damned bowl but rings," said one of the men-at-arms dicing nearby. "Saw him put them there myself."

Another shrugged. The men played on.

Ranulf played to win. Graeham was not surprised.

Finally, the party began to disperse to their respective chambers to prepare for the feast to come. That night would be only a preliminary to the celebration the following night of Allhallows, building up to the betrothal feast that would follow the next day.

The tumult of the castle in preparation for the feasting and festivities was in Graeham's favor.

His hood still close about his face, his eyes averted from anyone he might know, he accompanied Rorke along with several other knights to the family quarters. The other men-at-arms were there for the purpose of guarding the family in the corridors.

They would not notice when Graeham was taken inside Rorke's chamber that he would not return.

Rorke shut the stout, arched wooden door set in the thick stone. The family wing was a rectangular addition, part of the expansion Graeham's grandfather had designed.

It was here that the honeycomb of secret passages met the castle. They led to the cave and the sea. It wasn't through this chamber that Graeham had escaped the night Penlogan burned. He'd escaped through the lord's chamber. That would be Ranulf's chamber now.

But the tunnels burrowed throughout the private family wing.

Graeham's only question was whether or not Ranulf had discovered them. He held out no hope that they would find the letter he had left in his father's desk the evening Ranulf and Damon's men had arrived. It would have been foolish for Ranulf to keep it.

Graeham knew he had to depend on surprise to arouse a confession from his enemy.

Rorke slid the bolt home, securing their privacy. "Take me," he said grimly, "to the tunnels."

Graeham nodded, hoping they hadn't been found, sealed. He crossed the room, went straight to the tapestries between the narrow, arched windows, deeply recessed in the thick stone.

He swept the tapestries aside to reveal a seemingly bare stone wall.

But it was not bare at all, not to one who knew how to seek . . . and find its special grooves. There were grooves in the stone, places where the mortar seemed to separate. Notches to be pushed, in a certain order.

His grandfather had been an engineering genius on his own and had hired only the best masons— and had paid them well to keep his secrets.

He looked back at Rorke. The older knight watched carefully. Rorke was an enigma to Graeham. He had never known him as well as he had known Damon, and even now Rorke was a man apart, no matter how many people surrounded him. Graeham had noticed in the hall below, during the welcoming festivities, Rorke had taken no part. He had stood alone, watching, not participating.

It had to be painful, Graeham recognized, for Rorke to watch even the simplest of lovers' games, even knowing it was false, when the love of his life had been raped and murdered, her death beginning this ugly black spiral that still swirled around them all.

Looking into Rorke's eyes, Graeham saw how he would feel if he lost Elayna, truly lost her. If she died. He felt a chill fist grip his heart.

"We're going to find out who murdered Angelette," Graeham vowed grimly. "And we're going to make him pay."

Rorke's mouth tightened, and there was a brief gleam of emotion, then he was under perfect control again.

"I'll settle," he said, "for nothing less."

Graeham nodded, turned back, pushed the last notch, and pressed the heavy stone wall. He was rewarded by a groaning, and suddenly the stone wall—just a moment before an impenetrable barrier—swung open to reveal a gaping blackness.

CHAPTER
TWENTY-FOUR

If Ranulf needed money, the night's feast showed no evidence. From the salmon and currant dumplings to the spiced pheasant with apples to the meal-ending sensation of a four-and-twenty-blackbird pie, their host put on a show of wealth and power and confidence. If Gwyneth still carried her sword stick to dinner, as she had in years past, Elayna thought Lizbet might have grabbed it and whacked Ranulf over the head with it.

The sight of the birds trapped inside the pie shells, even temporarily, infuriated Lizbet, who loved birds far more than spectacle.

With the pies cut carefully open, the birds flew free, careening up to the vaulted rafters of the hall, singing as the crowd clapped below. Elayna placed a firm hand on Lizbet's arm below the table. She had no doubt her falconer-aspiring sister, usually composed, was about to launch into a tirade about the proper care and treatment of feathered creatures.

"The birds are not injured," Elayna hissed. "Let

it be. You know full well they are raised for just this purpose. 'Tis not your business to comment upon it.''

Lizbet's jaw set tightly and she glared at Elayna, though she held her peace. Clearly, she thought it was her business, and just as clearly, her estimation of her older sister had dropped another notch.

Elayna looked away, blinking back a sting of hurt. She couldn't explain now. No doubt Lizbet thought she was impressed by Ranulf's spectacles and his fine hall. In truth, it worried her.

Where was the money coming from?

Not from his demesne, judging by the state of Wildevale.

Ranulf had to be in debt up to his ears. And her dowry was his way out. Add that to the very real possibility that he was a murderer, and it all combined to form the image of a man who had nothing to lose.

The thought of Ranulf as a cold-blooded killer, a vile architect of a scheme whose proportions were yet unknown, was surreal. She knew the evening had to be painful for Damon. She'd noticed Belle watching her husband with worried eyes all day.

Elayna realized the rest of the family was leaving the table, and she followed them into a private parlor area behind the dais. The restored hall was magnificent, soaring stone walls lined with expensive tapestries, gold sconces to hold huge rushlights, and intricate glass art renderings in the soaring oriel that protruded from its upper end.

The stained glass was elaborate and lavish, no doubt procured at a high price. The oriel windows were new since Graeham's father's days, because the old panes had been blown out during the terrible fire that had ravaged the hall.

Ranulf had furnished the oriel as a small parlor, set off yet a part of the great hall at the same time.

Positioned near the dais, it created an intimate space for the lord to entertain special guests.

The family gathered in the oriel now, minus Rorke.

Rorke had not joined them for dinner. He had sent word through his squire that he felt unwell and would spend the evening in his chamber.

Elayna knew that Rorke and Graeham had planned to explore the tunnels of Penlogan, plotting the actions they would take tomorrow night, Allhallows, when the dead were said to walk the earth.

It was Damon's job to ensure that Ranulf stayed in the hall, entertaining his guests. He wasn't to be allowed to return to his private chamber till well past the end of the feast.

Rorke and Graeham needed ample time for their searching and planning.

She was to be allowed no contact with Graeham for the time being—and she ached to speak to him, touch him. The separation of the past four years was nothing in comparison to the separation of these last few days.

He was to remain secluded in Rorke's chamber until they sprang their trap.

Across the hall, Elayna could see the castlefolk and villagers setting up to play the traditional feast games. Children were bobbing for apples while older girls were paring them into long spirals and tossing them over their left shoulder. There were giggles and gasps as the spiraled parings landed and they examined the shapes of the parings into letters that would signify their future husbands' names.

A loud pop told her that someone was playing nutcrack by the hearth.

She deliberately chose a high-backed cushioned seat where she would have her back to the fire and prayed that Ranulf would not repeat his earlier interest in playing divining games. He had paid little attention to her during the meal, and so she hoped he'd tired of courting her for the evening. Some of the revelers had begun a carol-dance, of which she had no desire to join. So far, he was continuing to ignore her, but she felt vulnerable.

At any moment, he might recall their betrothal and act to reinforce the image of his true love for her.

For safety, she leaned over and plucked baby Ryen from Belle's arms. The boy was three months old, plump and rosy-cheeked, with brown hair. He would be a copy of his father, they had all already decided.

Two-year-old Venetia, rosy-cheeked as her brother but as blond as he was dark, took the opportunity to climb into her mother's now-empty lap. The little girl clutched a soft cloth doll in one hand, reaching up to pat Belle's golden coiled braids with the other.

Elayna held Ryen's warm, sweet body in her arms and yearned for a child of her own.

" 'Tis amazing how love changes the whole way you view the world and your place in it," Belle said softly.

Damon, along with Ranulf and his brother Kenric, was standing by the windows, talking about the quality of this year's grain harvest in comparison to the last. The men were giving no heed to the women at the moment.

Gwyneth, Lizbet, and Marigold were paying no attention either, as they had settled into a round of merrills using the board and bone game pieces they'd found on the small table in the oriel.

Elayna held Belle's eyes. "I'm sorry I never told you about Graeham." Her voice dropped to a whisper as she spoke his name. "When you first came to Castle Wulfere—"

"You were hurting more than I knew." Belle reached out to touch Elayna's arm gently. "And you are stronger than you think, then and now."

"I'm afraid—"

"I know," Belle whispered. "I know. But this love was meant to be. How can you think otherwise, when the two of you found each other as you did? I believe in miracles."

Elayna bit her lip, nodded, her throat thick with hope. She hadn't realized how comforting it would be to hear her own hope reaffirmed by someone else, especially Belle, who had overcome many obstacles to secure her own happiness with Damon.

"Thank you," Elayna whispered back.

"My ladies," came a fragile voice, and Elayna twisted in her seat to see Father Almund approaching the oriel. "How do you enjoy the season? 'Tis a bit morbid, think you not? I am always relieved when the All Saints' Day dawns following Allhallows."

"I suppose God must find prayers more fitting than singing for the dead," Belle said. "But the children do find singing and begging for soul cakes so much more amusing."

Father Almund's blue eyes twinkled and he lost his serious look. "Ah, yes, I suppose they must." He pulled a small cloth packet from the pocket of his voluminous tunic. He unwrapped it and exposed a half dozen flat, oval shortbread cookies made with currants, cinnamon, and nutmeg. "I sneaked these right from under Cook's nose," he said, holding the cloth packet out with one hand and patting his lips with one finger of the other. "It's a secret. Cook would slay me where I stand if he knew I'd stolen soul cakes from the kitchen before tomorrow night."

Soul cakes were a perennial favorite with children and even adults, sweet and crispy and saved always to be eaten only on Allhallows. Marigold, Lizbet, and Gwyneth made quick work of accepting their share while Father Almund distributed the remaining cookies to Venetia, Elayna, and Belle.

Elayna took the last one. Father Almund placed his hand on her arm for a moment, and she was surprised by how warm and strong she found his grip.

"Welcome home, Lady Elayna," he said, suddenly serious. "This castle has been too long without a lady. We have waited for this day."

Graeham's mother had died while he was a child, so Elayna knew it had been many years indeed since a lady's hand had been upon Penlogan-by-the-sea.

She didn't have time to think of a reply. Another voice broke into the moment.

"What, none for us?"

Elayna looked up to see Kenric gazing in mock pout at the old priest.

"You are soldiers," Father Almund responded teasingly, jovial again. "Far too grim and grave for the pleasures of childhood."

"Ah, that is where you are wrong, Father," Ranulf argued. "We soldiers need our hearts lightened more than anyone. Tomorrow night, I will expect you all to be prepared for a most traditional celebration. I myself intend to play King Crispin and you must all be my court."

King Crispin—really Saint Crispin, whose saint day was close to Allhallows—was usually played by the lord, who dressed in magnificent regal robes and directed the evening's events.

"Will we go souling?" Gwyneth asked, diverted from her game of merrills by the talk of tomorrow's revelries.

"Of course," Ranulf declared.

"Will we wear masks?" Marigold inquired.

Lizbet continued to concentrate on the board, evidently still piqued with Ranulf and Elayna and the world in general because she would rather be home training her tiercel than anywhere else, even if it involved souling and masks.

"Yes, masks too," Ranulf said. "And all the singing and begging and soul cakes you can stand."

Elayna looked beyond Ranulf to Damon. She knew if Ranulf hadn't planned to provide masks for the night's festivities, Damon had come prepared with a chestful of them.

Masks were a necessary element in their plans.

"Little wonder the dead wander on that night," Father Almund said. "All the singing and begging drives them from their graves."

"Do you think the dead really walk, Father?" Gwyneth asked.

Father Almund opened his mouth to answer but was cut off by a squeal from Lizbet, who had suddenly sprung into animation.

"Three in a row," Lizbet crowed, tapping down a bone piece across the board. Marigold and Gwyneth turned their attention back to the board, demanding a rematch, leaving the conversation to the adults.

" 'Tis a wonder we don't give our children nightmares with this holiday," Damon said, "but they do enjoy it."

"Yes, Father Almund is right, the holiday is morbid," Belle agreed. "But somehow still fun."

" 'Tis the time when spirits are most powerful and most lonely," Damon added. "I wonder that we celebrate that rather than fear it."

"Perhaps we do fear it," Kenric replied. "That's why we wear masks and sing songs, eat too much, drink too much, and dance the night away."

The young knight glanced at his older brother for a long moment.

The oriel was quiet. Elayna could almost hear the combined hearts in the intimate parlor beating, thumping, too hard, too loud, waiting. . . .

"Nonsense," Ranulf pronounced loudly. "Remember that it is also a celebration of summer's end, and of what nature has provided, not what it has taken away."

There was another silence.

"I'm tired," Elayna said, and she was surprised by how deeply tired she was quite suddenly. The anxiety was getting to her. She needed warm mead, a soft pillow, and a deep sleep with no dreams.

She said her good nights. Belle, her sisters, and the babies joined her in heading for the private quarters. Only Damon remained in the oriel. "To talk over old times with old friends," he said, and ordered a round of ale from a passing servant.

Elayna knew he would keep Ranulf and Kenric occupied as long as possible.

Graeham would have known each door, each secret opening, into the private family quarters by touch even if they hadn't brought a torch with them on their exploration.

He went straight to his father's former quarters. The lord's chamber was a spacious, well-furnished room, unchanged as far as he could tell from the day he'd last seen it despite Ranulf's occupancy. There was a huge canopied bed of dark wood with deep red bedcurtains. Ornately carved chairs, cushioned in the same deep red as the bedcurtains, sat on either side of the massive hearth. Several paintings adorned the walls—the miracles of Elisha and the story of Hezekiah on one side of the room, a battle scene from the Acts of Judas of Maccabeus on the other.

Through an arched opening to an alcove, he could see the large table his father had used as a desk.

He walked through the opening, ran his hand across the scarred, dark wood of the table. For a moment, he could almost feel his father's hand on his shoulder. He felt a strength move within him. *This was his home, his right, his heritage.*

A quick inspection of the drawers, including the secret compartment beneath the top one, revealed little of interest except a copy of the account rolls that showed Penlogan in serious arrears.

He tamped down the fury he felt at Ranulf's mismanagement of the ordered, prosperous demesne Graeham's father had left behind. Ranulf was a soldier, the second son from a poor manor— never destined for anything beyond what his muscle and might could win him on the battlefield. Yet he hadn't taken Penlogan-by-the-sea in battle. He'd taken it in a back alley below Blanchefleur when he'd devised the scheme that had landed Graeham's father in prison for Angelette's murder.

Why? How? The questions plagued Graeham. Damon had been blamed first—but there had been a huge outcry over his innocence. By the time Wilfred was accused, the relief at finding Damon innocent had muted further reaction—and the execution had been swift.

Somehow, some way, Ranulf had realized the advantage to be gained in Wilfred's death over Damon's—and he'd made certain through the discovery of the village warden's testimony that he was credited with the accomplishment of justice.

Whatever the answers were to his questions, they weren't here, at least not tonight.

They left the lord's chamber, and the farther

they went into the tunnels, the more Rorke was amazed at what Graeham's grandfather had engineered into the walls of Penlogan Castle.

"The perfect escape," Rorke said as they stood at last at the mouth of the cave. They bent their heads where the rock ceiling lowered near the entrance, then straightened as they came out onto the small rock promontory.

It was a sheer drop to the choppy sea below.

"I don't remember that night," Graeham said, thinking of Thomas, how much he owed his father's squire. "Thomas was a hero that night. He served my father well."

Below them, the sea churned under the gray-blue sky. No moon seeped through the thick clouds. A fierce wind whipped at their cheeks.

They stepped back into the interior of the cave, out of the direct attack of the elements, their necks bending in necessity due to the cave's low height.

The tunnel had joined the cave as it dipped down into the rock. The opening where they stood now at the mouth of the cave was like a small chamber—with room for supplies, even a couple of dinghies. One was missing, taken from the cave the night Graeham and Thomas had escaped.

The other was still here. There were several chests containing a mishmash of equipment—an ax, a small dagger, a lantern and a container of oil, a collection of leather canteens, oars, rope ladders, and other miscellaneous items.

Nothing appeared to have been touched. Graeham had no reason to believe that Ranulf knew of the secret world beyond the walls of the castle he'd stolen.

They headed back in the direction from which they'd come, one step closer to advancing their dire plan.

* * *

Elayna smoothed her hands over the pale green camlet gown. It was bordered in gold ribbon with pearls encrusted in the bodice.

The garment had been hastily sewn, designed by Marigold. Elayna would wear it tomorrow, then never again.

She laid the gown down again, draping it carefully against the chest at the foot of the bed.

There was a knock at the door.

She opened it to a young maid. The girl had calf-brown eyes that beamed curiously at her from beneath her snood as she set a steaming goblet on the table near the bed.

"I hope I made it as ye like, milady," she said, bobbing a curtsy. "Me mum always likes hers with lots of cinnamon, so I put lots in for ye."

Another maid, older and heavyset, had followed her into the chamber. She began plumping pillows and pulling down blankets.

"Her ladyship doesn't want to hear how yer mum likes her mead, Ada," the woman said flatly. "Don't be bothering her. His lordship wouldn't like it."

The young girl reddened, bit her lip, and looked down, as if ashamed. She glanced sideways, and for a moment, Elayna thought she looked afraid.

What kind of lord was Ranulf? she wondered. He had always seemed vaguely kind on his visits to Castle Wulfere. But she realized already that the man they had all known as Damon's friend was not the man in truth.

"I'm sorry, milady," she said, and bobbed again.

"It's all right," Elayna said. It bothered her, the girl's easy timidity. Her natural exuberance was too quickly reined in. If she did indeed become the lady of Penlogan, she thought, there would be a lot of work to do.

It wasn't just debt that had a stranglehold on this castle. The people here weren't happy.

Why?

The older woman finished arranging the bed.

"Is there aught else can be brought fer ye, milady?" she inquired, wiping a stray gray hair from her eyes.

Elayna shook her head. "No, thank you." She hesitated. She was eager for a moment alone to examine the walls, to see if she could find the secret door to the tunnels. Every room in the private wing opened into the tunnels, according to Graeham. But there was something else bothering her now. "Perhaps Ada could stay and brush my hair. I'm tired."

Fayette often brushed her hair at night at home, and she loved it, but she would normally have refrained from asking a stranger to perform the task. But she wanted a chance to speak to Ada alone. Truthfully, she had little hair to brush! But that wasn't the point.

The woman looked reluctant, but she didn't have the nerve to deny the request of the woman who was presumed to be Ranulf's bride very soon.

She nodded to Ada, who stood by meekly, awaiting permission, then left.

Elayna sat on the stool by the dressing table. Ada picked up the silver-handled brush and stood behind her. First, she plucked the circlet and veil from Elayna's head. The material had hidden the cut of her hair.

The maid gasped.

"Oh, milady, what happened to yer hair?"

"I cut it," Elayna said. She shifted around on the stool to look up at the maid's shocked eyes. "Go ahead, brush it. I really am tired," she said honestly, "and it might help me sleep."

She turned around again.

"Are ye fretting about the betrothal?" Ada asked, then stopped herself short, the brush freezing midway down Elayna's scalp. "I'm sorry, milady. I shouldn't be asking ye such questions. "Matilde is right."

Elayna supposed the older maid was Matilde.

"Why do you say that?" she asked.

"His lordship just wouldn't like it," Ada repeated the other woman's warning. "He gave us strict orders before yer arrival about talking to any of ye," she added.

"Oh, really? Why?" Elayna's curiosity was piqued.

Why wouldn't Ranulf want his staff to converse with her family? She was accustomed to being quite friendly with the folk at Castle Wulfere.

Ada didn't answer.

Elayna twisted to look back at her. The maid was looking at her with nervous eyes.

"No reason," Ada said. She tried to continue brushing, but Elayna took the brush from her hand and, shifting on the stool, spun around to take both of Ada's hands in hers, letting the silver brush drop to the floor with a thump.

"Why?" Elayna repeated.

Ada pulled away from her, wrung her hands. Her shoulders were thin in her plain, homespun kirtle.

"What is the matter?" Elayna demanded, softening her voice so as not to scare the maid.

"I can't say! I should not have told ye about his lordship's orders." The maid was in tears.

Elayna guided the girl back to the stool, this time seating the maid instead of herself, and picked up an unused bath cloth from the dressing table to dab at the girl's wet cheeks.

"I'm so sorry, milady," Ada said. She tried to get up right away, but Elayna insisted she stay seated until she had a hold of her emotions. "Ye're too kind, milady," she sobbed. "I'm ruining everything. If his lordship finds out—"

"He's not going to find out," Elayna said calmly. "I won't tell him, and it's just you and me in the room. Everything is just fine." She patted the girl's thin shoulder. "Now tell me why the servants aren't supposed to talk to us. Maybe I can do something to help—"

"Oh, no, milady, ye can't do anything to help!" Ada looked up at her, her face tear-streaked and skinny. Elayna guessed she couldn't be more than twelve.

"No one can help," the girl went on. "As soon as I'm old enough— As soon as me little brother is old enough—I'm running away. I don't like the notion of leaving me mum alone. Me brother is only five. When he's ten, I'm running away from Wildevale—and never coming back!"

She sounded extraordinarily desperate. Elayna knew what it meant to crave freedom from a life that was not your destiny, but Ada's words struck her different. Ada was speaking from fear.

"If I live that long," the girl added.

Elayna felt something cold clutch her heart.

"What are you talking about?" Elayna demanded.

"It's what we're not supposed to mention, milady," Ada said.

"What?" Elayna thought she would shake the poor girl in a moment if she didn't tell her.

"It's the night beast," the girl breathed.

She looked over her shoulder as if she expected some dark, monstrous creature to swoop down on her from straight out of the stone.

Elayna stared at her, stunned. "What?" she said blankly.

"The night beast," Ada repeated, still on a whisper. "He comes in the night and steals into our cottages. He's huge, tall as a castle wall, and black as night. He has wings as wide as the sea! He casts a spell on us so we can't move or speak. We can't fight him! He's too strong, too powerful. And he takes the young women into his talons and he's gone, away, into the night!''

Elayna almost forgot to breathe, she was so transfixed by the wild glow in Ada's eyes as she told the story.

It was a *story,* she reminded herself. It was crazy! Every place had its legends. This was Wildevale's.

"What happens to the girls?" she asked.

"They disappear! They're never seen again!" Ada was pale and shaking suddenly. "Never!"

Elayna reminded herself that it was almost Allhallows. Perhaps that explained Ada's strange behavior. The holiday *was* morbid, as Father Almund had pointed out. It could prey upon an imaginative mind.

"This was what Ranulf didn't want you to tell me? About the night beast?"

Ada nodded vigorously.

"His lordship said ye'd be scared, and there was no reason to upset ye when ye were about to be betrothed." She gulped back another sob. "I think ye should go, lady!" she cried in a rough whisper. "Go! Go tonight."

Elayna frowned. "Oh, Ada, don't worry about me. I'm safe here. My brother's guards are right outside, remember? Besides, I don't believe in legends."

Ada blinked. "Milady, it's not a legend."

Elayna felt a terrible prickle on the back of her neck. Dread.

"Of course it's a legend," she argued, trying to sound sensible. "There's no such thing as winged night beasts that steal into homes and fly away with young girls."

Ada was shaking her head.

She leaned forward and said in a desperate whisper, "Yes, there is, lady! Yes, there is! Else where is my elder sister? And Matilde's two daughters? And Cook's niece? And the armorer's wife? And all the rest? Where are they?"

Elayna paced the chamber before the low-burning hearth for a long time, thoughts roiling in her mind. She hesitated to get Belle, to bother her sister-in-law this late in the night.

She knew Damon would still be downstairs with Ranulf and Kenric in the great hall.

What she really wanted was to talk to Graeham, but she had tried in vain to discover the secrets of the tunnel door. She knew it had to be located behind the great tapestry on the exterior wall, but there was no opening it. She didn't possess the knowledge required, and she finally gave up.

Even if she found it, how would she find her way to Rorke's chamber—to Graeham?

Sleep was impossible. The mead sat untouched on the table.

It's the night beast, the night beast, the night beast.

Ada's insistent words and fierce eyes wouldn't leave her mind.

He comes in the night and steals into our cottages. He's huge, tall as a castle wall, and black as night. He has wings as wide as the sea!

The description was ridiculous, clearly fabricated. Surely fabricated. There was no such creature in truth. It wasn't possible. She'd described something of mythological proportions.

He takes the young women into his talons and he's gone, away, into the night!

They're never seen again! Never!

Elayna pressed her fingers to her pounding temples. What was going on here?

Where is my sister? And Matilde's two daughters? And Cook's niece? And the armorer's wife? And all the rest? Where are they?

Elayna tried to shake off the horrible prickling sensation that wouldn't leave her.

Something was wrong at Penlogan Castle, something Ranulf didn't want her to know about. Something he didn't want any of them to know about.

And she was very scared of what she was thinking.

If Ranulf had murdered Angelette, as they suspected, was it so impossible to believe she was not the first—or the last?

CHAPTER TWENTY-FIVE

It was a breath that woke her, a brush of air across her cheek, a touch—part of her dream, or not part of her dream. Elayna opened her eyes, bewildered, heart pounding almost out of her chest. *It's the night beast, the night beast, the night beast.*

A dark shape leaned over her, seemingly enormous from her position on the bed, a shadow silhouetted against the lowering fire, his body parting the bedcurtains. . . .

She would have screamed, but her gasp gave the warning and a gentle hand cupped her face.

"Elayna, sweetheart, it's me."

She sobbed her relief as his hand moved to skim her lips, her jaw, then kissing her on the cheek, the nose, the eyelids. . . . He discovered the squeeze of frightened tears from the corners of her eyes.

"I'm sorry," he whispered against her cheek. "I didn't mean to scare you."

"No, it's not your fault," she cried softly, and clung to him, feeling overjoyed and slightly foolish. Her imagination was running wild. She'd let Ada's tale take over her mind. But she was so glad to see Graeham, and for a moment, she didn't want to think of anything else. His arms were all that mattered. Clinging to his warm hardness, breathing in his scent, tasting his lips.

Her body reacted to his closeness, and so did his to hers.

"I couldn't stay away," he murmured thickly.

"I'm so glad." She arched her body into his, needing the reaffirming life and love he offered. "How did you get in here?" She was still fascinated by the tunnels. He had to have come in through her secret door.

But she wasn't surprised when he avoided giving her specifics. He was as protective as her brother.

He kissed her neck, raising goose bumps all over her skin through her thin chemise. "Rorke finally fell asleep" was all he said. "It's late, and I can't stay long. I just—" He kissed her again, hard, needy. "I had to see you."

His words inspired a sense of urgency. She was no longer a virgin, and she was ready to make love to him as the experienced woman she had become, and she wasn't waiting. He settled in beside her on the bed, and she used her legs to push him onto his back, then straddled him. He was dressed, but she made short work of dispensing with his clothes. She unbuckled his belt, slipped it away, then he rose up to help her remove his tunic. She curled down his hose and removed his shoes. Her own night chemise lifted easily over her head, and she floated it down to the floor.

She climbed on top of him again, pulling the bedcurtains closed behind her, and he groaned as she took him into her hands. She tormented him the way he had tormented her, with touches and kisses and anticipation of the delicious pleasure to come.

When she finally moved to place him inside her, he groaned desperately and she thought he would explode right away, but he was too disciplined for that.

He moved, and she moved with him, establishing the rhythm that was theirs alone. Hot tingles, deep, deep, deep thrust. Again and again until her insides tightened, tensed, and shattered, and then he could hold on no longer either.

The sense of completeness almost made her weep.

Afterward, they lay curled together, her back against his chest, his arm possessive around her waist, and finally, she told him everything Ada had said, hating that it would spoil the moment but knowing it was necessary.

The tale disturbed him as much as it had disturbed her. He didn't know what to make of it any more than she did.

He sat up beside her, a shadow in the darkness of the curtained bed. He was silent for a long time. She sat up, too, feeling cold despite the cozy warmth of their blanketed nest.

"It's not your fault," she said, suspecting suddenly where his quiet silence was leading. He had stayed away for years. He would blame himself. He was the true lord of Penlogan and these were his people.

"I wasn't here," he said grimly. "I started a new life. I left my people."

"You were nearly killed!" she pointed out. "You couldn't come back. Even now—if we hadn't found each other, if Damon hadn't been willing to listen— You were in danger. You're still in danger. You didn't choose your new life—it chose you. You said it yourself—it was God's will for things to happen as they have. This was the time you were destined to return. This is our destiny, now, today,

here. If you had come back before—perhaps you'd
be dead.''

She reached out, touched his hand, curled her
fingers between his. ''You didn't know about any
of this. You *couldn't* have known. And we *still* don't
know! This tale is fantastical. Something is wrong,
but a night beast? A monstrous winged creature
that steals young women in the night?''

''I don't know what it is.'' He shook his head in
the shadows. ''But I know about it now,'' he said,
his voice quiet and fierce. ''And I'm going to do
something about it.''

Damon and Belle were still dressing when she
arrived in their chamber the next morning, one
of Damon's men-at-arms dogging her every move
from the moment she'd left her guest chamber in
Penlogan's private wing. It was a short walk down
the corridor to Damon and Belle's room, but the
guard had strict orders.

She might have smiled to herself, thinking of
the secret visitor through the tunnels that she'd
had in her room despite all her brother's precau-
tions, if not for the fear swirling through her mind.
She and Graeham had agreed that Damon needed
to be informed first thing in the morning about
Ada's story.

Belle sat in a padded chair by the fire, nursing
baby Ryen, a small blanket thrown over her bodice,
the baby's legs peeking out below, his curled, dark
hair above. She refused to employ a wet nurse,
preferring to keep her babes close to her.

Damon was in the process of buckling his sword
belt.

Quickly, she told them everything, omitting that
she'd already had an opportunity to talk to Graeham. Damon listened, his harsh demeanor growing

darker, and he left immediately for Rorke's
chamber.

The information wouldn't change their plans,
but it added a sense of pressure. The mystery was
becoming more, not less, clear.

Belle retied the ribbons of her rose samite gown.

She juggled Ryen on her hip. A maid she'd
brought with her from Castle Wulfere emerged
from an anteroom with Venetia, her golden curls
bobbing around her plump, pretty face.

"The day begins," Belle said. Her gaze caught
and held Elayna's, worry etched in the lines of her
mouth. "Come with me to the chapel," she said
to Elayna. "It would do us good to start with a
prayer."

Every table in the great hall was adorned with
lanterns of turnips and squash, the insides hol-
lowed out, the sides carved with eyes, noses,
mouths, and thick candles set within to flicker and
glow. The night was full of light, for flames were
said to welcome good spirits and prevent evil ones
from coming near. Most of the turnips and squash
were decorated with friendly smiles, but a few were
carved with fearsome scowls, to the delight of the
children who squealed at the sight of them.

For this night, Penlogan Castle and the people of
Wildevale, invited into the keep for the celebration,
seemed willing to set aside whatever mystery stormed
over them.

Or perhaps, Elayna thought as she looked around
the full hall, they had been warned.

Beneath the smiles and squeals, she sensed anxiety in the eyes of Ranulf's villeins and castle staff.

She doubted she would be able to consume a
bit of the lavish feast spread before them due to
her own anxiety.

The pale green gown fit perfectly despite its hasty construction, yet it felt as if it were squeezing her like a vise. It was fear choking her though.

Allhallows was here. The dead would walk. The gown was the exact color and design of the gown Angelette had worn the night of her murder.

She smoothed her gown nervously, then reached up to touch the crispinette encasing her coiffure. It was an elaborate design, created carefully by Belle in accordance with painfully wrought memories shared by Rorke.

Every detail had to be just right.

Belle had parted her hair in the middle, then braided it into two plaits, working in lengths of false hair to make up for the shortness of Elayna's own hair. The plaits were brought forward, low on her cheeks, then turned back to encircle the back of her head, the ends of the plaits tucked neatly into one another. The entire arrangement was then encased in the gold network bag, or crispinette.

The hair felt strange. It wasn't hers in more than one way.

This was the way Angelette had always worn her hair.

Elayna wound her way through the crowded tables, heading toward the dais where Ranulf already reigned as King Crispin. She was the last one to join the family table. She saw immediately that Rorke, despite knowing what was coming, was affected by her appearance, and she wanted to run straight back to her room and tear off the clothes and coiffure, wanting anything but to hurt this good knight. But she could not. They were both doing what they had to do, and Rorke more than anyone wanted and needed to know the truth about Angelette's death.

Ranulf took in her appearance without comment. His look was unreadable, but he stared at her for a long time before rising, flourishing his scepter and bowing.

"My future queen!" he announced loudly, and a round of cheers came obediently from the nearby tables.

He was dressed in regal robes of purple and gold. The heavy chain around his neck was a medallion bearing the traditional emblem of St. Crispin, a boot.

"What the patron saint of bootmakers has to do with the dead is a mystery to me," Elayna heard Kenric say as she sat down to the trencher she would be forced to share with Ranulf, as would be expected due to their coming betrothal.

"The dead need shoes," Gwyneth pointed out from across the table, "if they are to wander the earth!"

Everyone laughed, and even Rorke seemed to relax slightly. Elayna was glad her sisters knew nothing of the evening's true plans. They would be safely abed, under lock and guard, before anything dangerous took place.

The remainder of the meal passed in a blur. She ate little and tasted none of it. Father Almund sat on the other side of her. She was comforted by his presence. He seemed to sense her distress, though he couldn't know its cause.

He held her hand and murmured trivial conversation close by her ear as if to distract her from whatever worried her.

"I was glad to see you come to pray this morning with your brother's ladywife," Father Almund said toward the end of the feast. "You must come often to my study when you are lady of this castle. I understand you have a deep love of books."

Elayna nodded, not distracted at all. She could think only of tonight, and Graeham.

"I have many fine illuminated manuscripts," Father Almund was saying.

"I'll come see them, thank you," Elayna said.

The priest laid a finger across his lips. "Perhaps it would be best to say nothing to your lord," he said, nodding to Ranulf. "Men, you know, sometimes find a lady's interest in books unfeminine. Soldiers," he said, shaking his head. "They lack refined tastes. They do not understand the beauty of words. They have no appreciation for such things."

Elayna nodded again, half listening, her gaze scanning the hall.

"If you ever have concern about anything, or a need for solace," Father Almund said, "you'll find my study a place for retreat, meditation, whatever you like. It is available for your use anytime. The decision to wed is a great one and should not be made hastily."

She looked at him now. From his tonsured head to his voluminously robed body, he exuded gravity. Was he trying to tell her something? Did he want to discuss her upcoming betrothal, warn her away from Ranulf? Was there something he wanted to tell her but was afraid to disclose if they were not alone in some private place?

Baskets were passed out to the children as the feast wound down. Ale flowed freely and overflowing platters of soul cakes graced each trestle.

Servants came around, distributing masks, some of cloth and covering only the eyes, sometimes the nose, of the wearer, others of pounded metal and painted with faces—both human and animal.

No one noticed as each knight of Castle Wulfere, stationed in various locations throughout the hall, donned the same mask, one that had been given to them before coming into the hall.

Elayna's mask matched the gold of her gown's

lining. It was one of the smaller masks, designed to hide her eyes and tied behind her head. She fixed it carefully so as not to damage her coiffure. The gold material was soft, and she could see easily through the slitted openings.

Ranulf, as King Crispin, donned no mask.

The girls, giggling in their various masks—Gwyneth in a hammered metal one painted with a fierce warrior's face, Lizbet wearing one designed like a hawk, and Marigold in a simple cat's mask—grabbed their baskets with the other younger girls and boys of the hall and took their places in the procession beginning to wind through the trestles.

Gwyneth, at fourteen, was among the oldest participating, but Elayna knew that her fun-loving sister, almost a woman and yet still very much a child, wouldn't miss taking part for anything.

Elayna suspected that Gwyneth was a little afraid to grow up. There was a woman dying to get out of her boyish sister's body, but Gwyneth wasn't quite ready yet.

"Souling, souling, for soul cakes we go," they joined in the song. "One for Peter, two for Paul, three for him who made us all."

At each table, the feastgoers passed out soul cakes for the children's baskets.

"If you haven't got a cake, an apple will do. If you haven't got an apple, give a pear or two."

The children had started with the lord's table, so Ranulf was already rising, beginning to move about the hall. Elayna watched Damon and Belle stand together, their protective eyes observing the scene.

"If you haven't got a pear, then God bless you."

At some of the tables, the soldiers teased the children, withholding the soul cakes till they begged.

As the children finished souling, they sat down in

a circle by the far hearth to consume their bounty. Many in the crowd were on their feet now, and as Elayna left the dais she found herself carried along with the flow until she was beside Ranulf again. He took her hand, held her arm up alongside his, and brought a slow hush to the hall.

"This night we ask the spirits our questions about love and life!" he boomed into the silence. "Shall we be happy? Shall we be sad?"

Yes! No! Calls came out across the hall in response.

Elayna's stomach coiled. She noticed Damon's knights weaving in among the crowd. Here, there. There again. The masks, not worn directly on the face but rather held to it by a metal grip at its base, were painted a deep, angry red, pounded and shaped into dragon's heads. *The red dragon. The heraldric emblem of Wilfred of Penlogan.*

Her gaze scanned the crowd of masked faces until she found him. Another red dragon. He wore a dark brown tunic similar to the tunics Damon's other knights wore this night, but she would know those shoulders, those arms, anywhere. They had held her warm and close and loved her last night.

Graeham.

She watched, her pulse taking up a heavy, dreadful beat, as he slowly moved the mask to the side, revealing his face.

Ranulf's hand, still gripping her, jerked.

She looked up at him. He was tall, taller even than Graeham, and formidable so near and holding on to her this way. She thought he would crush her hand if he squeezed it any tighter. He was frowning, tense, a shadow of confusion passing over his grim features, then it was gone and he seemed to shake himself from the strange moment.

Glancing back, she saw that the red dragon was gone.

A servant rushed up carrying a cloth with two whole walnuts. The boy held them out, dipping his head almost to the floor in nervous obeisance at the same time.

Ranulf released Elayna's hand and took the nuts. He tossed the cloth down at the boy, who grabbed it off the floor and scurried off.

Again, she saw the red dragon. Her red dragon. He was standing closer this time, only three trestle tables away.

Slowly, he moved the mask and waited for Ranulf's sweeping gaze to find him.

She glanced at Ranulf. His eyes narrowed, as if he were trying to figure out a puzzle.

"My lord," she said, her heart in her throat. Graeham was too close this time.

Ranulf looked at her, and the red dragon mask slipped back into place. One of Damon's knights slipped through the crowd, and Graeham slipped back, behind a pack of villeins. When Ranulf looked back, it was Damon's knight who stood there with his mask moved to the side.

Deliberately, the knight covered his face again, after giving Ranulf ample time to see that the first face and the second face were not the same.

Graeham continued to move about.

Ranulf's fingers pressed harshly into Elayna's shoulder. "Come, my soon-to-be bride. We must play our game. 'Tis Nutcrack Night!"

The crowd still watched, though murmurs and movements had begun. The game was taking longer than expected.

They were already near the hearth. He threw the two walnuts into the fire.

The nuts failed to burst.

Ranulf spun about angrily and ordered more nuts. The boy appeared again, and more nuts were tossed in. They burst this time, and Ranulf turned to Elayna, took her by the shoulders again, and shouted, "To the new lady of Penlogan!"

"To the new lady of Penlogan!" the crowd repeated. The ceremony over, the crowd dispersed into conversation, laughter, and their own games of divination. The noise level rose around them.

Red dragons shifted about the hall. Masks moved in unison, side to side, revealing brief glimpses of faces.

Ranulf frowned, his fingers pressing even harder into Elayna's flesh through the material of her gown.

"What the hell is going on?" he asked.

"I have no idea, my lord," she said.

He glared at her.

A red dragon mask slipped and slid behind him, over his shoulder, straight in her line of sight. Graeham.

There must have been some flicker in her eyes, something, because Ranulf let go of her and whirled.

The red dragon mask froze to the side of Graeham's face for a long, harrowing beat. Ranulf's gaze bored into Graeham's. Then the mask covered his face again.

He swore and suddenly drove through the crowd, his pace sending castlefolk flying from his path.

Soldiers of Wulfere shifted in and out of the crowd, surrounding the red-dragon-masked knight.

"What the hell is going on here?" Ranulf grabbed the front of Graeham's tunic with his fist. Damon appeared, forcing his way between Ranulf and the masked knight, causing Ranulf to drop his hold.

"These are my men," Damon said.

"Why are they all wearing the same masks?" Ranulf demanded.

Damon frowned. "What are you talking about?"

Ranulf turned. The other knights now wore masks of varying design. He spun back. The red-dragon-masked knight had disappeared. In his place stood a knight wearing a lion's face. The knight lowered the lion mask, revealing a young, unoffending visage. A stranger.

The lord of Penlogan shook his head, his face red with fury. "Where did the red dragons go?"

"What red dragons?" Damon asked.

"The red—" Ranulf swore again. "I don't know what in damnation is going on, but it had better cease."

Damon nodded to his men. Elayna watched as her brother continued his careful role.

"Are you all right?" Damon asked.

Ranulf shook his head again more slowly. "I thought I saw—"

"What?" Damon prompted.

"—someone dead." Ranulf stared into the crowd, searching.

Damon waited a hard beat. "Allhallows is getting to you, friend. The night the dead walk—it can prey on the mind."

Kenric had come up beside his brother moments before, in time to catch the scene as it had transpired.

"The red dragon," Kenric said slowly. He looked at Damon suddenly. "The emblem of Wilfred." His stunned gaze slashed to his brother.

"We've lost too many comrades, too many loved ones, in these past years," Damon said. "Perhaps that we are all together this Allhallows brings it back too closely."

Ranulf said nothing. Kenric nodded, his face set in lines as hard as his brother's.

"I think of Wilfred," Kenric said. "Always, I think of Wilfred when I stand in this hall."

Ranulf, Damon, and Kenric stood in silence for

a treacherous moment. Elayna watched, breathless, just outside their circle. Rorke was nowhere to be seen. She suspected he had disappeared, along with Graeham, in preparation for the next phase of their plans.

"Do not speak his name here, brother," Ranulf said sharply, finally. "He betrayed Damon. Damon could have died, spent a year tortured in the dungeon of Blanchefleur because of Wilfred. Do not ever mention his name to me again!"

Kenric's face blanched.

"Ghosts are walking," Kenric said, and pivoted on his heel to stomp away.

Elayna stared after him. What did he mean? What did Kenric know? There was something simmering, seething under the surface. One more mystery. There were too many mysteries. It was overwhelming.

She wished she could follow Rorke to her own bed, but there would be no rest this night. As much as possible, she kept by Belle's side, tending to the children as her excuse for avoiding her prospective bridegroom. She and Belle stayed in the oriel till the girls were tired and the babies were sleeping in their arms.

Kenric wasn't seen again. Ranulf continued to hold court, directing games, laughing too loudly, his eyes angry, scanning the hall constantly, rarely stopping, moving about, searching. He was looking for the red dragon masks. He wouldn't find them.

Relief flooded Elayna as the final festivity heralded the end of the torturous night. The only terrible thing about it was that Ranulf insisted she return to the dais and sit beside him to oversee it as the lord and wedded lady they were to become.

A candlelight procession rounded the hall three times. At each circling, the candle-carrying castlefolk bowed to Ranulf's King Crispin and his lady at the high table.

"Leave the candles lit till I have gone," Ranulf ordered the servants who had begun to blow out the candles still remaining on the tables. "Fools," he muttered under his breath. Elayna watched her family reluctantly leave the hall. She knew Damon would have guards waiting to follow her to her chamber from a discreet distance. For now, ceremony must be followed. The lord and lady must be the last guests to leave the hall.

"The candles scare evil spirits," Elayna said quietly.

Ranulf slanted a dark glance at her. "Are you scared, my lady?"

She swallowed. "No," she said with her chin tipped. "Should I be?"

He didn't answer but took her arm and guided her to the wing of family quarters. Outside her door, he stopped, his hard hand on her arm.

"Tomorrow we will be betrothed," he said.

There was something cold and cruel in his voice.

"Yes," she whispered, her heart thumping wildly. Just another moment and she would be inside her chamber.

"You will not run away again," he said.

Damon's guards had hung back, allowing her time and space alone with her soon-to-be-betrothed.

It was the first time the two of them had been completely alone, she realized. The first time he had spoken directly to her about her avoidance and delay of their betrothal.

"No," she said.

Before she realized what was coming, he placed a fierce, almost-painful kiss on her mouth. She came to life in time to prevent his searching tongue from piercing between her lips.

282 *Suzanne McMinn*

"Tomorrow," he said, breathing roughly as he released her mouth, "you will not deny me. You will never deny me again."

"No," she said, wanting only that this moment end.

"You are reluctant," he said. "I am not a stupid man. You are not eager for this marriage."

She said nothing.

"But I am," he went on. "And I always get what I want." He narrowed his gaze on her. "I always enjoy the game, and it must have an element of risk, must it not?"

He seemed to expect an answer, so she nodded.

"But I don't like to lose. I *won't* lose."

He kissed her again, as if to remind her that she belonged to him now. "Don't make me hurt your brother to have you," he said against her mouth. "Change your mind, run away, Damon dies."

That he revealed his true nature to her now told her how desperate his circumstances must be. He needed her dowry. He would kill to have it.

He left her there, alone and shaking. She didn't even feel her hand turn the knob. She almost fell into her room, into Graeham's waiting arms.

"What's wrong?" he said instantly.

Damon and Rorke waited behind him. They had gone to their own rooms, then into hers through the tunnels.

She explained quickly. Graeham held his anger in with difficulty.

"He will be stopped," Damon said grimly. "Tonight."

Rorke paced, the interminable hours of waiting putting a strain on him. Elayna knew this was most painful for him. Damon leaned his palm against the stone mantel of the fireplace and stared into the flames. She took Graeham's hand, and

together they waited as one candlemark passed
into another, and then it was time.

Together, they looked around at each other's
anguished faces, the danger fast upon them, and
knew they had no choice.

"God's will," Graeham said to them all, and he
was the first one into the tunnel.

CHAPTER
TWENTY-SIX

Graeham reached behind him for Elayna's hand and held on to her tightly as they moved through the pitch-dark tunnel, praying that they would all see the dawn.

He had fought to keep her out of this night's danger, but she had fought just as hard to be by his side. Finally, her brother had agreed to her plan when she had promised to stay out of harm's way.

She had convinced them she was an integral part of the plot, that she should be there. After all, the mystery started with Angelette. But most of all, Graeham knew that she wanted to be there, to be by his side. They were partners in this danger, and he couldn't deny her.

Damon and Rorke would stay even farther behind, in the tunnel, just behind the tapestry, with the tunnel door open so that they could hear but not be seen. Elayna was to remain near the tapestry, within her brother's protective reach if needed.

They arrived at the wall that would open into the lord's chamber. Graeham found the secret door by touch. They had brought no candle to guide their path. They couldn't risk its light being noticed once the wall was open and only the tapestry stood between Ranulf's chamber and the tunnel.

He squeezed Elayna's hand, then with his other hand reached up to carefully press the hidden points in the wall that would release the door. He let go of Elayna's hand then and pressed against the stone with both hands.

It slid silently open. The rough backing of the floor-to-ceiling tapestry met them. Graeham alone stepped cautiously against it, listening, his breath trapped in his throat, the moment nigh.

There was no sound from the chamber.

He moved carefully, slowly, tucking his finger around the edge of the tapestry, and looked into the room.

Ranulf lay prone on the huge bed, the curtains spread wide apart. Fire burned low in the hearth, lending warmth and flickering light to the large chamber.

Graeham waited several long beats. No movement. No evidence that Ranulf was awake, aware.

Elayna's gaze bored steadily into his when Graeham looked back to signal her. She nodded, ready. He wanted to tell her how much courage she had, and he was sorry he hadn't mentioned it before they'd gone into the tunnels.

He was sorry he hadn't told her that he loved her. Why hadn't he? He loved her with his heart and soul and every part of his body, and yet he hadn't spoken the words to her. He hadn't wanted to make a promise, to risk breaking another promise, but he'd been wrong. She had believed in him always, over all the years. It was he who hadn't

believed in her, or even in himself. It was he who
had been afraid.

He had been a fool. But not anymore.

Pivoting, he advanced toward Ranulf's bed,
eager more than ever to end this night, this mystery,
so that he could live the life he'd been born for—
to love Elayna, to lead his people, to guard his
castle.

He withdrew from the belt of his tunic the red
dragon mask. He looked back at Elayna. She waited
where they'd agreed, before the tapestry. From this
distance, she looked like a stranger. He'd never
seen Angelette, but he knew from Rorke's face
that anytime he looked Elayna's way, her hair and
costume were painful for Rorke to see.

Graeham hoped that in the night, seeing her
there, Ranulf, too, would feel Angelette's presence.

Ranulf would definitely feel his. He'd already
unsettled him. Ranulf had recognized him, finally,
the last time he'd moved the red dragon mask.

Of course, he surely thought he'd seen a vision,
or someone who just *looked* like Graeham.

He was about to find out he'd been wrong.

His sword—his father's sword, returned to Graeham by his father's squire that final night—felt
light in his hand despite its weight as he withdrew
it from its sheath. He almost felt as if his father's
hand were over his, helping him carry it. Carrying
him. All those years he'd practiced in the forest,
his father had been with him in spirit, he realized.
He'd been running from the past, but it had never
left him. Whether he'd known it or not, he'd been
preparing for this night for more than four years.

He pressed the tip of the sword against the flesh
of Ranulf's neck. With his other hand, he held the
red dragon mask over his face.

The other man's lashes fluttered, came open
quickly, startled.

"Don't move." Graeham pressed the sword tip until he saw a speck of blood seep against it.

"Who are you?" Ranulf demanded, bewildered, still sleepy and shocked. But Graeham could see the sleep falling fast from his face. Already, Ranulf was shifting against the pillows, rising in increments, uncaring that the sword trailed a line of blood as it scratched the skin of his neck.

Graeham pressed harder again, this time stopping Ranulf's movement. He could see the other man's eyes darting about, searching for his next move.

Ranulf's gaze came back to Graeham.

Slowly, Graeham lowered the mask, let the red dragon fall softly to the rush-strewn floor. Now he gripped the sword with both hands, his gaze locked on Ranulf's.

"Who are you?" Ranulf said, his voice almost shaking, but still he controlled it.

"You know who I am."

"You're a ghost. You're dead. I killed you."

Finally. The truth. It had been Ranulf that fiery night. *Ranulf.* One piece of the puzzle in place. But there were more.

Ranulf swallowed against the sharp tip of the sword. A thin line of blood trickled down the side of his neck.

"This is a prank," Ranulf added quickly, and he seemed to relax. He latched on to the idea. "This is an Allhallows trick. Get out of here!" he ordered.

Graeham laughed. "Ghosts don't respond to mortal commands."

"You *will* be dead if you don't get out of here," Ranulf threatened.

Graeham slid the sword down Ranulf's throat, settling it at the base and putting on a careful pressure.

"I'm already dead," he said grimly. "I've been dead for more than four years."

"Who are you?" Ranulf demanded again, still looking for some way to make sense of the scene.

"I'm Graeham of Penlogan," Graeham stated, his voice ringing in the high-ceilinged chamber. "You killed my father. You stole my home. Now it is your turn to die."

"The lord of Saville killed your father!"

"The lord of Saville executed my father because you brought a false witness against him," Graeham corrected Ranulf. "How did you do that? How did you get that village warden to speak that lie?"

"He wasn't lying," Ranulf countered. He pushed against the pillows, trying to sit up. It was a mistake. Graeham let the tip of his sword puncture the skin again, and a line of blood pooled against it. Ranulf gulped and froze. "He did see the murder," Ranulf clarified quickly, raspily. "He saw Angelette die."

His eyes shifted, moved, and Graeham knew Elayna had stepped into action.

From the corner of his eye, he could see her move before the hearth, displaying her silhouette, her hair and gown glowing. God, she looked like a spirit in truth.

"Angelette," Ranulf breathed, and the trembling in his voice was undeniable. The vision of her seemed to break him. "Not Angelette too."

"The dead shall walk," Graeham said quietly, returning his full focus to Ranulf. "Allhallows. You have been responsible for many deaths. Tonight they have come back to haunt you."

"I'm a soldier," Ranulf said. "The only deaths—"

"You're a murderer." He wanted to know about his father, about Angelette, but he couldn't forget the missing women of Wildevale. They preyed on his soul.

"I didn't murder your father!"

"You murdered Angelette. You were responsible for my father's murder. The lord of Saville tortured him—that was no true confession, and you know it! That was murder."

"I swear—"

Graeham had to fight to restrain himself from pushing his sword straight through Ranulf's neck. "Do not swear anything to me but the truth. Watch your words. I'm already dead— Do you think I care what I do to you?"

Ranulf swallowed visibly.

"There will be no lies now," Graeham said. "The night you came to claim Penlogan, you drugged the ale in my hall. You poured oil and pitch in the rushes. You set Penlogan aflame and you thrust your sword through my side and then told the world that I had done it, that I had burned Penlogan and killed myself."

Ranulf said nothing. Graeham pressed the point of the sword.

"Confess it."

"Yes!" Ranulf cried. "I wanted you dead! You and your father!"

"Why? My father loved you."

"Your father pitied me!" Ranulf struggled to rise again, and this time Graeham let him. He kept the sword to his neck, but he let the other man talk as he sat on the edge of the thick mattress. He needed Ranulf to talk. "Who was I? The second son of a knight from one of your father's poorest manors. He trained me, but I knew I would never have anything."

"My father gave you everything—your horse, your armor, your swords—"

"He gave me charity! I deserved more. I was the better knight." Ranulf's eyes blazed. "I was better than your father or you. Better than Rorke or Damon or my pathetic, do-good brother Kenric. I

was better than any of them—and yet still I would
have nothing when we returned from France. Every
battle won was a reward heaped upon your father
by the king. What about me?''

"You would have had your reward."

"What? A poor manor of my own, so I could
grow old and fat and pitiful, just like my father?
No, thank you," he spat out.

"So you set him up," Graeham probed.

Ranulf blinked, and looked as if he'd almost
forgotten Graeham was there. Did he think Graeham a ghost or a flesh-and-blood man? Graeham
didn't even know now.

"It didn't start out that way. It wasn't my fault."

Ranulf was shifting his eyes around the room.
From the corner of his eye, Graeham could see
Elayna had backed closer to the tapestry again, and
he was relieved. She was near her brother. He could
concentrate on Ranulf.

"It wasn't your fault that Damon was blamed."

"No, that wasn't my idea."

"What was your idea?"

"Your father." His eyes stopped their shifting
and bored into Graeham's. "There was such an
outcry for Damon's release. No one believed he
could have killed Angelette. But Wilfred had been
enamored of Angelette. Everyone knew that. And
when I found my chance—"

"The village warden—what did you pay him?"

"I paid him nothing," Ranulf said, a gleam of
pride lighting his eye. "He believes that's what he
saw. It wasn't hard to convince him. He did see
Angelette murdered that night."

"You."

Ranulf stared for a long time at Graeham. His
gaze shifted to the red dragon mask and back up
to Graeham's face.

He was fully awake and aware now, and he was

not fooled. "You're not dead," he said. "You're not a ghost. Somehow, I didn't kill you. How did you get away? Where have you been?"

"It doesn't matter."

Ranulf gave him a calculating look. "You're right, it doesn't matter."

Sharply, he swept his hand beneath the edge of the mattress, withdrew a sword of his own, and leapt at Graeham, attacking with an overhead cut. Graeham stepped out of the way with instinctive speed, making a swipe at Ranulf's stomach. Ranulf jumped back to avoid it, and Graeham pivoted, passed back, and took aim at Ranulf's shoulder. Ranulf raised his arm again for another overhead cut, but before he could bring it down, Graeham—balancing on his right foot—kicked him in the stomach with his left. Ranulf doubled over and fell back, hitting the stone wall. He raised his sword again, stumbled as Graeham pivoted toward him. Ranulf stretched out his arms for balance.

Graeham drove forward again, thrusting the tip of his sword directly against Ranulf's vulnerable middle.

"Drop it," Graeham demanded, "because I have no problem with cleaving you in twain."

Ranulf swore roughly, and the sword clattered to the stone floor. Something in Ranulf's eyes alerted Graeham to the watchers. Rorke and Damon had never been far away.

They had entered through the tunnel door. Ranulf's face held a stunned expression.

"Release him," Damon said quietly. "We have a lot to talk about."

"I have nothing to say," Ranulf said, but he was trembling and he gave no resistance when Rorke pushed him toward Wilfred's old desk and into a chair.

"You have a lot to say," Damon corrected him.

Elayna's brother's face was a harsh visage of pain. Graeham knew both Damon and Rorke had to be dealing with roiling emotion just then, but they were too disciplined to let it control them.

"And you're going to say it in writing," Rorke added.

"Why bother?" Ranulf said sneeringly. "It's already written down."

Graeham's chest tightened. He hadn't believed—

"You have the letter."

"Of course," Ranulf said. He seemed oddly proud, ready to discuss his accomplishments. "Where is the glory without any risk?" he said, repeating the motto of his battle years. "It was all too easy, you see. If I didn't keep the letter, it would have been like picking off a baby bird with a rock. I liked knowing I could lose. What if one day someone found the letter? Even after I was dead? It made life so much more exciting. Of course, I didn't plan to lose."

His face held an even stranger expression now, and Graeham felt a prickle run up his spine. This was too easy. What was Ranulf planning now?

Damon and Rorke looked at each other. Graeham could see their disgust.

"Your father wrote it all down," Ranulf went on. "But then, you already knew that, didn't you? I found the letter here, on your father's desk, after your death. Your supposed death." Ranulf laughed, and it sounded almost mad.

Graeham didn't explain that he hadn't had a chance to read the letter. He was so impatient suddenly, it took everything inside him not to put his hands around Ranulf's throat and demand that he hand it over.

"Where is it?"

Ranulf nodded at the desk drawers. Graeham

frowned. He'd searched the desk earlier, including the secret compartments.

Then it hit him. If his father and grandfather had built secret compartments, so, too, could Ranulf.

"In the lower drawer. Reach up. You'll find a latch. It releases a compartment in the top drawer."

Graeham followed the steps while Rorke and Damon looked on. Elayna stood near the open doorway, watching. He touched the latch, then returned to the top drawer and found the release and the crevice. It was so small, nothing bigger than the scrolled letter could have fit within it.

Elayna stepped toward him, eager, too, to see the letter.

"Stay back," Graeham said. He glanced from Elayna to Graeham. No matter how closely Rorke and Damon guarded Ranulf, he didn't want Elayna in arm's reach of him.

Ranulf's eyes narrowed. In the firelight, the garnet dragon fire winked on her hand.

"That tells only half the story, of course," Ranulf said slowly. "What happened that night at Penlogan—"

"Then you'll tell that part in writing," Damon demanded again. He met Graeham's eyes. "We'll go to the king and have the castle and title restored to you. My testimony and Rorke's is enough already, but a confession in writing would smooth the way."

Graeham gripped the letter. He nodded.

He started to open the scrolled letter, unable to wait any longer to see his father's last words. He'd been waiting too long.

Rorke and Damon looked at Graeham. "Open the letter. Read it."

There was a sudden movement from Ranulf. Rorke had been holding a short dagger against his neck and now Ranulf was struggling with him for control of it—but he wasn't trying to turn it on Rorke. He had hold of the hilt, his hands covering Rorke's.

"Let go of it!" Damon ordered.

"I'd rather kill myself than lose everything!" Damon swore.

"I need to talk to someone—"

"Talk to us, *friend,*" Damon demanded.

"I want to talk to Father Almund," Ranulf said, and any bravado was gone, as if it had just hit him how much trouble he was in. "I'm not saying another word, or writing anything, without the priest. I'm sorry. I'm so sorry." He was falling apart. His eyes were red, watery, and he looked as if he very well might slash his own throat at the first chance.

None of the men moved. Ranulf was unpredictable, and they were loath to leave one another until he was completely under control.

"Send the girl," Ranulf grated, his voice shaking and low. "Send the girl." He was almost pleading.

Graeham was only too glad to get Elayna out of there, away from the volatile Ranulf.

"Go through the tunnels, come out from your own chamber." Damon nodded to her. "Explain nothing. Bring Father Almund."

The chapel of Penlogan Castle was two-celled, the nave linked by an arched doorway to the chancel, where the altar stood and the liturgy was performed. The furnishings were minimum: a silvergilt chalice for the bread, a pewter chrismatory for the holy oils, an incense boat, a holy-water vessel, portable crosses, and a hand bell. There were stools for those who chose to be seated.

Elayna stopped, breathless, in the archway between the nave and chancel. Where were the priest's rooms?

"Father Almund?"

Her heart beat heavy in her ears. There were three doors along one side. She tried the first one and found it to be a small storeroom of vestments and altar cloths—possibly those kept for special festivals.

She tried the next door, and it opened into a narrow corridor with another door at the end. She rushed to the door, her soft-booted feet soundless on the stone. She pounded on the door. "Father Almund!"

There was no response. Could he be sleeping? This was an emergency. She pushed the door slightly, and it opened with a low creak.

The interior of the chamber was candlelit. A fire burned in the small hearth against one wall. The room was clearly a study, the one of which he'd spoken at the feast. Through an open arch, she could see a small cell with a narrow pallet for his bed and a chest for his clothing.

The pallet was empty.

A huge table with a matching set of carved chairs sat near the hearth and was clearly where the priest spent much of his time in this private area. There were books stacked everywhere—as he'd said, he had a large collection of illuminated manuscripts: prayer books, priests' manuals of rites, ordinals, psalters, hymnals, herbals, saints' lives, music books, and poetry. There were also sheets of parchment and erasing knives for the priest's own writings.

She ran back to the corridor. "Father Almund?" She went back to the chapel, tried the other door, and found it led outside to a small enclosed garden. Apparently, Father Almund enjoyed doing his own gardening.

The air was heavy, thick. She felt a plop on her cheek and realized it was starting to rain. Thunder drummed overhead.

She slammed the door shut again, shivering.

Where was the priest? The castle was quiet, most of the inhabitants long asleep but for a few guards posted at various points. Coming out from her chamber, she'd alerted Damon's men. They had been heading toward the corridor that held the lord's chamber while she'd fled in the other direction.

She wondered if she'd missed another connecting door and returned down the corridor to Father Almund's private rooms.

The door was shut. Hadn't she left it open? Her mind raced. She pounded again. "Father Almund?"

No response. She must have been wrong. Her chest banded tightly as she thought of Graeham, Rorke, and Damon in the lord's chamber with Ranulf. Anything could happen there. She had to find the priest, and quickly.

She pushed the door open again. The chamber was still empty, no one in the cell or at the study table. Wax candles dripped onto one of the bare parchment pages, and she stopped as she passed by it to move the blank page out of the way. It bothered her to see a good piece of parchment ruined.

Her gaze continued to scan the chamber, looking for any hidden recess or doorway that she'd missed, but she saw nothing. She had no idea where else to search for Father Almund. Penlogan Castle was huge.

She would have to go back, seek out Ranulf's guards, ask if they'd seen the priest. She turned, her gaze scanning the table, realizing something she'd missed before. The thick manuscript near the blank sheet of parchment had been closed, and now it was open, she was certain of it. Was Father Almund here somewhere? Had she just missed him?

She looked around, anxious. "Father Almund?" she called again.

Would he return in a few moments if she waited? She was impatient, worried about the events transpiring in the lord's chamber. She looked down at Father Almund's manuscript again. His script was bold and perfect, long practiced. Much finer than hers. She appreciated it for a full breath, her stomach churning with indecision and impatience before she took in what she read.

It appeared at first to be a book of sermons, with a largely printed admonition across the top. *Almighty God, to whose power and wisdom all creatures are subject, let the people hear thy will.* But as she looked closer, she realized it was dated—less than a fortnight earlier—and was more like a book of days, a journal much like her own. She flipped back through it and saw she was right. It was a journal. She set it back down, her gaze catching on the most recent entry. It clogged her breath in her throat as she read:

> *The night-winged beast, the devil appointed by the Lord, laid his spell upon the people. Then he came unto this unworthy damsel's house. The devil said, "Admit thy lust, thy sin, for only I can save thee." To which the wretched woman cried, "Nay!" and the beast stooped and took her into his arms, and strangled her even there. The night sky swallowed her up and he was saved from his own hell once more, the sin of women conquered another day.*

Ada's story pounded in her brain and her mind spun crazily. *He comes in the night and steals into our cottages. He takes the young women into his talons and he's gone, away, into the night!*

Elayna felt a small puff of air. That was the only warning she got. She turned in time to see the door to the private priest's room closing, Father Almund standing before it. His face was devoid of emotion.

He lifted his arms, his black vestments billowing at his sides like wings.

CHAPTER TWENTY-SEVEN

Graeham finished unrolling the letter. He'd waited so many years to find it, read it. He could hardly believe he was really holding it now.

His hands shook. He steadied himself with a deep breath and his eyes focused on the story his father told. Written in his father's last moments, it told the story of his shocking seizure by Saville's men and the torture he had briefly endured before giving in to the inevitable. He knew he was about to die. He couldn't bear the torture, and he had made his false confession.

None of this surprised Graeham, though it was comforting to have the proof in his hands. His father's confession had been forced, not given of his free will. But what came next froze his heart.

"Did you get there yet?" came Ranulf's suddenly calm voice. "To the rest of the story?"

Graeham tore his eyes from the parchment.

"Now do you see your mistake?" Ranulf went on. "Oh, you thought you knew everything, didn't you? You're so very brilliant. But not brilliant enough. Thought to trap me? I have trapped you now, have I not? Your ladylove—the woman who should have been mine!—is on her way right now to the lair of the true murderer of Angelette." He smiled, a cold, evil smile. "I took your home, your life, even the lives of Damon's men. But I didn't take Angelette's."

Rorke and Damon cast bewildered glances, and Graeham thrust the letter at Damon. "He didn't kill Angelette," he explained briefly, his blood roaring in his ears. "Father Almund killed Angelette. He confessed—to my father—when Saville allowed him into Blanchefleur to perform final rites! This"—he looked at Ranulf, no words to describe his feelings—"he somehow took advantage of it. He built on Angelette's death. They must have concocted this vile scheme to take Penlogan." His hands ached to throttle him. He wanted to stay and punish Ranulf this very instant, not wait for the king's justice, but all he could think of was—"Elayna!"

God, it was his own fault. Ranulf had seen the look in his eyes, heard the love in his voice. Ranulf had sent Elayna for the priest, feigned his own mental breakdown, to strike at Graeham one last time, through Elayna and Father Almund.

Damon paled, as did Rorke. Graeham was at the door, sword clutched tightly, when all hell broke loose behind him. He turned back but not fast enough. Ranulf pushed against Rorke, not caring that the blade they both held sliced his palms as he shoved backward. Rorke held on to the weapon but lost his balance. Ranulf called out, and guards—Ranulf's men—jumped to alert in the corridor, Damon's men close behind them.

It was an instant melee. Graeham fought his way through, Damon at his side. Through the clash, he could see Ranulf tearing off toward the tapestry, where he must have seen Rorke and Damon enter.

"Go! Find Elayna!" Damon yelled, holding off Ranulf's men as Graeham drove through the swarming men. The last glimpse he had of Ranulf was Rorke racing after him into the tunnels.

The winged night beast.

Elayna's mind sought to reject the thought as soon as it was formed. It was surely ludicrous—

"Welcome, my sweet lady, to my study," the priest said, and lowered his arms.

Folded his wings, she thought wildly.

"Father Almund," she said, her heart beating painfully inside her. Her voice came out threadlike, breathy. Her pulse was out of control and she couldn't think.

"You came to me," he said, his eyes fixed on her. "I knew that you would. You're the one. If only I'd realized it before, I wouldn't have had to wait so long. But you were so young. You have only now matured, blossomed. I told him to marry you, you know."

Elayna shook her head in confusion. "What do you mean?"

"My lord Ranulf," Father Almund said. "He had a dozen well-dowered ladies in mind, but I chose you. *I* chose you. I have the power. I've always had the power, you see. I order lives. I order deaths. It is the way it should be."

Elayna swallowed over the huge lump of fear rising in her throat. He was mad, entirely mad, and it was Ada who was quite sane. Ada's story, her fantastical story, was true. It still made no sense, but she didn't want answers. She wanted out.

She backed up, and bumped against the table that shielded the hearth and the tiny sleeping cell.

The only escape was beyond Father Almund. The door, the corridor, the chapel, and the castle.

Graeham and her brother and the guards pacing out their watches seemed very far away.

Father Almund hadn't moved, and she remembered how his grip had felt so strong when he had held hers the other night, and she realized she had been so very wrong about this old priest she had known for years. He wasn't frail at all.

His gaze glittered across at her. What did he plan to do with her? She realized she was going to have to find out, whether she wanted to or not, if she wanted to get out of there.

"What do you mean, you have the power?" she asked softly, battling to control the shaking of her voice.

Surely she could outrun him? But he stood in front of the door. She would have to fight her way past him.

"I never wanted to be a priest," he said calmly. She watched him remove a short gilt-handled dagger from the folds of his voluminous cloak. He held it in a nonthreatening posture, but she had no doubt that it was indeed a threat, a warning. "It was my father's charge for me. I was the fourth son, you see, and there was never a question of my future. I was content for a time. I served your lord brother's wife's family for many years and served them well. And I served the lord of Penlogan after that, and well. But what do you think was my reward for my years of service?"

Elayna blinked. "I don't know."

She continued watching him, her thoughts careening. He wasn't moving, and there was no way she could risk pushing past him with that dagger in his hand.

Her back was still to the table. She thought of the candles burning there. She could push them over, set the rushes—even his manuscripts—on fire in the process. Or, if he would only move away from the door, she could throw the candle between him and the door—if he moved so that she had a safe path out for herself. The fire wouldn't spread far, not within the quarters of the stone chapel, but it could give her the time she needed to get away.

She would have to circle the table. It would be too dangerous to turn her back to reach for them while they were behind her, she decided. And maybe he would move farther away from the door if she did too.

"He refused me the one thing I wanted," Father Almund said, his face still frightening impassive. "My love, my heart. My beloved."

Father Almund had sought to wed?

"The lord of Penlogan would not have prevented you from marriage," Elayna said. It was common for priests to wed. They often kept their own cottages and their own parcels of land, grew their own crops as well as tending their office.

"He would not let me wed the woman I wanted, the woman who was destined to be mine!" Father Almund said, and now his face changed. It flushed and hardened. He looked nothing like the gentle, kind priest she had known. He was a different person altogether, and she was afraid of him.

"I don't understand."

She had reached the other side of the long table. She wasn't near enough to the candles. She edged along the table in tiny increments. Father Almund had still not changed his position. Would her plan work?

"I was in love with the lady Angelette," Father Almund said.

Elayna froze, shocked by the confession. Angelette? But—

"She was mine. She was meant to be mine! They had taken Voirelle, occupied the castle," he explained, and his glittering eyes darkened, clouded. "She was staying there with her sister at the time. She was so beautiful, so perilously sweet. She had feelings for me—I know she did. There was . . . a connection. I felt it. She had to have felt it too. But he stood between us."

"Lord Penlogan?"

"He was in love with her too. Everyone could see that. It was pathetic," Father Almund spat out. "He knew she had no thought for him, and he was content to love her from afar, like a father, and let another steal her affections. He was a fool. I was not so content."

Elayna stared at him. Oh, God. *He killed Angelette.* But what of Ranulf? Her thoughts tangled. Angelette had loved Rorke. It had not been Wilfred's fault that she had not loved Father Almund. And yet somehow he had twisted it— He was mad, she reminded herself. Terribly mad.

"What do you mean? What did you do?" The story was still in puzzle pieces she couldn't put together.

"She wouldn't listen," he went on. His eyes were still distant yet locked on hers at the same time. "She laughed at me. She didn't believe I was serious. She told me she thought of me as a father. It was Rorke. He had seduced her, turned her into a whore!" He breathed heavily suddenly. "Wilfred would do nothing, nothing! I followed her, followed *them.* I knew all their secrets, their plans. I convinced Wilfred to plant the idea in the king's ear that Rorke was the finest tournament player in France and pit him against France's fiercest knight.

"It was the day he planned to run away with Angelette. The king ordered Rorke to participate in his tourney, and he had no choice. I planned to make myself available to carry the news to Angel-ette, but before I could speak to Rorke, he had arranged for your brother to keep their meeting.''

Elayna gasped, pressing trembling fingers to her mouth. This part of the story was all too familiar. Damon's race to meet Angelette, to warn her of Rorke's delay—and his own attack by a band of men who slashed his face, and then the discovery of Angelette near death, and his own imprison-ment and torture at the hand of Angelette's father.

"I arranged for that band of thieves who stopped your brother," Father Almund said. "Of course, they were supposed to kill him. They failed. Your brother was far too valiant for his own good. He only got himself in deeper trouble, didn't he?''

Elayna thought of the year Damon had spent in the dungeon of Blanchefleur, accused of Angel-ette's murder. She shivered in horror to think of how unnecessary it had all been, how cruel.

"I reached Angelette first. I made her mine, the way she was meant to be," Father Almund said. He moved, finally, stepping away from the door. Toward Elayna. "And then I punished her for her wickedness!''

Elayna's heart stopped, then it took up a new, pounding, heavy beat—so fast, she felt faint from it. She had to get out of there. He had raped and murdered Angelette. He had strangled God knew how many more women in the same way.

"And the others?" she asked, intent on keeping him talking.

She was almost in arm's reach of the candles. She was afraid to move too quickly, afraid he'd realize her plan. He was moving away from the door, and though that meant he now came nearer to her, it would provide the route to escape that she needed. A few more steps, and her way would be clear. She would topple the burning candle straight in front of him, and run.

"The others? Oh, you are a clever lady," he said softly. "So very clever. Like my Angelette. She was clever too. But not clever enough. I warned her, but she didn't listen. She didn't understand my power."

"Power?"

"To punish. Women must be punished. They are weak, easily swayed to sin. They are the devil's tools. Finally, I understood why I had become a priest. My duty was to punish the wicked."

Elayna felt a shudder wave up her spine. How long had he been insane? How had she never seen it? No one had seen it. No one but—

"Ranulf," she breathed, so stunned for a moment she forgot to think of her own escape. "Ranulf found the warden, the one who claimed it was Wilfred who murdered Angelette—"

Father Almund laughed. "I never meant Wilfred, or even Damon, to be imprisoned," he said. "It was happenstance. Bad luck, especially for Damon. Oh, the clamor of it. The outcry, would not cease. I traveled with Ranulf and other of Damon's men, men who had fought alongside the lord of Penlogan and fostered with him. I was there when they questioned every living soul in the village below Blanchefleur, and when finally they found one who had witnessed the event, it wasn't hard to convince him that the man he had seen was not me, but was the lord of Penlogan.

"Ranulf alone suspected the truth when he questioned the man. He would have turned me over to the lord of Saville—but it was then I began to understand my power. I convinced him of the advantage of seeing the lord of Penlogan executed for Angelette's murder. It was not difficult to make him see the light."

"But why—why Wilfred?"

"He was beginning to suspect," Father Almund said, shaking his head almost woefully. "He was starting to question the deaths."

"The deaths?"

"The girls. The girls in the villages we passed through, the castles we occupied, the inns where we stayed."

The girls. Her mind made a terrible leap. "The girls who—died?"

"So many of them to punish," Father Almund said. "They had to die—for her. For Angelette. She was a whore, and so were they. Only I could save them. I gave them holy rites and strangled them to prevent them from sinning again. You see—it was their punishment and their salvation at once."

Elayna couldn't believe what she was hearing, but at the same time it was making a sickening sense, the pieces clicking into place. Ranulf hadn't killed Angelette. Father Almund had killed her. Father Almund had been content to let Damon languish in the dungeon, but too many other people were not. Setting up Wilfred in his place was easy. Unlike Damon, he couldn't survive Saville's torture long enough for another outcry to rise.

And playing on Ranulf's greed meant that Father Almund held Ranulf in the palm of his hand, having been his kingmaker. He was free to fulfill his sick desires unchecked, to punish and punish and punish—

"Graeham." His name exploded from her lips. "Was it you, or Ranulf? How did you—"

"Graeham was a fool, like his father," the priest said, taking another deliberate step toward her. "No telling what he would have done, how he would have plotted to clear his father's name. There had to be finality. Ranulf had to have full control of the castle, and I gave it to him. While I was in France," he said, conversationally now as he made his way nearer, "I perfected a potion of poppies. A little weakens even the strongest man, a lot can kill him. I know just the right amount to cause sleep, hallucinations, wild half-awake dreams. Being a priest has its compensation. No one notices your doings. It was easy enough to poison the ale that night. Easy enough to ensure that neither Ranulf or I would drink it—though I let Graeham believe I had. Easy enough afterward to watch Ranulf kill him and let it be said that he killed himself amid a fire that destroyed the evidence. Who could say the truth but myself and my lord Ranulf?"

Elayna swallowed thickly. She had no intention of informing him that even now Graeham was alive and very near.

"Kenric," she said, remembering that there had been one other survivor of that deadly night. "He lived."

Father Almund shrugged. "I let Ranulf pull him from the fiery hall. He was his brother. He had a moment of weakness."

So Kenric was innocent. She felt a deep relief. One less betrayal for Damon to face, and for Graeham. The scene in the hall earlier between Kenric and Ranulf flashed through her mind. What had that been about? Did Kenric suspect his brother of these crimes?

"So all this time," she said, edging around the corner of the table, preparing to take flight, holding the priest's gaze steady. "All this time you controlled Ranulf. You gained Penlogan for him, and he gave you—what? Freedom? Freedom to keep punishing— After you killed Angelette, why didn't you stop?"

"There is yet wickedness!" Father Almund

hissed. "I watch them. They blossom into beauties and they cast their eyes about for men. They taunt and destroy. They are devils! I must seek them out and destroy them instead! They must obey me, and I will save them!"

"You give them the potions—"

"—then they are mine," Father Almund said, "to punish."

"And their bodies—why are their bodies never found?"

"The sea," he said. "They are carried away by the sea. But don't worry, my lady. I have other plans for you."

She gulped.

"What do you plan to do with me? Why did you tell Ranulf to marry me?"

She was still trying to distract him. She didn't want to know the answer. She knew enough. She had to get out of there, find Graeham and Damon.

With a sharp lunge, she pushed over the candle, sending it careening across the table. The force sent it flying past the manuscripts, but it burst into flame as it hit the ground, eating up the rushes. She heard rather than saw the result of her move as she tore toward the closed door. He hadn't bolted it, and her shaking fingers yanked it wide in a pulsebeat, but not fast enough. He had hold of her arm, dragging her back, dragging her into the rush-fire.

"You're my last chance!" he cried savagely. She fought him, kicking, screaming, until he held the dagger blade against her throat and she felt its cold bite.

She struggled for air, choked by the thick cloud of smoke filling the room. The rushes were popping and spitting fire in an ever-widening circle.

"You are the one," he said into her ear, yanking her against his chest, her back to him, one incredibly strong arm clamped around her waist, the other holding that sharp blade to her throat. "Last year, we visited Castle Wulfere again, Ranulf and his men, and I saw you, how you refused all suitors, and I realized you were the one pure woman, the one I've been waiting for all along."

Her mind reeled. She remembered the visit. It had been near May Day. She scarcely recalled that Father Almund had been in attendance. But he'd been there, watching her.

"I knew you wouldn't want to marry Ranulf," he continued, "and you don't have to worry. I never intended for you to wed him. I'll save you. We'll save each other."

Smoke hurt her throat. Already, a tapestry was afire, flames rushing up the far wall. The table was engulfed, the manuscript pages sparking and spitting. A spark landed on her cheek, and she gasped.

"We have to get out of here," she pointed out desperately. "Please! You don't want to burn."

The smoke was fast filling the room.

He lifted her up as if she were nothing, and her thoughts careened ahead, knowing this was her chance. In his escape from the fire, she would escape him.

Then something—his shockingly powerful fist, she realized belatedly—crashed into her temple and the smoky room went entirely black.

The chapel lay empty, but the smell of smoke, acrid in the now-hot air, led Graeham down the open door at the side of the nave and into the long private corridor. *Dear sweet God, was Elayna in there?*

He couldn't see down the passage for the smoke that billowed up it, but he heard a noise and felt

a breeze, and in the fresh air that came in saw a
shadowed shape disappear through an open door
to the outside. Behind him, he heard shouts, soldiers. He didn't know if they were Damon's men
or Ranulf's. Not waiting to find out, he ran after
the shape, gulping in the clear air of a tiny garden.
It was dark, rain gushing down around him. He
was drenched in heartbeats.

The shape was there, across the small garden,
racing up a staircase cut into the stone. The figure
carried something over his shoulder, another
shape—Elayna? The figure reached the wallwalk
and disappeared.

"Stop!" he called against the boom of thunder,
and his heart in his throat, chased across the garden, up the stone steps.

Elayna woke to the hard rain on her face and
the cold embrace of Father Almund's arms holding
her tight. And the sound of a voice, a man's voice.
Graeham?

She had to have imagined it. But it didn't matter.
He gave her strength even from afar. She had too
much to live for. *They* had too much to live for.

She had no idea where she was as she fought
her way out of Father Almund's arms. The sky was
wild around them. Lightning exploded over her
as he dropped her hard on a castle rampart. She
fell back onto the stone, the sky swerving crazily
overhead. Lightning flashed again, revealing the
village perilously far below as she turned her head.

Then he was hauling her up again, shoving her
over the edge.

"Let me go," she cried, pushing at Father
Almund. His cloak billowed out from his body and
she felt as if she punched at air.

"Come on, sweet Elayna," he spat at her low and

deadly. "Fly with me! It's the only way you can be saved! It's the only way we can be saved together! Your purity, my power."

Did he believe the stories the villagers told to make sense of the madness wreaked upon them? Did he truly believe he was a night-winged beast, a creature of fantastical proportions who could seize women in his talons and fly over the land? Was he that insane?

"No!" she screamed, gripping onto the stone, looking for any purchase that would hold her steady, keep her from flying over the wall—to her death—with him.

"You're the one!" he demanded, pressing the blade against her throat again. "Fly with me, and we will both be saved."

"No!"

He roared and smacked her so hard against the stone that she saw stars in the wet, black sky.

"Fly, Lady Elayna! Fly!" His eyes were hot, and it was like looking into hell for her. She started to roll away, and the dagger came out of nowhere again, sharp and fast, and she felt something shear across her shoulder bone, something that spurted hot and icy at once.

She saw a shape behind him then, from the corner of her eyes. *Graeham!* But it was too late. There was no more time. She felt a mighty shove, and then there was only the dizzying view of the storm-flashing sky and the sensation of falling, falling, falling.

Instinctively, she reached for the rock protrusion, the only handhold she could hope to gain. Rain washed down her face. She tried to throw her other arm up for better purchase, but it felt as if it belonged to someone else. Pain shot from her shoulder, almost causing her to black out again, but she fought to remain conscious. To black out would be her end. Slowly, agonizingly, she brought her other arm around the crenellation and held on for dear life.

Her legs dangled uselessly below, and she clung, fighting to find a way to raise her body over the edge and unable to manage the feat. It was taking all her strength just to hold on. Where was Father Almund? He had disappeared. Had she imagined Graeham?

Then she heard his voice again—it was real!—and almost sobbed, but she was afraid to so much as breathe in her precarious position. But she heard Father Almund's voice too, and he was back, leaping to the wall's edge, his booted foot stamping down onto one of her hands. Pain crashed through her, but still she held on. Graeham was near! She couldn't let go now.

The billowing shape of Father Almund rose over her, and then he was gone, leaping over her, his arms reaching out, tearing at her. He grabbed hold of her hair, and she felt a hard yank, but other arms were reaching for her now—warm, secure, solid, loving arms, and as Graeham pulled her over the side of the castle wall to safety, all that fell with the priest were the false braids that had been pinned to her head.

The last thing she remembered seeing were Father Almund's eyes, glittering and mad. His thin, wind-tossed voice echoed in her ears, "*Angelette*!"

Then Graeham's soft arms and even softer voice, over and over. "My sweet, sweet Elayna. You're all right. You're all right. Thank God. I love you."

It was all she would ever need to hear to drive out her nightmares. It was all she had dreamed of for so many years.

"I love you too."

EPILOGUE

Recovery came in small increments, one day after another, and Elayna learned to appreciate the journey. Finally, her impatience had been tamed—almost.

Her husband patted her rounded belly as they sat in the great bed of the lord's chamber—a room completely renovated since the evil day they had confronted Ranulf there—and felt the first flutters of life inside her and ached to hold that tiny life in her arms in sooth, and not have to wait another four months.

"Did you feel her?" she cried, gazing up at Graeham beside her, joy lighting her heart as much from the life inside her as from the life within him.

It had been hard won, this joy, and she treasured it more than she would have believed. Even now, there was yet much to be grieved. Graeham's father, so cruelly lost. And the people of Penlogan Castle and the village of Wildevale, so savagely scourged. And even those closest to them—Damon, hurting for the foster lord he'd believed to have betrayed him and now knew had been betrayed himself, and Rorke, grieving afresh for Angelette. And Kenric, shocked and stricken at the treachery of his brother.

They had learned that the reason Kenric had left Castle Wulfere two years earlier was that he had sensed something wrong at Penlogan, something wrong with his brother. He had come to find the truth but had found it too late.

Now Ranulf was gone too. He could be nothing but dead—having gone over the cliff at the mouth of the tunnel. Rorke and Damon and their men had chased him to that sheer drop, and without time to manage a boat, or even to throw a rope ladder over the side, rather than be captured Ranulf had jumped into the churning sea. His body hadn't been found, but the storm had been wild. There was no way he could have survived the drop into that mad sea, the horrible dashing his body would have taken against the rocks.

Graeham had achieved a kind of peace, slowly, through the pain. He was home, with his love and his life and his people.

And the future.

If life wasn't perfect, Elayna thought, it was as close to it as she could imagine. The king had restored his castle and title and cleared his father's name. Graeham was home for good, and he'd brought the people of Cradawg with him, welcoming them into Penlogan and filling Wildevale with their merry company, bringing the village as well as the castle back to life.

Meldrik had set up shop in a tavern overlooking the sea, and men were fishing again. And the women were smiling. The healing had begun. It would make a great story. She smiled as her gaze passed over the stack of parchment on the desk. She'd already begun.

"Him," her husband corrected her with a low curl of a smile. "Him. I don't think I am strong enough to raise any daughter you would bear. She will be intractable, stubborn, unmanageable. I'm scared already. I've been talking to Damon."

She laughed, enjoying his teasing, his own new-found hope and happiness. She snuggled closer on the high-blanketed bed. It had been six months since they'd wed, and still she hadn't gotten tired of feeling his arms around her. She knew she never would.

"I'll tell you a secret," she said, and pulled her sweet, dear husband close, "the midwife says it's twins—and I pray, if 'tis God's will, they are both girls!" In sooth, she didn't care what sex her babes would be, but teasing her husband to smile was its own reward.

Graeham just shook his head, still grinning. "Then I am lost," he said, "for my beautiful wife knows how to shape God's will." He placed a warm kiss on her lips. "And for that, I will be grateful the rest of my life."

Elayna kissed him back, a little tearful suddenly, sometimes still overwhelmed by how much they had been blessed.

"Me too," she whispered against his mouth. "I'm grateful too."

ABOUT THE AUTHOR

SUZANNE MCMINN writes contemporary and historical romances from her lakeside home in a small Texas town. She has three young children, and she is a middle school English teacher. To learn more about her books, visit *www.SuzanneMcMinn.com* or write to Suzanne at P.O. Box 12, Granbury, TX 76048. Happy reading!

If you liked MY LADY RUNAWAY, be sure to look for Suzanne McMinn's next release in the Sword and the Ring series, MY LADY KNIGHT, available wherever books are sold in December 2002.

As untamed as the wildflowers in meadows beyond Castle Wulfere, Gwyneth knew that womanly pursuits such as embroidery and song suited her brother's new wife, Belle. Gwyneth preferred hunting with the castle's knights, and the solid power of a bow and arrow in her hands. Only one thing inspired a dream of femininity in her—Rorke of Valmond, a man who viewed her as a troublesome child. She never imagined that he would return from war after years away and see her as a child still, or that her rash behavior would hasten them to the altar. For Gwyneth wanted more than a husband in name only—and she vowed to be the woman who would steal Rorke's wounded heart.

COMING IN DECEMBER 2001 FROM
ZEBRA BALLAD ROMANCES

__A ROSE FOR JULIAN: Angels of Mercy
by Martha Schroeder   0-8217-6866-2 $5.99US/$7.99CAN
Taking a position with Miss Nightingale is a dream come true for Rose. One
patient in particular—Julian Livingston, an earl's son—inspires dreams of
another kind. They are impossible dreams, for Rose believes that Julian will
despise her if he discovers the shameful truth of her past. Can Julian convince
her that he loves the woman she has become?

__JED: The Rock Creek Six
by Linda Devlin   0-8217-6744-5 $5.99US/$7.99CAN
Jed Rourke, a Pinkerton detective, finds a compelling reason to stay in Rock
Creek—prim and sensible Hannah Winters. Hannah's brother-in-law has been
charged with murder and she insists on helping solve the crime. Working with
a woman is the last thing Jed planned on, but with Hannah, teamwork may just
lead to a walk down the aisle.

__REILLY'S HEART: Irish Blessing
by Elizabeth Keys   0-8217-7226-0 $5.99US/$7.99CAN
Meaghan Reilly has never let being female stop her from doing anything, and
now studying medicine is her only dream. Until Nicholas Mansfield, Lord
Ashton, walks back into her life. Meaghan is certain that the nobleman is her
destiny. If only Nick would ignore the duty that has brought him to Ireland and
instead, embrace the passion between them . . .

__THE THIRD DAUGHTER: The Mounties
by Kathryn Fox   0-8217-6846-8 $5.99US/$7.99CAN
Mountie Steven Gravel wonders if business is the only thing on Cletis Dawson's
mind. At every chance, marriageable middle daughter Emily is thrust into his
path. Yet it's not gentle Emily who draws Steven's eye, but the oldest girl,
Willow. Stubborn Willow is hardly willing to be courted—unless Steven can
unlock the secrets in her wild heart.

Call toll free **1-888-345-BOOK** to order by phone or use this coupon to order
by mail. *ALL BOOKS AVAILABLE DECEMBER 01, 2001*
Name _____
Address _____
City _____ State _____ Zip _____
Please send me the books I have checked above.
I am enclosing $ _____
Plus postage and handling* $ _____
Sales tax (in NY and TN) $ _____
Total amount enclosed $ _____
*Add $2.50 for the first book and $.50 for each additional book. Send check
or money order (no cash or CODs) to: **Kensington Publishing Corp., Dept.
C.O., 850 Third Avenue, New York, NY 10022**
Prices and numbers subject to change without notice. Valid only in the U.S.
All orders subject to availabilty. **NO ADVANCE ORDERS.**
Visit our website at **www.kensingtonbooks.com.**

BOOK YOUR PLACE ON OUR WEBSITE AND MAKE THE READING CONNECTION!

We've created a customized website just for our very special readers, where you can get the inside scoop on everything that's going on with Zebra, Pinnacle and Kensington books.

When you come online, you'll have the exciting opportunity to:

- View covers of upcoming books
- Read sample chapters
- Learn about our future publishing schedule (listed by publication month *and author*)
- Find out when your favorite authors will be visiting a city near you
- Search for and order backlist books from our online catalog
- Check out author bios and background information
- Send e-mail to your favorite authors
- Meet the Kensington staff online
- Join us in weekly chats with authors, readers and other guests
- Get writing guidelines
- AND MUCH MORE!

**Visit our website at
http://www.zebrabooks.com**